Also by Jonathan Carroll

THE LAND OF LAUGHS
VOICE OF OUR SHADOW
BONES OF THE MOON

SLEEPING IN FLAME

DOUBLEDAY

NEW YORK · LONDON · TORONTO · SYDNEY · AUCKLAND

SLEEPING IN FLAME

JONATHAN CARROLL

Published by Doubleday, a division of
Bantam Doubleday Dell Publishing Group, Inc.
666 Fifth Avenue, New York, New York 10103

Doubleday and the portrayal of an anchor
with a dolphin are trademarks of
Doubleday, a division of
Bantam Doubleday Dell Publishing Group, Inc.

Library of Congress Cataloging-in-Publication Data
Carroll, Jonathan, 1949–
Sleeping in flame / Jonathan Carroll. —1st ed.
p. cm.
ISBN 0-385-24957-8
I. Title.
PS3553.A7646S54   1989
813'.54—dc19   88-26036
CIP

"Metaphors" copyright © 1984 by Diane Wakoski.
Reprinted from *The Collected Greed, Parts 1–13*
with the permission of Black Sparrow Press.

"A Space in the Air" by Jon Silkin reprinted from *Selected Poems*,
Routledge Chapman and Hall, Inc.

"The Night Comes Every Day to My Window" from *Monolithos: Poems
1962 and 1982.* © 1962 by Jack Gilbert. Reprinted by permission of
Graywolf Press.

BOOK DESIGN BY CLAIRE M. NAYLON.

Without the insight, imagination, and support of Martina Niegel, this story would still be a held breath.

For Ryder Pierce Carroll—
where the heart begins

There lives within the very flame of love
A kind of wick or snuff that will abate it;
And nothing is at a like goodness still,
For goodness, growing to a plurisy,
Dies in his own too much . . .

—Shakespeare, Hamlet,
Act 4, Scene 7, 113–17

Isn't that a large shadow on the road
running parallel to us or our dream?
Is it loaded?

—Joseph McElroy, Women and Men

SLEEPING IN FLAME

PART ONE

STEALING HORSES

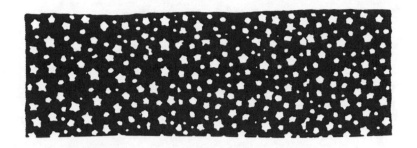

CHAPTER ONE

1.

It took me less than half a lifetime to realize that regret is one of the few guaranteed certainties. Sooner or later everything is touched by it, despite our naive and senseless hope that just this time we will be spared its cold hand on our heart.

The day after we met, Maris York told me I had saved her life. We were in a café, and she said this through the folds of a black sweater she was pulling over her head. I was glad she was lost in the middle of that pullover because the statement, although true, made me feel much too brave and adult and embarrassed. I didn't know what to answer.

"It's quite true, Walker. The next time I saw him he would have killed me."

"Maybe he just wanted to go on scaring you."

"No, he would have tried to kill me."

The voice carried no emotion. Her big hands lay open and still on the pink and blue marble table. I wondered if the stone was cold under her palms. If I had been really brave I would have covered her hand with mine. I didn't.

Every once in a while my friend Nicholas Sylvian calls, in a huff, and says he wants us to make another movie together. He's got some new moneybags lined up to finance one of the many projects we've discussed. When that happens, I usually stop what I'm doing and give him my full attention. Life with Nicholas is fun and exciting, and sometimes very peculiar. I think in our past lives we were probably related in some close and aggravating way—revolutionaries who couldn't agree on tactics, or brothers in love with the same woman. We always fight a lot when we're together, but that's only because we love the same things, despite seeing them from different angles.

This time there was a Herr Nashorn in Munich who was very interested in producing *Secret Feet*, our adaptation of an obscure short story by Henry de Montherlant to which I owned the rights. The scoop was, Herr Nashorn wanted us to fly to Munich that weekend and talk the whole idea over, courtesy of Nashorn Industries.

So at 6 A.M. on Saturday, forty-five minutes before our flight was due to leave, Nicholas picked me up in his little white delivery truck. The first time I saw that odd vehicle, I asked my friend what had possessed him to buy it.

"Because it looks like the kind of truck the Pope tours in."

When I got into the Popemobile that dark morning,

Nicholas looked at me and said, "We've got four problems. One, I don't have any gas. Two, I think I forgot my passport. Three, the radio says the traffic out to the airport is impossible. Four . . . I can't remember, but I'll think of it. Do you have any money for gas?"

There was no fourth problem, he had his passport, and we made it to the airport on time. When we were settled on the plane and had ordered coffee, he lit a cigarette and smiled to himself.

"Listen to me, Walker. No matter what happens with this Nashorn meeting today, there's a woman in Munich I've got to call. She's an American sculptress you have to meet. You'll love her." He said no more about it for the rest of the trip, but kept the same smile on his face.

The idea excited me. I had always liked blind dates. If nothing else, it was an interesting way of discovering what people thought of you. How often do we have the chance to see what we are in a friend's eyes? On a blind date you're told "You'll love her. I think she's very much your kind of woman." And whether she is or not, you end the evening knowing something new: As far as this friend is concerned, you're the "sexy blond" type. Or a "smoky brunette who has to be convinced" kind of guy.

My wife and I met on a blind date and that date led to seven good years together. In the end we separated after both of us spent time in other people's beds for greedy, bad reasons, and even worse results. The divorce consisted of two raw, mean people saying sordid half-truths about each other.

Why did things go wrong? Perhaps because wonderful as it can sometimes be, you can be sure marriage is at all times a quirky, difficult thing to maintain. In certain ways, it is very much like the solid gold family heirloom watch your father gives you for graduation. You love looking at it and owning it, but it isn't like the twenty-dollar liquid-crystal thing made of plastic and rubber that needs no maintenance to keep perfect time.

Every day you have to wind the gold beauty to make it run right, and you have to keep setting it, and you have to take it to the jeweler to be cleaned. . . . It *is* lovely and rare and valuable, but the rubber watch keeps better time with no work at all. The problem with twenty-dollar watches is that they all suddenly stop dead at some point. All you can do then is throw them away and buy another.

I realized this after my marriage wound down and stopped. It made me feel stupid and bitterly sad, but by then things were way beyond fixing, and neither of us wanted to see the other again.

My wife Victoria (a name I still say slowly and carefully) remained in the United States after our divorce and entered graduate school. I am sure she is a serious, diligent student.

The worst part of being alone was memories often cornered me and wouldn't let me get away. A pumpkin-colored coat in a women's boutique froze me in front of the store window, remembering a meal with Victoria in Cyprus where most of the things on the table were that same Halloween orange. Or waking with a fierce cold, and the first thing you think of is, the last time I had one this bad, someone right here was genuinely worried about how high my temperature was.

In the year after the divorce, I returned to Europe and wrote two good screenplays for films that had only an outside chance of ever being made. But that wasn't bad because the work kept me busy and eager to see what the final drafts would look like.

There are long quiet periods in life that are very much like waiting for a bus on a nice day. You don't mind being there so much because the weather is sunny and nice, and you're in no hurry. But after a while you start looking at your watch because there *are* more interesting things you could be doing, and it really is time the bus came.

Maris just read these pages, and indignantly said I hadn't once mentioned where all of this happened. I told her I was going to get around to that; I had been saving Vienna for a place in our story where I would be able to describe it in the roundabout, leisurely way it deserves. But since there is less and less time now, perhaps she is right.

Victoria and I had come to Vienna eight years before, newly married, full of zip, curiosity, and enthusiastic love for each other. I was acting in a low-budget spy movie being filmed there. I'd gotten the role because I have the looks of a vaguely sinister pretty boy. In my short acting career, I'd played a cowardly Nazi soldier, a show-off baseball player, an arrogant college student, and a mad killer in a Hawaiian shirt. The Vienna role, which turned out to be one of my last, was that of a golden boy–Ivy League diplomat in the American Embassy who just happened to be a Russian spy.

One of the first things that struck me about Vienna was the funny-sounding street names: Schulz-Strassnitzkigasse, Ottakringer Strasse, Adalbert Stifter Strasse, Blutgasse. Usually you took a big breath before saying one of these names so you wouldn't run out of air halfway through the pronunciation.

Everything was clean and gray and too heavy with history. Round a corner, and there would be a white plaque on the side of some building describing Schubert's birth here, Freud's office there.

American cities shrug at their brief histories. There are few signs of pride in past tenants or events, notwithstanding the kitschy Disneyland atmosphere of places like "Colonial

Williamsburg." It is as if the places are saying no, we're not so old, but who cares? Look how far we have come. Look what we've got *now*.

Like so many European cities, Vienna has an old heart and is arrogantly proud of its long, confused life. Its art school rejected the candidacy of young Adolf Hitler. Yet some years later, the Viennese greeted him with delighted fervor in one of their most revered places, Heldenplatz (Heroes Square), a few days after he had invaded their country. In the first years of his life, Mozart blossomed fully in Vienna into the exquisite short-lived orchid he was. Then, only a couple of decades later, he died there and was dumped into a paupers' grave somewhere outside the city walls. They're still not sure where.

Because so many old people live there, the city's personality is a reflection of theirs: careful, suspicious, orderly, conservative. It is a town where you needn't be afraid, where taking a walk is still a great visual pleasure, where real cream is used in the cafés.

Victoria and I had never been to Europe together, so being in Vienna in those first days of our marriage was one long adrenaline rush to wonder.

Nicholas Sylvian was the director of the film, and our friendship began quickly when we discovered how similar our tastes were.

When shooting for the day was over, we often went together to the Café Zartl where we talked about rock and roll, how both of us had at one time wanted to be painters, and only as an end-of-the-evening subject, how to make our movie better than it was.

The producers had taken a chance on Nicholas because he was still relatively young and, until then, had never made a "big" film. But his lovely documentary about old Russians living in Vienna, *Opa Suppe (Grandfather Soup)*, had won a

Golden Bear at the Berlin Film Festival and caused a lot of talk.

Women loved Nicholas because he was completely attentive to them and seemed to promise every good trait they ever wanted in a man. But he was volatile and moody, and quick to wipe you off his list if he ever felt you weren't with him all the way.

I learned all of this in the three months it took to shoot the film. And working with Nicholas Sylvian, director, I learned I was a mediocre actor. I knew I would be able to play golden bad boys for a few more years, but that didn't matter: I didn't want to spend my life working hard to be just *okay* at what I did, no matter what it happened to be. After a time, when I felt I could trust my new friend with a few big secrets, I told Nicholas my doubts.

"No, Walker, you're not a bad actor. You've just got that perverse face up against a sunny temperature."

"You mean *temperament?*"

"Exactly. It takes a really great actor to overcome that. A man can have a baby's face and be a villain in the movies, but it's hard to be the reverse. People in the audience don't believe it. In real life it's okay, but not in the movies.

"You don't want to be an actor anyway. I keep waiting to see that script you wrote."

"How did you know about that?"

"Victoria told me. She said you're dying to show it to me, but won't because you're too afraid."

"I'm not a writer, Nicholas. As soon as I show it to you, I start pretending I am."

He shook his head and rubbed his nose at the same time. "You don't have to be Tolstoy to write a movie. You were a painter once. Writing for the movies is like giving the eyes direction. Dialog comes second in this kind of writing. Only guys like Lubitsch and Woody Allen get away with great language. If you want great words, read a book. Let me see the script tomorrow."

After I had finished my part in the film, we decided to stay in Vienna to enjoy some of a spring that had arrived in the quick, unexpected way it often does in Central Europe: two days ago sleet, today summery-slow pink clouds, and all tops down on the horse-drawn carriages.

Nicholas didn't like my screenplay, but surprisingly, *did* like the way I wrote. He said I should start another. That gave me heart to leap into another story idea I had hiding in my shadows.

Every morning I kissed my sleeping wife good-bye and, full of inspiration, marched out the door of our apartment, notebook and fountain pen ready to go.

Two blocks away was my beloved Café Stein where, after coffee strong as a stone and a fresh croissant, I would get down to work on my newest *magnus opum*. The waiters glided by in a professional hush. If I looked up and caught their eye, they'd nod approvingly at the fact I was writing in their café. They carried silver trays that caught the early sun's rays, which threw silver back against the smoke-stained walls.

Anyone who doesn't want to be an "artist" in Europe, raise your hand.

If you are very lucky, you're allowed to be in certain places during just the right season of your life: by the sea for the summer when you're seven or eight and full of the absolute need to swim until dark and exhaustion close their hands together, cupping you in between. Or in another country when there is both an exciting *now* and enough dust and scent of the past everywhere to give fall light a different, violent color, the air a mixed aroma of open flower markets, people named Zwitkovitz, a passing tram's dry electricity.

Victoria and I were very lucky. While I wrote my movie, she discovered the Wiener Werkstätte group, which resulted in her eagerly enrolling in a Viennese architecture and design course at the university.

A month, then two, came and went. Whenever we discussed leaving Europe and returning to the United States, a blank look crossed both our faces, and we either smiled or shrugged: Neither of us was ready to go, so why even talk about it?

One day a friend of Nicholas's called and sheepishly asked if I would be interested in acting in a television commercial. They would dub a German voice over mine after filming, so all I would have to do would be to smile convincingly and mouth how much I loved feeding *Frolic* to my bulldog.

Things worked out well, and I talked with a number of people on the set. A few days later one of them called and asked if I wanted another job.

For the next two years, my modeling for magazines and television commercials allowed us to continue living in Vienna. By then, both of us had made contacts all over the place. Victoria had been hired as a researcher by a professor at the School for Applied Art. In addition to modeling, I was working at an assortment of free-lance jobs, including a commissioned script for Nicholas.

Since we had first met, he had made a reputation as a smart, able director who put together good-looking highbrow films for very little money. Our spy film had been his only real shot at a big commercial success, but it had done only so-so. He worked all the time, but never on as large a scale as he wished.

Along the way, he had married a woman who designed furniture and had a last name so long and impressive that even she couldn't put all of her money in it. Unfortunately, Eva

Sylvian didn't like Victoria Easterling (and vice versa), so most of the time just Nicholas and I went out together.

He knew so many different people—opera singers, neo-Nazi politicians, a black American who owned the only Mexican restaurant in all of Austria. Nicholas wanted you to meet all of his friends. They were the greatest gift he could give: He wanted to give you to them. Some of these people became friends, others simply filled the evenings with funny lines or pompous chatter.

At first, Victoria wanted to hear all about these gatherings, but as time passed, only about who famous was there, or the juiciest morsels.

We had so many things together, Victoria and I. A life fully shared three-quarters of the time. But from the beginning, my wife and I plotted our courses on separate, albeit adjoining, maps. I don't know if that's what led to the death of our marriage, but I don't think so. Those different courses made our time together richer and more precious. When we met in the evening, it was to give each other the gift of our day, how it had opened, what it meant or had done to us.

But in the midst of one of those death-throe arguments you have at the end of a long and successful relationship, Victoria said we were guilty of having given each other too much room, too much rope, too much time away. I said that wasn't true. We were guilty of having grown lazy about things that should have been checked and rechecked all the time; adjusted quickly when we saw the gauges registering in the red zone of the heart. I am not being facile, either. Life itself is fine-tuning. Marriage, that, times two.

Life starts to go bad when irony begins. Or is it the converse? The ironies in our life began with my first lover outside marriage: a classmate of Victoria's from the university who came to our apartment one night to discuss a project they were doing together on Josef Hoffmann.

Victoria's first lover? Naturally, an actor I introduced her to, who owned a lot of Josef Hoffmann-designed furniture.

Having an affair is like trying to hide an alligator under the bed. It is much too dangerous and big to be there, it sure doesn't *fit*, and no matter how carefully you try to conceal it, some part of the beast inevitably sticks out, is seen, sends everyone running and screaming.

The last time we traveled together was to America to get a divorce. Victoria said divorce was never having to say you're sorry . . . again.

After it was over, my family urged me to stay with them in Atlanta awhile, but I used pain as my excuse to escape to Vienna: My friends were there, my work, everything. So I returned to the town as if it were an old best friend who would put its arms around me and, over drinks, listen sympathetically to my problems.

I was thirty, and that is a turning point for anyone, even those not freshly divorced and out on the track again.

Nicholas and some other nice people were wonderful. They squired me around, fed me lots of delicious meals, often called late at night to make sure I wasn't leaning too far out the window . . .

At one of those dinners, someone asked me if I knew how flamingoes got their color. I didn't. Apparently those funny, long-legged birds are not naturally that psychedelic coral pink. They're born a sort of dirty white. But from the beginning, they exist on a diet of plants rich in carotene, "a red hydrocarbon." If you are a flamingo, you turn from white to pink when you eat enough carotene.

Anyway, the image fascinated me. I kept thinking I had gone through almost a decade with Victoria, largely unaware of either our original colors or the shade our relationship had eventually turned us after all that time together.

And almost more important, what color was I then, back

in Vienna, alone? To go from a good marriage to a stranger's bed was a pretty big change from a "carotene diet." It is not only God who is in the details, it is also very much us.

It was time for me to pay attention to those details. Next time around, assuming I would be lucky enough to have another chance at a shared lifetime with someone, I would know the color of my skin (and heart!) before offering it to another.

Did that mean carrying a hand mirror with me at all times so I could see myself from every angle? No, nothing so drastic or inane. Self-examination is usually a half-hearted, spontaneous thing we do when we're either scared or bored. As a result, whatever conclusions we reach are distorted either by a clumsy urgency or a listless sigh. But in my own case, I simply wanted to be less surprised by what I did *after* I did it.

About six months after I returned to Austria, luck, like a boomerang, came flying back to me on a wide slow arc. The movie I had been commissioned to write was shot. For some unknown, delightful reason, it did great business in Italy and Spain. Its success led to another Nicholas Sylvian–Walker Easterling collaboration that happened at just the right time. I also liked the idea of this new one more, so the actual writing came much more easily. It was a romantic comedy and I was able to plug many of my own good memories into the story. Another time, those memories would have left me feeling blue and failed. But integrating them into a film world that ended happily, with a long kiss and a fortune in the pocket of the lovers was the best way to relive that part of the recent past.

The film was never made, but it led to another producer, another script, and a basic assurance that, for the time being, I would be able to rely on the writing profession to keep me going.

I bought a small, sunny apartment on Bennogasse, two black leather chairs that looked like matching pistols, and a blind cat from the *Tierheim* that somewhere had picked up the mysterious name Orlando. He came when I called and spent the first week in my new home walking carefully through the rooms like an astronaut just landed on a new planet. He was the salt-and-pepper gray of week-old snow, and spent most of his day asleep on top of an old baseball glove I kept on the edge of my desk. Orlando's greatest, his only, trick was knowing when the telephone was going to ring before it did. If he was asleep on the desk, a few seconds before the call came he would lift his head suddenly and move it left and right, as if a fly were somewhere in his neighborhood. Then, *ring!* I liked to think that being both a cat *and* blind made him privy to certain small cosmic secrets. But the longer we lived together, his early-warning telephone look appeared to be his only talent in that direction.

I also tried to make the days more orderly and worthwhile. Wake up, exercise, eat, write, go for a long walk. . . . In certain ways I felt like a lucky survivor; someone just out of the hospital after a dangerous operation or terrible illness.

A direct result of all this reshuffling and reappraisal was that, despite meeting a number of attractive and interesting women, I did not want to get involved in any kind of relationship then, not even just to "fool around." Sex with new faces held little appeal in those days, although that had been one of the prime causes of my dead marriage. There were so many other things that needed to be sorted out and understood before I visited the Land of Ladies again.

Four months later I was married again.

2.

The whole ride in from the Munich airport Nicholas talked about the woman he wanted me to meet. It was characteristic though, because whatever Nicholas liked, he liked whole-heart-edly and described in glowing, mountainous terms.

"Do you know Ovo, the fashion photographer?"

"Sure, he's the guy who does models parachuting out of planes in ball gowns, doesn't he?"

"That's right. Maris York was his main model for two years. You'll know her face when you see it, I'm sure."

"Is she beautiful?"

He frowned, hesitated before answering. "Beautiful? I don't know about that. She is six feet tall, has hair as short as yours, and brown eyes that are a miracle. But no, she's not what most people would call beautiful. But she's the kind of woman you see someplace and wish you were going to spend the rest of your life with."

I laughed and nodded to show I was impressed. He wasn't finished.

"She drives an old Renault R4 with no heater and the radio is always broken. The wires stick out of the dashboard. You love her even more for that car."

"Have you ever been together with her?"

He looked at me as if I had said something terrible.

"Hell no! It would be like blowing out the candles on a birthday cake."

"What is that supposed to mean?"

"Walker, some people you touch and some you dream about."

Herr Nashorn looked like a goldfish in aviator glasses. We had coffee and cake in his office and talked about films we'd all enjoyed. It was get-acquainted chatter, and we were all waiting to see who would be the first to mention our project.

In the middle of the gabbing, Nicholas stood up abruptly

and asked if he could make a telephone call. He winked at me, and started dialing from a phone in the corner of the office.

While he called, Nashorn began talking to me, so I couldn't really hear what my friend was saying. But when he reached her, his voice went low and sexy, and his face was truly happy.

"Herr Nashorn, where are we eating lunch, and at what time?"

"The *Vier Jahreszeiten*, I guess. About two o'clock."

"Good." Nicholas held the receiver up and pointed to it. "Do you mind if I bring a guest?"

We waited half an hour before ordering. She didn't show up. The food came, we ate and talked, she didn't show up. Nicholas went twice to look for her, but came back both times shaking his head.

"It's not like Maris to do this, damn it. I wonder if something is wrong. It has me worried."

"Did you call her?"

"Yes, but there was no answer."

After lunch we went back to the office and spent the afternoon talking, but Nicholas was clearly preoccupied with his friend and not much help selling our picture. Every half hour he got up to call again. Nashorn didn't like these interruptions one bit. He kept shooting exasperated, annoyed looks at one or another of his associates every time Nicholas excused himself to go to the phone.

I did what I could to keep the ball rolling, describing wonderful scenes I already had in mind to write, suggesting actors I thought would be right for the different roles. Whenever someone made a suggestion or comment, I listened carefully and even pretended to take notes.

Someone said you should never be a housepainter because

others all think they know how to do it and, as a result, will always be telling you how to do it better. The same is true with making movies. Some of the things said in the meeting that afternoon were so dumb and off-base that I frequently had to gulp to keep my exasperation down.

Fortunately, Nashorn was very interested in making a movie, and despite Nicholas's strange behavior, our meeting ended with the boss of Nashorn Industries smiling and actually rubbing his hands together.

"This kind of work is what I like. Lay the plans and then get going. I think we can pull something together here, Mr. Sylvian. And Mr. Easterling, you have the right ideas for the screenplay: clever, funny, and sexy. Don't forget those sexy parts though—that's what makes people like me go to the movies!"

Everyone shook hands, backs were patted, and finally we were out on the street in an adamant winter rain before either of us spoke again.

" 'Don't forget the sexy parts!' Nicholas, are we really going to have to work with that dope?"

"He's just an asshole, Walker. Don't worry about him. We'll take his big money and make our own film. Come on, I've got to find a phone. I want to try her one more time before we go to the airport. What time is the flight?"

I looked at my watch. "A little under two hours."

We walked some blocks in the rain before spying the ghostly yellow block of a lit phone booth. While Nicholas called, I stood outside and tried to shield myself from the mean, icy drops that were coming down like ball bearings.

He reached her and gave me a big thumbs up. But he spoke only a few words before shouting "He did *what?*" and slamming his hand hard against one of the walls. The booth shook.

With the phone to his ear he looked at me and said, "The fucking guy tried to kill her!"

I didn't know which fucking guy he was talking about, but assumed he meant the man she was living with.

"He killed me" is one of the more overused phrases of our already hyperbolic times. As a result, it has lost most of its punch. People use it to say "killed" in business, in bed, on the golf course. I've learned not to pay attention when people use it, but the look on Nicholas's face behind the wet glass said there was no fooling around here.

He spoke for a short time into the receiver, looking at me while he mumbled and nodded and tightened his lips repeatedly. Suddenly, he hung up with a bang and came out.

"We've got to meet her at the Käfer. She'll be there in twenty minutes."

The streets were jammed with five o'clock traffic but we found a taxi. It was a brand-new Mercedes full of that great mystical new-car smell.

"Do you want to talk about it?"

He nodded. "She's been living with a French guy for about a year. Luc something. He thinks he's a director, but the only films he's ever made have been industrial shit about how to work a computer or a storm window. I don't know where she got him, but I never liked him. He's about five feet five, spends most of his time lying around home complaining, and walks around in T-shirts in winter so you'll see his muscles. A real weekend Rambo, you know?

"Anyway, she got smart about two months ago and threw him out of her house. Since then he's been following her everywhere she goes. Stands outside her apartment all night, shows up in every restaurant she goes to, calls her up and threatens her—"

"Threatens her? How?"

"Hey, listen, a couple of days ago he broke into her place and tried to rape her! Tore off her clothes and threatened to stab her with a pair of scissors if she didn't come across. Jesus Christ, she's such a sweet woman. Wait till you meet her. How could somebody do that? She was able to talk him out of it, but then today he grabbed her on the street and started hitting her in the face. Said *no one* ever left him. Can you believe it?"

"I can believe it if he's a madman. How did she stop him?"

"Started screaming. Luckily, a couple of cops showed up. He ran away! *Ran away.* The guy is forty years old and he runs away! But when she went back to her apartment, he called her and said he was going to get her, no matter what she did."

Nicholas patted my knee and shook his head. "A nice man to get involved with, huh?"

The Käfer is a Munich "in" spot of the first order. It is full of people wearing leather, jewels, or very little. During the last part of the cab ride Nicholas cheered up some, and was smiling again as we went through the door of the restaurant.

It felt as if all the people there were waiting: for their date, for the right moment, for whatever they felt was their due. I have always felt uncomfortable in places like that, places where no one tastes the expensive food or drink because they are too busy watching the door to see who comes in. I was thinking about that as we made our way across the room to a staircase leading to the bar.

As we were about to start climbing, Nicholas turned to me and said something exciting, but which later turned out to be eerily prophetic.

"Walker, now you are going to fall in love with a unique

woman." He said no more and moved up the stairs. I followed, curious as hell.

The bar was small and crowded. People were making lots of noise, drowning each other out. Watching the action and looking for a unique woman, I lost sight of Nicholas, who had drifted off to the left somewhere. It was very hot in there, and I decided to check my coat at the stand on my right. Moving toward it, I had to go around a high metal table that was there for people who couldn't find space at the bar.

Standing at that table was a very tall woman dressed all in black except for a round red velvet hat that looked like something a bellboy would wear. The first thing that entered my mind was how wonderful it would be if she were waiting for me. Her face was cloud white, her eyes dark, large, and memorable. The funny hat was pushed forward and down tight on her head, but thick eyebrows said she had black or very dark hair. She was smoking an unfiltered cigarette. When her eyes saw me they were indifferent. This woman definitely *wasn't* waiting for me. I tried to hold those eyes with mine, but she suddenly saw something over my shoulder that made every feature on her face brighten.

Someone put his hands on my shoulders from behind and I felt myself pushed toward her.

"Nicholas!"

"Hello there!"

They embraced and I watched her pull him in with a giant bearhug. So what? *This* woman was Maris York. Sometimes life hands you a big tip.

"I am so glad to see you."

"Me too, pal. Maris, this is my friend Walker Easterling."

She continued to hold his arm while we shook hands. She gave me a good shake: strong, totally there.

"It's good to meet you, Walker. It was so nice of you to come."

It astounded me how poised and happy she looked. A couple of hours ago she had been attacked, but now she stood there like the unruffled hostess at a diplomatic cocktail party.

"Hey, what's that?" Nicholas pointed to a dark mark below her right ear.

"A souvenir from Luc. I think my jaw is going to be a hell of a sight tomorrow. I'll look like a boxer who lost."

"Wait a minute. Let me get some wine and then we can talk about everything." He walked to the bar. Maris watched him closely. When she turned to me she was crying and smiling at the same time.

"Please excuse me, Walker. I just—" She put a hand to her eyes and brusquely rubbed tears away. "It's so good to see you two. After Nicholas called this morning I was so happy. Then this stupid thing had to happen." She rubbed her eyes again. "I was really lost today. I thought I was going to drown."

"Are you all right now?"

"I want to be all right, but I'm still pretty bad. I wish we could have met under different conditions."

Nicholas came back with a large bottle of white wine and three glasses. "So, have the police caught him yet?" He handed her a glass with wine to the top.

"No, and I don't think they will, either. If I know him, he's on his way to France by now. He's been in trouble with the police before. Whenever something bad happens, Luc zips back to Paris. He's got family there. At heart he's a big scaredy-cat."

That did it. That she should call the man (monster?) who'd so recently tried to kill her a "scaredy-cat" made me love her. Believe me, it was that simple.

The keys that unlock the heart are made of funny materials: a disarming phrase that comes out of the blue, nowhere, a certain sexy walk that sends you reeling, the way someone hums when she is alone. My father said it was the way my mother danced with him.

Nicholas and Maris continued talking while I stared at her and tried to figure out what to do. When I tuned back to their conversation, he was asking what she was going to do.

"Stay with a friend. I want to leave town as soon as possible because I don't know when he'll be back. I don't know where to go yet, so I'll have to figure that out first."

"Do you want some money?"

She reached over and touched his cheek. "No, but thank you for offering. When I was home I took all of my cash and checks and passport, just in case. I'm not going back to that apartment. I'll call my friend Heidi and have her move my things to a warehouse, or something. Wherever Luc is, he won't leave me alone anymore. I didn't tell you a lot of the things that have happened. I used to think he was just angry and hurt, but he's really crazy, Nicholas."

"Why don't we take you with us to Vienna?"

I said that.

Both of them looked at me with the same expression: Huh?

Nicholas drank some wine, then looked at his watch. "He's absolutely right. Let's go, Maris. We've got forty-five minutes."

She put a hand to her mouth. Oh! The moment before she spoke was ten years long. What the hell would I do if she said no? What would the night be like back in Vienna without her? She looked from Nicholas to me, to Nicholas again.

"I think I want to do that."

"Then do it. Let's go."

Her coat was short and black and made of some kind of satiny material. I watched her pull it around her shoulders as we got ready to go. She turned and looked at me.

"Is this crazy? Should I do it?"

"I guess it's no crazier than anything else today, you know? Does Luc know you're friends with Nicholas?"

"Oh yes, but he'd never expect me to go to Vienna on the spur of the moment like this. It's not my style; I'm not usually very spontaneous."

"Then you're all set."

She took a deep breath and nodded, more to herself than to me. "Yes, you're right. Thank you."

Nicholas took her arm and started for the stairs. I followed, wondering what part God or fate or luck played in this script. There was still a fear around my heart that she would suddenly stop and say she couldn't possibly go. Maybe without thinking I walked behind them on purpose, to catch her if she began to fall back into uncertainty, or ran up hard against the wall of risk she was facing.

A few weeks later I asked Maris what she was thinking that night as we walked out of the restaurant. She gave a strange answer.

"I was thinking about a woman I know who entered contests. For years she clipped coupons and filled out forms, did all those things you do to enter contests. A real fan. Well, one day she won. Won first prize. It was a three-day trip across Colorado in a hot air balloon. Gourmet picnics, see the mountains from up high, the works. Nice, huh? The day she was to go up, she had to meet the balloon in a big field somewhere that bordered a national forest. When she arrived, there were all kinds of cameramen and TV reporters there to record the festivities. She loved that because she's kind of a ham. So now the prize was even better than she'd hoped. How many times does that happen in life? First, she'd won the contest, then she was going to be on the six o'clock news. Everything was *wunderbar*.

"There were four people in the balloon, and once they were all on board, the thing took off. The television cameras were rolling, everyone was shouting good-bye and waving, the pilot had broken out a bottle of champagne. . . . Then the balloon caught on fire. Don't ask me how. The whole thing just went right up, *swoosh!* They were about two hundred feet in the air. No, that's too much, but they were very high, according to her. The balloon started disintegrating and dropping pieces of burning canvas on them.

"My friend and two of the other people panicked and jumped right over the side. Those other two were killed as soon as they hit the ground, but by some miracle my friend hit a tree and was slowed or deflected. She didn't die, but she spent the next three years in a hospital and walks with two canes now."

"God, what a story. But what does it have to do with the night we met?"

"That night I was wondering if flying off to Vienna so spontaneously was going to be like my friend jumping from the balloon."

"From the frying pan into the fire?"

"No, because the fire was all around me. Luc had burned that day to the ground. I thought that even if I came down and hit like an egg in Vienna, it'd be better than going down in slow mad flames."

We drove to the Munich airport in her old red car. It was as Nicholas had described—a mess. The ashtrays were packed, the back seat sported a big rip, books were scattered everywhere. I spent most of the trip trying to read the titles by passing streetlight. I wondered if she was a slob, but I was so happy about what was going on that I didn't care. Nicholas asked her to turn on the radio, but she said it had been broken the week before. He leaned over the backseat and winked at me.

"Hey, *Kleine,* how come you never bought a nice car? You

make enough money. This thing looks like something out of *Mad Max*."

While shifting gears, she gave him a poke in the ribs. "That's not very nice. What am I supposed to do, be like you and buy a Porsche? An M.L.C.?"

He looked at me again. "What's an M.L.C.?"

"A Mid-Life Crisis car. Every man I know who drives one is either a twenty-year-old brat who got it from his daddy, or a forty-year-old who wants to have a last fling before admitting he's bald and looks silly with a gold Rolex and a teenage girl-friend."

"I'm not bald. I don't have a teenage girlfriend."

She looked at him, and although she was smiling, raised her eyebrows questioningly. "Maybe not, but you bought that car as soon as you turned forty. Don't forget, Nicholas, I was right there when you got it."

There was a kind of sexy, teasing tone to their banter that made me seriously doubt what Nicholas had said earlier about their not being lovers. Before the ride was over, she had said a number of things to him he wouldn't have allowed others to say without becoming very angry or defensive.

She drove the way she spoke: nervously, a little too fast, but clearly in control. I kept forgetting what she had already gone through that day. It was as if we three were out for a night on the town and not, in fact, helping her to flee a lunatic who had gone for her with a pair of scissors.

"I'm going to call Uschi from the airport and see if you can stay with her."

I quickly tried out three or four sentences in my head. "She can stay with me, Nicholas. It's no problem." "Hey, stay at my apartment, Maris. I'll bunk out on the couch if you don't mind sleeping with a cat." I tried several and then wisely de-cided to keep my trap shut.

At the Munich airport she put the car in a long-term

parking slot and we scampered through the fast-moving traffic to the main terminal. It was nine at night and there were few people in the building. While Maris bought her ticket, Nicholas went off to find a telephone. I stood far back from the ticket booth, not sure if she wanted me nearby. When she was done she came right over.

"I haven't flown in so long. I've always hated to. It scares me right down to the bone. I usually take five Valium and sink into a dead stupor an hour before flight time. That's my way of handling it. No Valium this time."

"You don't look like the kind who'd be afraid of flying."

"Just watch my knees when we take off."

"I know! We'll sit on either side of you in the plane so you can have stereo arms to squeeze if you need to."

"You know what's so nice about this whole experience, Walker? That something so reassuring and . . . human could come out of so much bad. I thought when I went to meet Nicholas it would be for an hour and he'd make me feel a little better. Nothing more than that. But afterward I'd have to go back to being frightened and unsure of what to do next. But you've so wonderfully taken all of those decisions out of my hands. You just said 'We'll take care of you' and you have. I can't tell you how grateful I am. And you don't even know me!"

I almost couldn't look at her. "I hope I will."

It was raining when Nicholas pulled up in front of the Arrivals section in his white truck. Maris laughed loudly and clapped her hands.

"It's the Good Humor man! Where's the Porsche, in the back?"

I had forgotten there were only two bucket seats in the little truck, so Maris had to ride back to town on my lap. She kept asking if she was crushing me. It would have been fine with me if the trip had lasted a few days.

Uschi Hellinger had worked with Nicholas for many years, doing all of the costuming for his films. She was probably his best female friend, and he often referred to her as his sister. I liked her for many reasons, especially because she was always dead-honest with me, but also generous and quirky. When I returned to town after my divorce, she was one of the kind ones who had kept a loving eye on me.

She lived in an atelier in the Third District, and answered the door that night in a flannel nightgown as red as a fresh poppy. I didn't know her connection to Maris, but the two of them whooped happily when they saw each other and embraced hard. A glass table in a corner of the room had a big spread of food on it. None of us had eaten in a long time, so the next half hour was devoted to consuming everything on that table, while Uschi grilled us about what had happened in Munich.

In the middle of Sachertorte, Maris began to cry. She was exhausted and the day had finally closed down on her. I have rarely seen a person in so much obvious pain. Hunched forward, hands spread over her face, there were so many tears that they actually dripped through her fingers onto the floor. Uschi got right up and put her arms around her, their heads together in what looked like prayer, or mourning.

Nicholas looked at me and gestured with his head for us to go. We got up at the same time and went for the door. I turned there and looked back into the room. Uschi looked up, smiled briefly, and then turned her attention back to her friend.

3.

The next morning I woke to an almost total loss of memory of what had happened the day before. It was only when I was pulling on my pants that everything came back in such a Technicolor rush that I could only stand there and look blankly at the wall across the room.

I don't know why this lapse occurred, but I had a hunch. Seven hours before my mind, like the rest of my body, had also dropped all of its "clothes" on the floor before crawling wearily into bed. Overtired by all the things the day had demanded it take in, or consider, reject, memorize . . . my brain had simply had enough and wanted some empty hours to itself. And like a heavy drinker the morning after, it rose to the call of the day only because it had to.

Orlando broke through my remembrances of things past. Standing in his magenta cat box in the bathroom, he loudly announced that it was time for breakfast, since he had already finished his morning ablutions, etcetera.

I walked barefoot into the kitchen and opened him a can of something tasty. One good thing about Orlando; he wasn't a picky eater. Avocadoes or raw liver were his favorites, but he made a happy meal of almost anything I put in his bowl. He always ate very slowly, pausing sometimes between bites to think about what he was eating. If you said something to him while he was chewing, his mouth would stop moving and, blind though he was, he would look in your direction and wait for you to finish before he went on.

While preparing my own coffee and toast, I ran yesterday through my mind: backward, forward, and lots of stop-action. It reminded me of an athlete reviewing previous game movies in order to spot both his opponents' and his own weaknesses and slip-ups.

When the phone rang, I was thinking about something Maris had said to me on the plane trip home. "Today has been the kind of day that tires you out the rest of your life."

The phone had rung four times before I picked it up.

"Walker, have you called her yet?"

"No. Should I?"

"Of course! Don't you know how lonely and frightened she is?"

"Nicholas, it's nine in the morning! I don't think she's lonely and frightened yet. Listen, we talked about this, but I'm going to ask again: Is it really all right with you if I ask her out?"

"Absolutely. I know what you're thinking, but we really never went very far. Don't be paranoid before you begin."

Before I called I brushed my teeth.

"Hello, Maris? This is Walker Easterling."

"Hi! I just got back five minutes ago. I went out and bought everything I need to camp out here indefinitely: a toothbrush, soap, and mascara. I even went to a toy store and bought a couple of LEGO sets."

"LEGO? What do you do with that?"

"Didn't Nicholas tell you? That's what I work with. I do LEGO constructions. I build cities with them. LEGO, balsa wood, sometimes papier-mâché. I'll show you sometime. I build my own cities for a living and people actually buy them."

"Do you show in galleries?"

"Oh yes. I had a big one in Bremen a while ago; sold almost everything. It made me so happy and lazy that I didn't do anything for two months. Then I realized I had run out of money and it was time to start working again. Unfortunately, that's when Luc started in on me."

"Maris, do you have any free time today? Can I treat you to a coffee or lunch?"

"I was going to ask you the same thing."

"Really? Do you think we could do it now? I waited breakfast, hoping you'd say you were hungry."

We met a half hour later on the Graben. One of Vienna's main walking streets, it is always a nice place to be, full of relaxed strollers, outdoor cafés, chic stores. I arrived early and, on impulse, walked into the Godiva candy store and bought Maris two chocolate golf balls.

As I was coming out, I saw her bustling down the street toward Saint Stephen's Church, our designated meeting place. I watched her for a moment. An idea struck me, and I moved fast to catch up. When I was about ten feet behind her I slowed, wanting to see other people's reactions to this tall woman in a red hat.

I wasn't disappointed. Men watched admiringly, women gave two looks: the first of recognition, the second a quick up-and-down appraisal to see what she was wearing, or what she'd done with her makeup or clothes.

I touched her elbow from behind. Instantly, she touched my hand with her own before turning to face me.

"It must be Walker. Ha, it *is* you!"

"You're pretty trusting. What if it hadn't been me?"

"If it hadn't been you? It had to be you. Who else do I know on the Graben today?"

"But how can you be so trusting after all that craziness in Munich you've been through?"

"Because I want to keep trusting people. If I become scared and suspicious, then Luc really has won, even when I'm so far away from him. Where should we eat? Is the Café Diglas still alive?"

To my surprise, she was thirty-five years old, much older than she looked. Her father was one of those trouble-shooting engineers who carts his family around the world with him while supervising the building of a university in Paraguay or an airport in Saudi Arabia. There were two children in the family: Maris, and her older brother Ingram, a disc jockey in Los Angeles.

She had gone to international schools in six different countries before entering the Tyler School of Art in Philadelphia at eighteen to study painting and sculpture.

"But the school and I were like oil and water. From the beginning, I wanted to work with all kinds of crazy things like LEGO, and crayons, and those little rubber soldiers you buy in a plastic bag at the supermarket. You know the kind I mean? That's all I really wanted to do, but they didn't go for it at all. So I did the typical dumb-ass thing and quit after two years. I went to Hamburg instead because one of my greatest heroes lived there—Horst Janssen, the painter. I figured that if he lived there, then that would be my starting point. I went one summer and stayed. Took jobs in bars and restaurants, whatever I could find. I learned how to speak good German by taking orders and having to tell people how much their bills were.

"I was working in a bar called Il Giardino, which was where all of the models and photographers in Hamburg hung out after work. Right in the middle of our busiest time, around eleven-thirty one night, a man came up and asked me to hold a bouquet of white roses. Actually, he didn't ask, he just sort of handed them to me and walked away. I had a giant tray of empty glasses in one hand and suddenly all these beautiful flowers in the other. I didn't know which to put down, so I stood in the middle of the floor and started laughing.

"The man came back with a camera and started taking pictures of me. I hammed it up and posed like Betty Grable, or as best I could with all the glasses and flowers! When the guy was done, he handed me a card and told me to come to see him the next day. It was the photographer Ovo. You've heard of him, haven't you? Well, the most shocking thing was, I discovered the next day Ovo was a woman! When I got to the studio, there she was right in the middle of all her assistants and models, and it was so obvious she was a woman . . . I felt terrible for ever having thought otherwise!"

Maris went on talking about her modeling career, about three months spent in Egypt, about living with a famous German opera singer. There were enough experiences and adventures for three separate lives. Her thirty-five years were so full and consummately interesting that it struck me, more than once, that she might be lying. I had known great liars before and had enjoyed their tales. But if this were true about Maris York, then it was both heartbreaking and dangerous. Had her Luc attacked her the day before because she was a beautiful psychopath who couldn't distinguish between what was and what she wanted things to be? Even worse, had this Luc even attacked her in the first place?

Proof came in a sexy way. While talking about life with her opera singer, she casually mentioned that he had asked her to prove her love for him in a bizarre way: He wanted her to be tattooed on the small of her back with a single musical note. She said she'd asked him which note, and then gone right out and done it.

Nervously, I asked if I could see it. She smiled at me, but it wasn't a particularly friendly smile. "Are you a music lover, or do you just want proof?"

"Maris, your life sounds like a nine-hundred-page Russian novel. It's all just too much. I mean—"

Before I finished, she leaned forward and jerked her black

sweater up and over her head. She was wearing a white T-shirt underneath, and this she rucked up just a little to show her back. And there it was—one bright purple musical note against the white smoothness of skin.

A long silence followed between us for the first time that morning. I thought it was because she was angry at me for doubting what she had said. She began to put the sweater back on, at the same time saying, "You know, you saved my life yesterday."

I didn't know what to answer.

"It's quite true, Walker. The next time I saw him, he would have killed me."

She knew Vienna because she had often come with her opera singer when he performed at the State Opera. On one of those visits she'd met Nicholas and Uschi. The three of them became close friends. After her affair with the singer died, Nicholas asked her to come back to Vienna to work as a set designer on one of his early television shows.

"He has been my lifesaver more than once, as you can see. I wish there was some way I could repay him, but he gets very grumpy when you say thanks for anything he does. Years ago, I made a city for him and filled it with characters from his movies. He liked it a lot, but that's the only thing he's let me do in return for his kindness. What a strange man. He wants you to love him, and that's so easy, but when you show it, he doesn't know how to handle it; it's a hot potato for him. Do you know the German phrase, 'You can steal horses with him'? It means a person you can both make love with all night, passionately, then wake up with the next morning and be completely silly. And he never makes you embarrassed or self-conscious about anything you do."

"That sounds like the perfect lover. Is that the way things are with you and Nicholas?"

"No, oh no. We've never touched each other. I have a little fantasy in the back of my head that maybe things would be like that if we were together, but neither of us has ever made the slightest movement in that direction. I think we dream about each other, but never want to go beyond that dream. It'd be too horrible if we tried something in real life and it was bad."

She looked sadly at her hands. "I've always loved that phrase, 'You can steal horses with him.' Do you think it's possible to find someone like that?"

"It's like Halley's Comet."

"Halley's Comet? How?"

"It comes around once every seventy-five years or so. You have to have a big telescope to see it, and be in exactly the right place."

"And you think it's that way with love?"

"Yes, genuine, twenty-four-carat love. I think it's easy to find the *ingredients* for love, but then it depends on how you mix them. There's so much work involved." I counted things off on my fingers as I cited the different points. "First you have to understand and accept. Then, you have to be best friend, always. Work on overcoming what they don't like in you. Be bighearted when it's so much easier to be small . . .

"Sometimes the spark for real love is there from the beginning. But too many people mistake that spark for a flame they think will last a long time. That's why so many human fires go out. You have to work so hard at real love."

My voice fell when I saw a big smile rise on her face. "I'm sounding like an evangelist on television."

She shook her head and touched my hand. "No, like someone who believes what he's saying. But I'm smiling because I was just thinking of God. When I was a little girl I

went through a long period when I *breathed* God and religion.
I could have posed for those religious postcards they sell in
Catholic bookstores. But my favorite thing then was to write
letters to God. I'd have long chats with Him on yellow paper.
When I'd finished one, I'd go immediately out on the balcony
of our apartment and burn the letter. I was sure it'd go right to
heaven. I worked hard at loving Him, you know? Just like what
you're describing. I'm glad you said that."

We went on talking until each of us had so much information
about the other that we tacitly agreed to stop for a while to let
it all sink in.

The day had started out overcast but decided on drizzle
by the time we left the café. It was early afternoon and I was
hungry, but since we'd just spent three hours sitting, it wasn't
the right moment to suggest a bite in a cozy restaurant. We
walked out toward the Ringstrasse.

The air smelled of wet streets and car exhaust. Maris
walked fast, taking great long strides as she moved. While trying to keep up with her, I looked down and noticed for the first
time how large her feet were. Everything about the woman was
full size, impressive.

In contrast, my ex-wife Victoria was a small woman who
prided herself on being able to buy shirts in the boys' department at Brooks Brothers. Her hands were slim and pretty; she
liked to have her hair done once a week. She often wore dark
fingernail polish to bed.

Maris was by no means raw or unfeminine in the way she
looked or carried herself, but seemed to know she was impressive "as is." She didn't need to have perfect skin or fresh eye-
liner on to stop your heart.

"You have wonderful feet."

"Thank you. They're the same size as my father's."

As soon as she said this, she saw something that suddenly made her break into a run.

About half a block down the street, a woman was hitting her child. That was bad enough, but she kept slapping him so hard that the little boy would have fallen down if she weren't holding his arm.

Maris sprinted toward them. People stopped to watch her zoom by. With no idea of what she was doing, I hesitated for a moment, then followed. When I got there, she had already grabbed the woman by the arm and was shaking her.

"Are you *crazy?* You don't hit a child like that!"

"Don't touch me! I'll call the police!"

The woman was as tall as Maris but much broader. She had a face like a month-old melon, and bulged through every seam of her clothes. The child hung limp in her hand, but his face was all fear and flutter. Something in his expression said Mama had done this before.

"Yes! Call the police! Do! I'll tell them what you're doing to that child!"

A number of people had gathered to watch. The woman looked around for support. All she saw was indifference or hard faces.

"Look at how frightened your son is! How can you *do* that?"

The boy started to cry. Without looking, the woman shook him and told him to shut up. Maris took a step toward her. A fistfight was one second away. Maris stuck a finger in the woman's thick cheek and said if she did that again, she was going to get hit.

Now, *no one* talked to this Mama that way. Looking Maris straight in the eye, she shook the child again. Maris slapped her face. The other's eyes flared, then narrowed. She kept looking at Maris while she shook the child again. Harder.

Watching the two women, I didn't see the man until he'd

stepped forward and grabbed Mama by the back of the neck. He was nondescript, middle sized, *bürgerlich.* He held the woman so tightly in one hand that she couldn't turn around to look at him when she tried. He ignored her, and spoke to Maris.

"Go away now. I'll take care of it. The kid's mine, not hers."

"Do you love him?" Maris looked at the man, then the boy.

The man nodded instantly. "Yes. He told me she did these things, but I didn't believe him. She's always nice to him when I'm around. That won't happen again, the bitch. I'll kick her fat ass if it does!" Letting go of her neck, he gave her a tremendous slap across the back of her head. It sounded like two hollow wood blocks hitting. She staggered forward, let go of the boy, fell down. The boy squealed in delight and clapped his hands.

"And you *know* I'll kick your ass, don't you?"

Maris walked quickly away, looking once over her shoulder for me. I gave one last look at the family. Papa had the boy in his arms. Mama was just getting up off the ground. Her knees were smeared with mud, and she was trying to smile at anyone who'd look. They were real George Grosz people, and it was plain this event would do little to change any of their lives. In a day, or a week, this important tension and recognition would lose its purpose in the fog of meanness and stupidity that enclosed their lives.

I went after Maris. She was walking even faster than before, hands deep in her coat pockets. When I caught up, I touched her elbow. She turned quickly.

"Why didn't you stop me, Walker?"

"Why? You were right."

"You're sure? But I hit her! It's so embarrassing."

"Of course you shouldn't have hit her, but so what?

Maybe it was time someone bopped her. Give her back some of her own medicine."

Her expression said she was unconvinced. She started walking again. "I would never hit a child. *Never.* No matter how bad it was."

I wanted to change the subject. "Do you want children?"

"Oh yes, although I'm getting a little old for it. At least two." She smiled and slowed a little. "Two girls."

"Girls? What would be their names?"

Her smile widened. "Names? I don't know. Jessica and Kenyon."

"Are you okay now about what happened back there?"

"Not really. My teeth are still chattering a little. Would you take me someplace happy? Do you know what I mean?"

I lit up at the idea. "I know exactly! There are three places I go in Vienna when I feel bad. I'll take you to all three."

We caught a tram and rode it around the Ring. Even in the rain, many people were out walking. Open horse-drawn carriages, full of sightseers, wheeled slowly down the middle of the street.

At Schottentor we got out and walked the Herrengasse into the center of town.

There are baroque palaces on the Herrengasse: the Spanish Riding School, the National Library, and the Albertina Museum. The Café Central, where Freud and Lenin drank black coffee and disturbed the universe, is one street over.

Some mornings, if you're lucky, you can see trainers leading the white and gray Lippizaner horses from their stables on one side of the street to the performance ring on the other side. The sound those hooves make on the stone pavement is indescribable.

When we passed the entrance to the Hofburg Palace and were about to go left onto the Kohlmarkt, Maris stopped and looked up at one of the statues in front of the gate. I thought she was going to say something about it or the palace, but I was wrong.

"My God, life is hard, isn't it, Walker? Did you ever play one of those computer games, like *Donkey Kong* or *Lode Runner*? They're terrible, because the better you get at them, the more adept, the harder they get and the faster they go. You never get rewarded for your achievements—more like penalized!"

"Is that an analogy to life, or are you still trying to figure out why you hit that woman?"

"Both! Yesterday Luc was hitting me, today it's me hitting someone else. Don't you want to get better at life? Learn from your mistakes, make the right decisions, not feel guilty, use your energy in a good way . . ." She shrugged and sighed. "How far are we to your first happy place?"

"Five minutes. It's a barbershop."

"Grüssgott!"

"Uh oh. The American is here!"

We walked in and sat down between an old man and a teenage boy.

The two barbers, owners of the shop, were identical gray-haired twins who forever kept up a sarcastic, funny patter with their customers. The place was Vienna's equivalent of a Norman Rockwell barbershop; talk of sports, women, and the stupidity of politicians abounded. Usually there was a group of regulars in there for nothing more than the insults and good feeling.

"Who's your pretty friend, Herr Easterling?"

How could I say we'd dropped in for a little cheering up because my new friend had just hit another woman?

But Maris winked at the barber and asked if she could have a haircut.

He was surprised, but gestured grandly toward his chair. She plopped down in it and asked for a trim.

Another man walked in, in a hurry, but stopped halfway across the floor when he saw her in the barberchair.

"That's the best-looking guy I ever saw in this damned place!"

Conversations started up again after that, and the good-hearted nastiness of men comfortable with each other returned. Maris said little but smiled the whole time. It was clear she enjoyed being there.

When the barber was finished cutting her hair he carefully brushed her off, looking thoroughly pleased with himself.

Outside again, Maris briskly rubbed her head a few times and stopped in front of a store window to check her reflection.

"They're nice in there. They all get a big kick out of each other, don't they?"

"Yes. I always come out of there feeling good."

She started walking. "I would too. What's your next happy place?"

The next was a pet shop on the Josefstädter Strasse that sold some cat and dog stuff, but also used bicycles, handmade birdhouses, and diving equipment. The owners were an old couple and a sad-eyed Saint Bernard that must have been twenty. The dog had his own full-length couch, from which he never moved. I never understood how the place survived, because no one was ever in there, and the goods for sale had the lopsided look of things that had sat in the same spot for years.

The people always asked how Orlando the cat was getting

on, so we talked about my roommate for a few minutes. But then, when things got quiet, out of desperation I bought an enormous bag of kitty litter I didn't need.

Trying to see it through Maris's eyes, first-time eyes, it was both strange-looking and sad. The store smelled of coal stove, big dog, years-long failure, and dusty everything.

She asked, "What can I buy for your cat?"

"Well, it's a little hard, because he's blind and can't really play with most toys."

She asked if they had a ball with a bell inside. The man brought out one as exhausted-looking as the dog. I hadn't the heart to tell Maris that Orlando already had one and hated it. It was beneath his dignity to chase a tinkling ball.

After that we went to lunch and watched the sky clear to blue through the windows of the restaurant. It was a quiet meal. I didn't know whether that was because of the fullness of the morning, or because somewhere along the line things had gone flat for her. Maybe that flatness was my fault, but I also kept forgetting: Literally, the day before, a man had tried to kill her.

"You know what I liked about that pet store?"

"You liked it? I thought I'd really bombed out with that 'happy place.'"

"Not at all, Walker. I liked the way they treated their dog like a pal and not a pet. I bet they don't have children. Dogs are the kids we've always wanted. They're totally devoted and want to live with you until they die. Not like children who can't wait to take off as soon as they grow up and don't need you anymore.

"You know what I've been doing for the last five years or so? Writing a daily letter to my daughter, even though she's not born yet. So she'll know what I was like when she grows up. I think it's more important than anything. Kids *have* to know who their parents are, and were."

"When would you let her read it?"

"When she is sixteen or seventeen. Old enough to understand what I was saying."

"You're crazy about children, huh? How come you've never had any?"

"Because I never met a man I loved enough to want to share that experience with. I don't care if we were married or not, or even if the relationship ended later. It's only important that at the time we decided to have the child, we were so completely involved with each other that it'd be the absolutely right thing to do."

She looked out the window and ran her hand through her new haircut. "I've been talking the whole time, haven't I?"

"I'm glad."

"I can't tell if that's good or bad. It usually takes me a long time to talk like this with a man. Especially one I just met. But maybe we didn't just meet, you know? Someone came up to me once and said 'Weren't you my wife in our last incarnation?' It was the best come-on line I'd ever heard."

"What happened to that man?"

She looked calmly at me. "It was Luc. The one who . . . hit me yesterday."

"It's four hundred steps to the top, Maris, maybe more. Then we have to walk for another fifteen minutes, straight up. Are you sure you want to do it? It really doesn't matter to me. Honestly."

We stood at the bottom of a staircase in the Thirteenth District. To our right was the Lainzer Tiergarten, a private hunting reserve of Kaiser Franz Josef in the time of the Habsburg Empire. Now it's a big, lovely park, where strange animals roam free, and you can come face to face with a family of wild boars if you're lucky. It was weeks since the park had closed for the winter. But after Maris insisted on visiting my third happy place, we drove to this far-off corner of Vienna to see . . . a field.

She looked at the steps and then at me. She let her tongue hang out as if she'd made the climb three or four times that day already. "So what's up there that's worth four hundred steps?"

"It won't sound interesting if I tell you. You have to see it for yourself."

She pulled her tongue back in. "Is it the Emerald City?"

"Better. I've never shown it to anyone. I only go there once in a while: Only when I'm either completely happy or totally sad."

"Sounds interesting. Let's go."

She started fast up the stairs, but by the halfway point I could hear her breathing hard. She finally stopped and put hands on hips. "Walker, I'm not in love with climbing four hundred stairs. How come you're not even winded?"

"I used to do a lot of mountain climbing when I first came here. One of those grizzled old guides showed me how to walk vertically."

"Teach me." She dropped her hands and gestured toward the stairs, ready to move again.

I walked ahead and spoke to her over my shoulder. "Walk more slowly than you think you should. Don't take giant steps, because that'll just tire you. Walk slow and steady, and breathe like that too: slow and steady."

"It sounds like a meditation from Bhagwan's *Orange Book.*"

I turned and mugged at her over my shoulder. She reached out and gave my jacket a friendly tug. It felt as if she'd stroked my hand: the same little electric shock that comes whenever someone important touches you the first time.

We climbed and climbed. The steps were covered with

layers of gray and brown leaves so dead they didn't even make that skittery, crackly, dead-leaf noise. Everything had gone out of them, and they were soft under our feet.

A few other people passed on the way up and, invariably, said the inevitable *"Grüssgott!"* when we passed. God's greetings. It's a small, nice piece of Austria I have always noticed and liked.

At the top of the stairs, Maris turned around for the first time and looked behind us. Above the treetops of the Tiergarten you could see wet rooftops and smoke from chimneys, slices of sun reflecting hard off windows everywhere, like flashy clues to God's whereabouts. The air had been washed clean by the rain, and we'd climbed high enough above the city for there to be totally different smells around us—pine, fresh earth that had never been out of shadow, wet plants. After the stairs came a dirt path that wound up and into a forest. Without hesitating we kept on, walking side by side. A man with a soccer ball under his arm and a Great Dane close by came marching smartly down the path. The dog looked like a silver-brown ghost in the dim light through the trees. *"Grüssgott! Are you going up to the hill?"*

"Yes, we are."

"It's wonderful there now. We've just been playing ball on the field. Only a few people around, and the view is clear all the way to Czechoslovakia." He tipped his hat and the two of them moved off down the way.

"It sounds like something special up there. You're still not going to tell me?"

"No, Maris, you have to see it. It's not that much longer now. Only a few hours." I smiled to reassure her I was kidding.

Before leaving the forest, we passed a giant antenna for O.R.F., the Austrian National Broadcasting Company. Its high, intricately worked steel and busy electrical noises were completely out of place here. She looked at it for a moment, shook her head, and moved on. "It looks like some invader from Mars sitting here, trying to decide what to do next."

Two men came out of the little office at the base of the antenna. Each had a sandwich in one hand and a beer in the other. Both stopped in midstep and midbite when they saw Maris.

"*Mahlzeit!*"

They seemed so tickled by this lovely woman in the middle of nowhere wishing them a good meal, that they grinned like the cartoon characters Max and Moritz. They tipped their bottles to her, and nodded to me their approval of my companion.

"That wouldn't be such a bad job; working up here on top of the world."

"Wait, you haven't seen anything yet."

It was another few minutes before the hill evened out into the giant open field that gave onto the most beautiful panoramic view of Vienna I knew. I'd discovered the place years before, but it was true I almost never went there. There are certain experiences in life we should hoard so we never forget to savor them when we have them.

I didn't want to look at her until the full impact of the view sank in. The late afternoon sun, perfectly round and sad yellow, had begun its slow slip to the horizon. The light at the end of a clear fall day is wise light: melancholy, able to pick out the most beautiful or important characteristics of anything it touches.

Without thinking, I said that to Maris as we stood there, and I was glad I did, but also a little embarrassed.

She turned and looked at me. "Walker, this place is superb. I can't get over how much has happened in the last twenty-four hours. I can't. Yesterday at this time I was talking to the Munich police about what Luc had done to me. I was crying, and scared to death. More scared than I've ever been.

Now, today, I'm up here on Mount Olympus, feeling comfortable with you." Her voice changed completely. "Can I say something else?"

"Sure."

"I think something is going to happen between us. The feeling is already there for me, and it's only the first day we've spent together. I don't know if you want that, though. I don't even know if I should be telling you."

I took a deep breath and licked my lips. My heart felt like a truck trying to burst out of my chest.

"Maris, the first time I saw you I thought it would be the greatest thing in the world if that woman in the red hat were waiting for me. As far as I'm concerned, something's been *happening* between us since then."

That's when we should have embraced and held each other tight. But we didn't. Instead, both of us turned away and went back to looking at Vienna below. But despite our not touching then, it was a moment I will remember the rest of my life. One of those extraordinarily rare moments when everything important is so clear, and simple, and easy to understand. It was a moment like the view of the city: perfect, tinged with a light so pure it made me sad, transient.

In the next months, we would grow so close and empathetic that she once joked she wasn't breathing air anymore, she was breathing me. All that happened, and I will tell you about it, but those minutes on top of the hill were somehow the best. They were our Eden, they were what set everything else in motion. Finally, they were what ruined us.

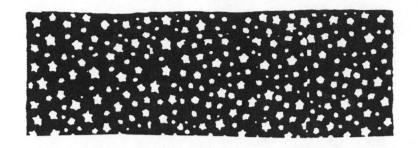

CHAPTER TWO

1.

When we were driving back downtown, Maris asked if she could see my apartment. There was nothing in her voice that said she had anything more in mind than normal curiosity. She'd been so forthright about her feelings that I didn't freeze up at the request or lick my lips like the Big Bad Wolf. She wanted to see my place, and that was that. After we got out of the car and were walking down the street, she took my hand and slipped it with her own into her pocket.

"I liked the barbershop and I loved the hill, but why did you take me to that pet shop?"

"Because the owners love being there. I sense it every

time I go in. They love the dog, they love talking to their customers, they probably love it when no one's in there but them. So few people like what they're doing these days. People don't do their job well because they hate it or are bored by it. I like to see people enjoying what they're doing with their lives. There's a bank near here I go to just to watch the teller handle money."

We were at the door to my building and I stopped us just short of it. The door was fifteen feet high and made of carved wood, a beautiful thing.

"Look at this door. Sometimes when I'm going in I stop and look at it because the guy who made it obviously did the job with love."

We walked down the long hall to the entrance to my part of the building. Then up three stairs to the ancient elevator that made so much noise ascending that I often worried whether I'd reach my floor or not. We got in and I slid the door closed, pressing the button for the fourth floor. The thing clanked, groaned, and lurched up. Maris gave me an alarmed look.

"Don't worry, it does this every time."

"That's not reassuring."

When it stopped on my floor she opened the door fast and got out faster. "That thing should have been in *The Third Man.*"

At the door to my place I fumbled with my keys, and realized I was more nervous than I'd thought. But I finally found the right one and turned it in the lock. As soon as I did, Orlando gave his normal "welcome home" meow on the other side. He must have been standing right by the door, because it hit him with a small thump when it swung open.

"Do you always greet your cat like that?"

On hearing a foreign voice in his kingdom, he stopped dead and "looked" in Maris's direction. He was a friendly fellow, as cats go, but wasn't used to other creatures (besides me) being in the house.

"Let him smell you, then he'll be okay."

He walked over and gave her the once-over sniff test. Satisfied she was neither enemy nor large mouse, he began his normal weave around and through her legs.

"Can I touch him?"

"He'd like that."

She picked him right up and gently patted his head. He didn't purr, but I could tell by the set of his empty eyes that he was content to let this happen. Holding him in her arms, she walked into the living room. I followed, feeling like a real estate agent eager for a sale. It was important that she like where I lived, liked the space and objects with which I had chosen to surround myself. Sitting down in one of my expensive chairs, she looked slowly around, checking out the room from that low altitude.

"Which of these do you sit in when you're alone?"

"The one you're in."

"I thought so. The leather has the most wrinkles. Le Corbusier was such a goof. These are the greatest-looking chairs around, but there's nowhere to put your arms. He talked about the necessity for absolute simplicity in things, then designed snazzy furniture like this that's simple, all right, and totally impractical! It's the same with his buildings."

"That's true! I'm always looking for something to do with my arms when I'm sitting there."

She put Orlando down and worked her way out of the chair. "Sure. And they cost a small fortune, too. Do you have any pictures of your family?"

Nodding, I went to my desk and took out a large envelope filled with photographs. I felt a little exposed handing it over, though, because of the pictures of Victoria in there, the pictures of Victoria and me clowning for the camera, the pictures of me in costume for movies and ads I'd done. Besides the wrinkles on my face and personality, those shots were really the only concrete remnant, proof, to Maris York of my last few years. There was a pullover in the closet bought on a trip to Paris with my former wife, spoons in a kitchen drawer we'd chosen together at the Vienna flea market. But Maris didn't know that. Besides these photographs, she would only know Victoria, or my past, through my stories, but those were so shadowed and colored by my biases, secrets, and hurts . . .

"Is this Victoria?"

"Yes."

"She looks a lot like I thought. Your description was good."

She saw my parents, their house in Atlanta, my stepsister, Kitty, in the kitchen making brownies.

"Did you ever read anything about handwriting analysis?" She was holding a snapshot of me at the age of ten in a Little League uniform. I shook my head.

"The most interesting thing about it is that experts say you can never tell people's personality via handwriting until you've read five pages of their script. There are certain big companies that give a test when you apply for a job where you're required to write longhand for five pages. Then they give only the fifth page to a graphologist or psychologist and get their opinion. I think it's the same with a person's picture album. You've got to look at the whole bunch before coming to any conclusions. Right now I'm thinking 'How come he doesn't talk much about his family? Why does he only have a couple of pictures of his stepsister?' Things like that. But I know I have to go through all of them and see what they're of before I can get any clear idea of you."

"Would you like a drink?"

I must have said it in a strange voice, because she looked up quickly. "Are you angry, Walker?"

Looking at the floor, I shook my head. "It's funny how you can be thirty years old and still embarrassed about things that happened when you were young. Things you didn't have anything to do with, but they still have their hooks in you.

"I was adopted, Maris. I was found in a garbage can outside a restaurant in Atlanta. A bum discovered me while looking for dinner one night. He's the closest I ever got to who my real parents were. But by the time I found out his name and where he lived, he'd been dead for years."

An expression of pain and great wonder spread across her face. "Is that true?"

"That is true. I have a great family. I love all of them very much, but I have no idea who the real ones were. And you want to know something? Victoria always believed that's why I became an actor: so one day my real parents would see me up there on the screen and know their son. I don't know how they'd recognize me after thirty years, but she was sure that was one of the reasons why I worked so hard at succeeding in the business."

She came over and took my hand. "And that embarrasses you? It's like a German *Märchen!*"

"If it were a fairy tale it'd be all right, but it's a real life, Maris. *My* life!"

"It is not. It's the beginning of a life. What you've done since then is what matters. Look at all those people who were born with everything, but then muck it up completely. They're the ones who should feel guilty. From what little I've seen and you've told me, you're a decent man with a good supply of perception and sensitivity."

"And my divorce?"

"Don't be silly. Something like 50 percent of adult Americans have been divorced at least once. How did it happen?"

"We cheated on each other too many times."

"That's not so nice, but it's one of the dangers of living

today. Everything is open and easy, and you don't have to put much time in to get all those exciting things our parents told us came only after hard work and a lot of real love. I think our generation is still getting used to the fact that sex has been relegated from the main course to an appetizer on the menu. It's too bad, but it is. We just have to accept that and move on."

"But you said you're interested in me. Doesn't my being divorced make you skeptical about my staying power?"

She walked over and put her hands on my shoulders. "I'm skeptical, I'm scared, I'm excited. You don't get killed one day and then fall for someone the next. But that's what's happened, isn't it, Walker? What can I do, put on a crash helmet and duck?"

I leaned forward and just barely kissed her lips. She kissed back, but then her body began to tremble all over. Her mouth moved into a smile beneath my own.

"I'm sorry I'm shaking. It's been so long since I did this. It's been so long since I *wanted* to kiss someone."

I took her full into my arms and stopped the words with a real kiss. Her fingertips pushed on my shoulder blades. I could feel her breasts against my chest. I ran my tongue slowly down the line of her jaw to her throat. She shook harder, flattened both hands against my back. Her throat was soft and warm. When she swallowed, I felt her Adam's apple move beneath my tongue. She smelled of hours-old perfume and a human heat that made me want to shove my hands under her clothes, touch the skin it cooked from. Our kissing became less tender, more bold and wet. She kept shaking, but it was all one with our moving then, so I ignored it.

I turned her so her back was to me. Kissing ears and hair, I slipped both hands under her sweater and ran them slowly up a slim rib cage to her breasts. She put her hands over mine, not so much to stop as join them on their first, tentative move across her body. Surprisingly, she began to hum. It got louder the longer I touched her. Then she sang in a quiet, deep voice, " 'Now is that gratitude, or is it really love?' "

"Is this passion, or are you giving a concert?"

She turned and faced me, smiling. "Do you know the rock group, Oingo Boingo? That's their song. It's exactly how I feel right now. What you're doing makes me so hot. Is that because it feels good, or because *you're* doing it?"

"Both, hopefully." I started pulling her sweater up and off. As soon as it was off and tossed on the floor, the quaking of her body increased. Looking me in the eye, she quickly shrugged off her undershirt. She wore no bra. Her breasts were large and I wanted to kiss them. But bared so quickly, I was suddenly afraid even to touch them. They didn't seem the same ones I'd held in my hands an instant before, when her black sweater and white shirt acted as stern chaperones.

Sitting down on the floor, she untied her shoes and took them off. "Come sit here with me."

As soon as I did, she started unbuttoning her pants. But before she could go further, I pressed her gently back onto the floor. The carpet was dark brown. It lit up her pale skin like a lamp. She smiled at me, put her arms up, and wiggled her fingers.

"Come hug me."

2.

Several hours later, Nicholas Sylvian called.

"Walker, where's Maris?"

"Right here, Nicholas. What's the matter?"

"Good. Her asshole boyfriend Luc just called me. Said he knew she was in Vienna and wanted to know how to reach her."

"Christ! What'd you tell him?"

"I told him to fuck a bird. I don't know anything about where she is. Do you?"

"What'd he say to that?" Maris slid closer to me in bed. I turned the receiver so she could hear, too.

"That's the problem. He said he was coming to town tonight to find her. Called me a shithead, and said if I didn't tell him where she was, he was going to *get* me!" He laughed. I heard him light a cigarette and blow out smoke.

"Where will he look?"

"I don't know. In the phonebook? Who cares. I just wanted to tell you what was happening. How is our beautiful friend?"

Maris took the phone from me. "Nicholas, don't be so cool about this! Luc's crazy, and stupid enough to really try something bad. Maybe he'll do something to your family."

"Maris, remember that movie, *Babyskin,* I made with Weber Gregston as his assistant? When it was over, he gave me a Colt Python pistol as a present. A crazy but very sweet *Geschenk.* If the little Frenchman comes, I'll shake it at him and tell him to go away."

She hit her head, exasperated. "You idiot! And what if he goes to your house when you're not there? Have you thought about that?"

"Yes, I have. Just enjoy yourself and stay close to Walker now. Let me talk to him again, please."

"I'm here, Nicholas. But she's got a good point, if he is as nuts as she says."

"Did I ever introduce you to Goldstar? The meanest man I ever met. European boxing champion years ago, but now he works as a stunt man. Looks like Gorbachev. He's at my house now and he'll stay there a couple of days. If Rambo comes, he'll have to shake hands with Goldie before he gets in. Everything is taken care of, believe me.

"You want to go to dinner tonight? I made a reservation at Frascati for nine o'clock. Let's go eat some scampi, huh?

"Maris, if you're still there, stop listening."

Shaking her head, she rolled to the other side of the bed and started petting Orlando, who was perched on a pillow.

"Is she okay, Walker?"

"She's fine. We had a great day together."

"That's good. Let's finish it with a good meal."

Ristorante Frascati was one of the few gifts I'd ever been able to give Nicholas that he didn't frown about. The décor was a mixture of bad paintings of Venetian scenes and uncomfortable chairs. But the food was the best Italian in town, so it had become one of his regular hangouts.

Maris and I arrived a few minutes early and were chatting tiredly when he breezed in. Nicholas Sylvian was a celebrity in Vienna. When he entered a restaurant there was much fawning by waiters, whispers, and subtle pointing by pretty women and jealous men as he made his way across a room.

"I've already ordered a hundred scampi and two bottles of Orvieto for me. Maris, you look much happier today. Did you meet his cat? Only Walker would *buy* a fucking blind cat!"

He looked around the room to see if he knew anyone. The artist Hrdlicka was sitting in a corner with a group of people. When he saw Nicholas, he made a funny face and tipped his glass our way.

Nicholas waved back. "I just bought a bronze figure from Hrdlicka that cost as much as a house. It'll take five men to put it in my living room. Then I'll never be able to get it out of there again. The greatest piece you ever saw, so I had to have it. End of discussion. Where's the wine?"

"Did you hear anything more from Luc?"

"Nothing. He's just playing macho. What did you two do today?"

Maris told him about everything except her confrontation with the woman, and our time in my apartment. He watched closely and seemed to enjoy her company thoroughly. Her earlier fatigue disappeared and was replaced by a happy vibrancy and animated gestures.

Again it struck me that they had an important history together that I wasn't any part of. Fall hard in love, and immediately you want to know everything about them. Whom did they love most before and why, what things delight them, where do you fit into their soul . . . Nicholas was probably the best friend I had. He'd helped me survive some of the worst days I'd known when stumbling through my divorce and after. But in the restaurant that night he was a worry: a strong, fascinating man, who knew much more about this woman than I did. If we'd been alone, I'd have asked him questions about her I was hesitant to ask Maris directly. In bed, earlier, she'd told me many intimate things that showed she was willing to enter into a lovers' trust with me. But which of those intimate details did Nicholas know, too? Both said separately they'd never had an affair. Yet despite those assertions, certain looks crossed the table between them that were as thick and voluptuous as whipped cream. Paranoia often rides into town right behind love and makes a beeline for all the same soft spots. Nicholas had "given" me Maris, and I felt enormous gratitude, but that was a long yesterday ago. Today I had to be the only one she wanted to steal horses with.

"Have you decided what you're going to do yet?"

"I think I'd better stay here awhile and think the whole thing over. You know?"

"I spoke with Uschi. She said you could stay with her as long as you like."

"That's kind of her. But I want to find an apartment as soon as I can. Do you know of any place?"

He shrugged. "Not right now, but I'll ask around. There's always something. What about all your things in Munich? Are you going to get them?"

"Yes, but not soon. I know Luc will watch my house for a while if he's still there. So I'll wait a few weeks and go back in the middle of the night or something with a truck. Maybe I'll ask your friend Goldstar to go with me."

She got up to go to the bathroom, touching Nicholas on the shoulder as she passed. When she was gone, he pointed his fork at me and squinted.

"All right, tell me everything."

"She's the best."

"Did she calm down? Is she all right?"

"I think so. Hearing Luc might come made her nervous, but generally, she's okay."

"You've got to take care of her, Walker. Promise me you'll do it."

"That's easy. I haven't felt so good with a woman in a long time. It's really been a happy day."

"I noticed! When I came in, you two looked like little birds in a Walt Disney movie. You know, where they put their heads together and thousands of red hearts come rushing out?

"Did she tell you about the cities she builds? They're amazing. Like nothing you've ever seen. Someone in Hollywood saw her show in Hamburg and asked her to design a whole space city for one of those *Star Wars* movies."

"Really? Which one? She didn't say anything about it."

"Because she didn't do it! They offered her enough money to live on for a year, but she said those films are dumb."

"What's dumb?" Neither of us had seen her return.

"I was telling Walker why you didn't do that *Star Wars* movie."

"Why? Because they make science and space look terrific. I hate that kind of propaganda! The whole idea they're projecting is, let science do whatever it wants and soon we'll be whizzing happily around in our very own rockets. Everybody'll get to wear a pink aluminum foil suit. Isn't that wonderful? I don't think kids should get excited about aluminum foil suits, or laser cannons, or stun guns. And I don't think science knows what the hell it's doing these days. It scares me."

"Hello, Nicholas, you asshole."

A blond woman in her early forties, overdressed in ten different designers' best, strode up next to his chair. She broadcast a thousand-watt look of anger, hurt, you-owe-me. Nicholas looked at her and smiled wanly. *"Servus,* Evelyn. How are you?"

"Not so good, Nicholas. Could we talk a minute?"

He got up and walked with her toward the front of the restaurant. I looked at Maris to see what she made of it. She watched them go, then spoke quietly.

"There must be a lot of women in this town furious at Nicholas. He has a bad habit of making women fall in love with him and then forgetting about them."

"Does that bother you?"

"When I loved him romantically it tore my heart out. Now it just makes me sad for him. He wants so much for people to love him."

"What's wrong with that? I want people to love me, too."

She reached across the table and touched my hand. "That's not the same, and you know it. We're always trying to fit some name to our lonely. Winning people's love is Nicholas's. And that's okay, but not if you toss it aside once you've won it."

"What do you mean, 'fit a name to our lonely'?"

"Everyone says 'I'm not as happy as I'd like because of this reason or that. If I can beat it, then I'll be content.' Nicholas doesn't think he's loved enough. So that's his goal: get interesting people to love him, and he believes he won't feel so scared or alone when he goes to bed at night and looks into the dark. Then he wins their love, but it's never enough. Not ever. It confuses him, but he still thinks it's the right way, so he keeps doing it.

"Don't you know the name of your lonely, Walker?"

I recoiled slightly. We had talked intimately all day, in bed and out. Yet this one question scratched long fingernails across some psychic blackboard inside, leaving me both jarred and strangely moved.

"I don't know how to answer that." I tried a smile but it died.

She touched my hand again and shook her head. "Don't take it the wrong way. I didn't mean it like that."

Fortunately, the waiter came for our order so I didn't have to say anything more. Instead, I watched Maris ask his opinion on several things, her small mouth a moving plum of color.

Why had her question so disturbed me? What *was* the name of my lonely? The confusion about my real parents? Wanting a life partner, but then betraying the one I had had for no valid reason? Had I fallen so quickly for Maris York because, deep down, too much of my life was empty, one big lonely that needed filling fast?

"Jesus, do you know who that was? Evelyn Heckler! I didn't recognize her. She changes hairdos as often as I change shoes." Wine glass in hand, Nicholas stood next to the table, apparently not interested in sitting yet.

"What did she want? She looked completely pissed off at you."

"She was! Her husband Pierre directed that awful film, *Full House.* Did you see it? The worst! I don't know which was more horrible, the direction or the script. I said that in a magazine interview a few weeks ago. Pierre doesn't talk to me anymore, but this is the first time I've seen Evelyn since it came out.

"I also made the big mistake of having an affair with her once. Every time we went to bed in her house, she had drawings her kids had done all over the walls of the bedroom. Do you know how depressing it is to do it when you're looking at Fred Flintstone?"

He leaned over Maris, kissed the top of her head, then finally sat down.

Dinner came a few minutes later and we all leaped on it at once. Those poor shrimp didn't stand a chance. While we ate, I told a long silly story about Los Angeles that kept both of them laughing through most of the meal.

I had gone to college in Lost Angles and been both happy and tan there. But four years of the city convinced me that was enough, despite its being *the* place for actors.

Everything both clever and shitty has already been said about that shiny part of the United States. But I'm sure they'll go on talking about the state until it cracks off and falls into the sea one fine day. Whether it is a beautiful woman with a hidden killer disease, or a genuinely wonderful place teeming with interesting, imaginative people and possibilities, I think it gets all this attention because no matter what's said, it never fulfills anyone's expectations—high or low—and thus remains the ultimate tricky enigma.

Dinner ended with espresso, grappa, and big handshakes from the management. Out on the street again in front of his car, Nicholas embraced each of us.

"I have to go look at a cassette of an actor they want me to use in the new film. All I know about him is he has a big nose.

"Maris, I'll ask about an apartment for you tomorrow. Walker, call me, huh?"

We watched him work his car out of its parking place, and drive slowly down the narrow street.

I turned to Maris. "Would you like to go back to Uschi's now?"

"I think so. It's been a long day, you know?"

"But a good one! Two amazing days in a row. How often does that happen?"

Taking my arm, she put her head against my shoulder. "I want to see all the films you made. Do you have copies? Will you watch them with me? Can we fool around tomorrow, too? Can I have your telephone number? Will you be my friend?"

She turned and stood in front of me, nose to nose, still making requests. I gently put my hand over her mouth and nodded yes to everything.

The evening was nearly asleep by the time I left Uschi's apartment. Streets were empty, save for an occasional lone wolf taxi cruising slowly by. Vienna is a city where most people go to bed at ten o'clock. You rarely see anyone walking around past midnight, and those you do are usually going home. I stood in the doorway of her building pulling up my collar. Dog-tired, all I basically wanted was to go straight to bed. But a small part of me was still keyed up and demanded something more before calling it a night. A café down the street was still open, so I decided on a quick brandy there and then home.

Walking that way, a figure suddenly loomed before me down the street. It took a moment to see that it was a man riding a bicycle. The bike was completely decked out in a mad, glittering jumble of streamers, mirrors, saddlebags, bumper stickers, antennas, and everything else. The man had a long Rumpelstiltskin beard. He wore one of those round fur hats that cover most of the head and ears and remind you of woodchoppers in Alaska. Pedaling hard enough to make the bike sway from side to side, he came flying toward me as if death, or sanity, were right behind him. The street was quiet but for the whizzing sounds of the bike and the man's loud breathing. I was so tired that I didn't know whether to go left or right to avoid him. He kept coming and I kept standing there. As he got closer I saw more and more of his features. His face was lined and scored. A long, narrow stalactite of a nose hung above a mouth (he seemed to be smiling) full of dark teeth that went in every direction. I still hadn't moved when he was ten feet away and coming fast.

"Rednaxela! Welcome!" he shouted as he passed within inches of my feet, so close that I could smell his garlic, sweat, and craziness. He didn't look back once he'd gone past; just drove straight up to the corner, a sharp right there and . . . gone.

I looked at that corner awhile, then up toward Uschi's apartment, then at the corner again. It was time for Rednaxela to go home.

3.

I pulled the handbrake up tight, gave the motor one last goose, then turned it off. The Renault shivered and coughed, as if angry the trip was finally over. But Maris and I weren't. We had driven all night from Munich through a snowstorm straight out of *Doctor Zhivago*. What was worse, the car had no snow tires, heated only our feet (sort of), and the windshield wipers marched to the beat of a truly different drummer. Four times we'd had to pull off the dark and treacherous autobahn to scrape icy slush off the windshield. The last time, outside Linz, the car wouldn't start again when we climbed back in. Nietzsche said there are times when things get so bad you either laugh or go crazy. Another option is to sit in a cold

Renault R4 that won't start and eat *Extrawürst* sandwiches at four in the morning.

The car was loaded to the gills with her things, which included seven large LEGO cities, a stuffed Russian crow, and a state-of-the-art Atari computer that looked like something the Pentagon used. The cities and crow made sense, but the computer was a surprise. It turned out she used it to sketch and design the cities before she built them.

As soon as I got out, my neck and back felt as though I'd been hefting cement bags for the last nine hours. Bending over and touching my toes a few times, some of the hairier moments on the road came back to give me the creeps. I looked through the car window and saw she was doing stretches, too.

"Remember how that border guard looked at your crow?"

"It was the only thing that interested him. I'm sure he thought I had heroin or something inside. Walker, you know how much I appreciate your helping me."

"Would you have done the same thing?"

"You know I would."

"Right. So I just did what you would have done."

"Don't be so gallant. You did me a really big favor and I appreciate it a lot."

"That's good. Let's start unpacking your things."

"Don't you want breakfast first? Let me treat. We can go to *Aida* and have hot *Töpfen golatschen.*"

"If I fill my stomach now and get warm and cozy, I'll go into coma. Let's take the first couple of loads up to your place and then have coffee there."

"*Gut. Sowieso.*"

Although she spoke fluent, unaccented German, having lived there so long, it almost always surprised me when she slipped unconsciously into Deutsch. Once, when I asked her what language she thought in, she said both.

"Okay, Ms. Sowieso, let's go."

After studying the real estate section of the newspaper every day for two weeks, Maris had found a small, recently renovated studio apartment in a Biedermeier house on the edge of the Wienerwald. The owners were a rich, unpleasant couple named Schuschitz who immediately announced that the big untidy lawn behind the house was not for her to use. I told her no one with that name and that much pettiness deserved her rent money, but Maris said she was sure they'd all get along fine after awhile. And she was right.

I took the computer out of the car and gingerly made my way across the icy street to the front gate. She unlocked it, and then went back to get a load from the car.

It was seven o'clock in the morning and the sun was just up, but the hard cold stillness and heavy gray sky were not the best welcome home to our first day back in Vienna. As I struggled up the outside stairs to her apartment, Diplom Ingenieur Schuschitz (as the big brass plaque on their numerous doors announced) came toward me.

"So, Frau York finally decided to bring her things and stay awhile, eh?"

He had the face of a man who was sure he had all the answers and would be happy to tell them, if only you were smart enough to ask. But I knew his wife had all the money from her side of the family, and treated him with the sweet dismissal due the fool she'd married a long time ago when they were both young, she was naive, and he only was good-looking.

I was about to say something unpleasant when Maris came up close behind me.

"Frau York, that's not your computer is it? What do you do with something like that?" he asked.

"I'm working on schematic physiology right now, and need the machine to do the representative zero zone equations. It's much faster that way."

He looked puzzled, then hunted: If he stood there a moment longer, we'd discover he didn't know a thing about "schematic physiology."

Smiling like a nervous rat, he welcomed her home and hurried past.

I waited till I heard the gate close behind him, then said over my shoulder, "I didn't know you were good at zero zone equations."

She laughed a little. "Sure, he's an ass, but remember, I have to live in their house. Anyway, that's how you treat people like that: Make 'em know how dumb they are, and they go away feeling a little less pleased with themselves."

For the next hour we toted Maris's old environment into her new one. It was another way of getting to know her. She liked rough-edged singers like Tom Waits and Screaming Jay Hawkins ("You like cool music, but I want to hear the kind that tears your heart out"), heavy, laced shoes and boots, obscure novels in both English and German. I'd helped pack these boxes in Munich, but we did everything in a hurry so as to be out of there as quickly as possible. To tell the truth, she'd been calmer than I then, but I wasn't ashamed of that nervousness. From the moment we rode west out of Vienna two days before, I'd had a deep-seated feeling I would do something both extreme and regrettable if Luc showed up.

In the month we'd been together, Maris slowly told the tale of her relationship with him. Too much of it reminded me of the ingredients in the witches' pot in *Macbeth:* fillet of fenny snake, a toad dead under a rock thirty days, sweat from the body of a just-hung man. She resented the comment when I said it, but there was no avoiding the fact she'd tied up with a high-level psychopath with a Ph.D. in creative sadism.

They'd met through a mutual friend, and from the beginning Luc had done all the chasing. Charming and clever and vulnerable (she thought), he called constantly, sent exotic flowers, took her to meals he paid for with borrowed or stolen money. They slept together for the first time in a seven-room apartment in Schwabing he said was his, but later turned out to belong to an old lover he threatened to beat if she didn't get out for two days and leave him the keys. He told Maris truths like that when their own relationship had degenerated into a series of ominous scenes and dangerous possibilities. One afternoon he came over to her and a date at Schumann's and sadly scolded her for not telling this man she had AIDS. Just because she was dying didn't mean she had the right to kill others, no matter how bitter she was.

"He sounded so heartbroken and *convincing*, Walker. The other guy ended up thanking Luc as if he'd saved his life."

"What did you do?"

"What can you do? Say you don't have AIDS? That's a hard accusation to follow, you know?"

Somewhere in those cardboard boxes was a film he'd made about her entitled *It's Incredible!* It showed the cities, her working on them, people talking about them at one of her shows. The film was all right, but pedestrian. If it was any indication of his ability as a film director, it didn't say much. When they started having trouble, he took the film and added a new section: He stole her favorite piece of work, and filmed himself pouring gasoline over it and burning it.

"Why didn't you just leave? Or tell him to get the hell out!"

"I did, but he had a key."

"Change the lock."

"I did! But he got a locksmith and had a copy made when I wasn't there. I changed it three times. The last time, I had one of those expensive unpickable locks put in. When I came home that night, he'd squeezed Krazy Glue into the hole and even *I* couldn't get into my place."

The brakes failed on her car. When she took it to be

repaired, the mechanic said there was a good possibility they'd been tampered with.

These stories went on and on until I got completely exasperated. "For Christ's sake, Maris, why didn't you go to the police? You were being fucking terrorized!"

"In Germany, all you can do is go to the police and make out an *Anzeige*, which is the same as lodging a formal complaint. But if no one's around to witness the event, you're out of luck until there've been lots of those *Anzeigen* made against the same person. Then the cops start looking into things. I did one when he hit me the first time, but you know what the cops said? Even after I'd shown them the bruises he'd left on me? How could they be sure I hadn't hit myself just to get him in trouble! Thank you very much, Munich police. You can't imagine how helpless women are under the law in most countries when it comes to things like this, Walker. That's why they're so hesitant to go to the police after they've been raped or attacked."

"But I thought that whole policy was changing."

"It is, but it isn't changed yet."

In the boxes were a wonderful silver ballpoint pen from the 1940s, a Claude Montana leather jacket the color of a chestnut, a pack of tarot cards wrapped in a piece of black parachute silk.

"Do you read the tarot?"

"Yes, but please don't ask me to do it for you yet. I'm a little afraid of what it would say about you and me."

"Are you good at it?"

"Sometimes. It's always there to hold your hand, but then you grow too dependent on it and don't look for the answers on your own. It helps best when you don't need it so badly."

"What happened when you asked it about Luc and you?"

"The card that always came up was the Tower. *Das Turm.* Do you know what it means?"

"Bad things?"

"Life crashes down. Ruin, usually. It's a card that scares me whenever I see it."

"You won't read for me?"

"Not yet. Also, please don't take the cards out or touch them, Walker. No offense, but there's a funny kind of magic associated with that. The only one who's supposed to handle them is the one who reads them. It's an old law of the tarot."

People I'd known had had their cards or palms read, their astrological charts made up. To me, it was a convenient, vaguely questionable and frightening way of finding out about the day after tomorrow or how to handle it. Part of me believed, part didn't. What held me back most was the thought that fate was a much more illusive and teasing creature than we liked to admit. Why should it reveal its next move so readily and easily, in a line across the hand or the figure of a man with a few swords going through his body? Maris later assured me the only thing the tarot did was give suggestions about how to handle our lives and our next moves: the final decisions were certainly up to us. But by then she had read my cards and the Tower showed up in every hand she dealt. By then I believed completely in fortune telling, but it gave no suggestions, only told me again and again who I was. And that there was no way out.

An hour later we were standing in the middle of her apartment surveying a Matterhorn of boxes and things stacked everywhere. The doorbell rang. While she went to answer it, I pulled a large book out of a box on the architect Charles Jencks. I heard a child's voice and assumed it was one of the Schuschitz children. I wasn't thrilled. They'd discovered Maris and her kindness as soon as she took the apartment, and had been coming to visit at all hours of the day, sometimes to our embarrassment.

I didn't like children very much but didn't feel guilty about it. Maris said she couldn't believe that, and attributed the feeling to my own strange beginnings. But that was too simple. Children are a world in themselves, and as an adult you either want to live in that world or not. My stepsister Kitty had two children and I enjoyed their company whenever I visited Atlanta. But Uncle Walker could bring presents and wrestle around with them like crazy because he knew they were part of a visit, not a lifetime. Yet I knew that if Maris and I were to remain together, kids were an essential part of her future. We talked about it until the cows came home, which I took as a tremendously positive sign about us, because she got more and more emotional about it the more we discussed it.

"Did you bring your cities, Maris?"

"I did. I brought the cities *and* all my thousands of LEGO, too. We're going to make a whole universe!"

She came back into the room with the boy and girl, both lovely looking, both bratty as hell. They knew they had Maris wrapped around their little fingers, but with the same perceptive antenna children have about adults, they were sure I was big competition. We three checked each other out coolly. The boy even squinted his eyes at me in dislike.

"We have to go to school now, but I said we should come down to welcome you home."

She knew the kids were naughty, but smiled at them with pure delight. Her love was helpless and all-encompassing. "If I had some sweeties I'd give them to you, but I haven't been shopping yet. Walker and I just got in. Come back after school and we'll have a little party."

They accepted this and, after checking out some of the

more interesting things she'd already unpacked, went out again.

"You really don't like them, do you?"

"Whenever they come in here they *want* something from you. No kids should be like that, Maris. They're too used to being given everything and expecting it as their due. No, I don't like that."

"Oh, Walker, haven't you ever read Freud or any of those people? Kids expect things as their due because no one's told them different yet. The worst thing that happens to kids is the shitty day they discover the world doesn't give a damn. It happened to all of us, so why not indulge them a little till then? That's only fair; it's what our parents did with us."

I touched her hand. "I don't love them, but I love your love for them. I know what you're saying. You're right."

She went to the bed and started taking boxes off it. I knew what she was doing. It made me as excited as the first day we'd been to bed. I walked over to help. She grabbed me around the neck in a headlock and pulled me down with her. The sheets were freezing cold when we slid beneath them, naked, minutes later.

In a few days she had everything in place and the apartment was completely her. On the walls were large prints of Tamara de Lempicka women, Michael Graves buildings, a blow-up of a *Vogue* photograph of Maris dressed as a giant green cactus. The shelves were filled with interesting or funny things that said their owner had a taste for the silly as well as the beautiful.

The first time we ate a full-fledged meal there, she brought out a photograph and put it in front of me.

"It isn't nice, Walker, but I want you to see a picture of him just in case he ever comes around."

Luc had curly brown hair and a slightly cleft chin. Sad

eyes, sweet eyes. He looked a lot older than I'd imagined, but wore the clothes of a fifteen-year-old—scruffy white sneakers, bleached jeans, a "Best Company" yellow sweatshirt. Maris had worn the same shirt often. Seeing it on him sent a small prick through me.

"I know that shirt."

She took the picture and looked at it. "He wore all of my clothes. We're about the same size. It drove me crazy. Did I tell you about the underwear? When things really started going bad between us, he would take my underpants and wear them. He thought it was a very hot thing to do."

"Come on, he wore your *panties?* What the hell for?"

"Because he knew I hated it. He wanted to get me angry."

"And you let him do it?"

She looked at me sternly, her hands on her hips. "What was I going to do, Walker, hide them all from him? Or say 'Hey, take off my underpants this instant, or else!' "

I cracked up. The tone of her voice, those hands on her hips, and what she was talking about, just cracked me up. Both of us broke into that kid-silly laughter that happens when you're too tired or giddy to be in control of either yourself or your emotions. Forty-year-old Luc walking around her apartment in a pair of lilac panties with little white flowers over the crotch was too much.

While we laughed, I unconsciously took the snapshot and put it straight up by one of its corners on the tip of my finger, as if to balance it there. But when I took my other hand away, the picture stayed perched, vertically, on the finger. It didn't move, not even a bit. Fascinated, I wiggled my whole hand, but the card stayed straight up. I looked at Maris, but she was staring goggle eyed.

"Walker, how do you do that?"

"I don't know. It's just happening."

"Come on, tell me. It's wonderful! Can you do other tricks?"

Uncomfortable now, I took the picture off my finger then put it back. It stood just as straight as a moment before. I took it off and put it on—again and again, until I got the jitters. Maris was enchanted.

That night I dreamed I was an infant lying in a crib of gold and fur. A woman with very long amber hair spilling around her face was looking down at me. Although I was very young, no more than a few months old, I understood her when she spoke.

"I've done everything, but I never knew there were so many names: Klodwig, Mamertus, Markwart, Nepomuk. People coming from everywhere, everywhere, with new names: Odo, Onno, Ratbod, Ratward, Pankratius . . ."

She put her face in her hands and began to cry.

That is all I remember of the dream. When I woke, Maris was lying asleep across my left arm, so I could barely feel my fingers out there on the edge of my body. It was strange, a night thing, knowing part of you was near but gone at the same time.

4.

I was making a commercial for mineral water the day Luc arrived in Vienna. But somehow I knew he was there. From the moment he stepped off the train at the Westbahnhof and started looking for a phone booth, I knew. And that didn't really surprise me; I'd had the feeling all along I would instinctively know when he approached Maris's and my planet. He was simply too dangerous a force: a meteor careening out of control, that gave off all kinds of waves as it sped across space toward us.

He arrived at seven in the morning and by seven-ten was on the phone with Nicholas, demanding to know where Maris was. Nicholas was a heavy sleeper and usually didn't go to bed until very late. It isn't hard to imagine how he felt when he realized who was calling. Eva Sylvian said she had no idea who it was because Nicholas spoke to the Frenchman in a quiet and reasonable voice. The only strange thing was he said *"nein"* every few words. Eva was only half-awake when the call came through, but she said she distinctly remembered Nicholas saying no at least ten times in the short conversation.

Where was she? Nicholas had better tell him right now. *Nein.*

Just give him a phone number where she could be reached. That way she could decide for herself if she wanted to see him. *Nein.*

Did Sylvian realize what Luc could do to him if he kept up this shit? *Nein.*

Und so weiter.

Nicholas was flying to Tel Aviv the next day to meet with an Israeli producer. Because he'd be gone a while, we three had had a farewell coffee together a week before. Naturally, Luc came up in the conversation. But after screaming with laughter at the Luc-in-Maris's-underwear story, Nicholas brushed him off as if he were a fly on his hand. Even if "that idiot" did show up, he would be taken care of. Maris asked how, but only got a smile and a vague shrug for an answer. My director friend loved intrigue and strange situations. Our adventure in Munich had made him happy for weeks afterward. In retrospect, I know he was delighted to have Luc in Vienna that day, because Nicholas had been planning a scene with him ever since we'd returned.

So, instead of packing his bag for Israel that morning, he

surprised Luc by making a date to meet in front of the Burg Theatre at noon. Eva was wide awake by then and watched her husband across the bed smile like a bandit who has just cracked a safe. He made two other calls before getting up and whistling all the way to the shower. Life was about to become art.

The whore's name was Helene *Köstlich* (Delicious) who, from afar, looked a good deal like Maris. Nicholas had also given her a photograph so that when the time came, she could make herself up to look as much as possible like the woman in the picture. He'd used Helene to play a bit part in one of his films, so she was glad to do him a favor.

Goldstar owned an old but perfectly kept Jaguar sedan that had been given to him the year he won the European boxing championship. Behind the wheel he looked like an Easter Island statue with arms. Originally, he'd offered to beat Luc up, but Nicholas wanted something more interesting than that: He wanted theatre.

He called Helene Delicious, told her to put on the "Maris look," and dress in the sluttiest outfit she had. Today was the day! Goldstar picked both of them up and drove to the Burg Theatre. Although it was the middle of December, he was attired in an all-white polyester suit and a hideous matching red tie and shirt Nicholas had supplied for the occasion. The three of them must have looked like they were going to a photo session with Diane Arbus.

When they arrived at the theatre, Luc was nowhere to be seen. Ten minutes later he came ambling out of the Café Landtmann next door, cool as could be. Nicholas got out and happily walked over to meet him. Luc looked his way, then at the car. From that distance he could only dimly see the woman inside. Was it Maris? In a gold lamé dress with a neckline that fell below his line of vision? Topped by a foxy Tina Turner wig? And who was the gorilla sitting next to her? "Maris" waved at Luc at the same time the gorilla started climbing out of the car. Nicholas had directed Goldstar to take his time so his entrance would be that much more impressive.

Luc asked what was going on. Nicholas innocently said Maris had agreed to see him, but first he would have to ask permission of "her friend," who was fast approaching.

The conversation that followed between the two men went something like this, after Goldstar took out a knife and held it open to his own nose.

"You want her back? You can't have her. That ends that discussion. You want to fuck her? First you have to fuck with me.

"She told me about you, asshole. You like to slap girls around and then walk around in their underpants? Why don't you come to work for me, too? I'll let you wear all those things —bra, silk panties . . . We'll even buy you some Tampax too: to put up your ass! I bet you got a nice ass, huh? Tight, very fuckable."

To Luc's credit, he stayed calm and asked nicely if he could speak to Maris a moment. Goldstar turned and yelled the request back to the car. Helene Delicious rolled down the window and gave them the finger.

"I guess that means no, Luc." Goldstar folded the knife and put it back in his pocket. "Maybe she doesn't like guys who kick her ass, then wear her underpants. You got to be one or the other, you know? You got to be one or the other, right, Nicholas?"

On the phone to us later, Nicholas said Goldstar overdid it a little, but it worked. Maris said it sounded like he overdid it about 500 percent. But I could tell she was both tickled and relieved. No matter how brave a front she'd put on since the bad days in Munich, knowing Luc was simmering in his crazy juices somewhere on the same continent worried her terribly. At night she spoke in her sleep. Although I didn't tell her, what she said was too often loud and frantic and disturbing.

Walking into a restaurant, she'd seen someone who looked so much like him that she'd started to bolt. Only at the last moment did she realize the man's hair color was completely different. Maris isn't the kind of person who runs away from things. I sensed this from the first, and it's still so now.

After Helene gave them the finger and Goldstar walked away, Nicholas asked Luc if there was anything else he wanted. The other looked confused and disoriented, but couldn't let it go. He had come so far for . . . this?

"How could she be a whore? *Maris?*"

"She's not, Luc. She's living with him, and that's the way he likes her to dress. I think he'd kill anyone who tried to touch her, especially you. I guess she's told him everything. What was that about your wearing her underpants?"

"How could you bring her to him? A *pimp?* How could you do that?"

"What did you do for her, Luc? Beat her up? Scare her to death? Why do you think she's even with him? She doesn't want you near her life. You're her trouble, man, not him."

"Fuck you, Sylvian."

Nicholas turned around and shouted to Goldstar, "Luc wants you to fuck yourself, Goldie."

Goldstar honked the horn twice, scrambling out of the car again. Helene tried to restrain him, but couldn't. He rose, and rose, and rose from the spotless Jaguar, looking like a demonic Mr. Clean. Pointing a long finger at Luc he bellowed, "Go home, little shit frog. Go home before I eat your fucking face."

When it seriously looks like Mr. Clean is going to eat your face, you get out fast. That's what Luc did, but not before saying to Nicholas, "I'm going to get you."

"What did he mean by that?" Maris worried.

Once again, I'd turned the receiver so both of us could be in on the conversation at the same time.

Nicholas chuckled. "Maybe he'll report me to the Directors' Guild."

"He's a crazy man."

"Maris, he looked so goddamned confused by what he was seeing, that it's going to take him a couple of months to recover, believe me. He was scared, honey, what else could he have said? He thinks I've got big pimp friends who can't wait to kick his ass!

"Leave it alone, forget it. You won! Walker, tell her to stop worrying. Go out and celebrate. I've got ten things to do now so I'll be ready to go tomorrow. You know what I don't like about Israel? Breakfast. You can't put milk in your coffee, then they give you raw onions and tomatoes. God, what a country! I'll send you a postcard of a tank. Let's go to Frascati when I get back. Tell me I'm your hero, Maris."

"You know I love you anyway, Nicholas."

There was an embarrassed silence, then, "Yeah, me too. Take care of each other. I'll see you in a few weeks."

"Do you want me to take you to the airport? It's no trouble."

"No, Eva will take me. She likes to drive out and play her radio. Bye-bye."

The next morning the Sylvians arrived at the airport an hour before Nicholas's flight. It wasn't like him to be such an early bird, but he knew El Al was very slow and careful about inspecting luggage and passports before they let you on the plane. He couldn't afford to miss the flight, so he played the good boy.

As he was checking in, an old Mercedes pulled up to one of the doors on the upper level of the airport. Several Arabs with submachine guns and hand grenades got out and ran into the building. Eyewitnesses said it was such a shock to see them there, that no one really started doing anything until after the men opened fire and threw the first grenades at the El Al counter. The same thing was happening in Rome at Fiumicino Airport.

The bullet that tore off part of Eva Sylvian's ear was probably the same one that kept moving—straight through her husband's head. One in the head, one in the stomach. If you have ever seen that grisly picture they ran in *Time* of the many dead at Vienna airport, Nicholas Sylvian is the man in the dark suit splayed like a dropped doll, still clutching something in his hand. It is his passport in the leather billfold Maris and I gave him at our last meeting.

We heard about the attack in an electronics store while out shopping for a new VCR. The first report was that the road to the airport was closed to all traffic because of an "incident." We paid no attention because the Austrians love to interrupt their radio programs with traffic reports at all times of day. But a few minutes later the first detailed news of what had happened started coming in. Maris said she noticed the whole place stopped and, as one, everybody turned toward whatever radios were on in the store. These things didn't happen in Vienna. They simply didn't. No one looked at anyone else— only the radio speakers had the answers we wanted.

In that shock-time when the enormity of what had happened began to come clear, I was first outraged at the sheer wrongness of the act. Shoot randomly into groups of people at an airport? For what, a political cause? What about the politics of humanity? Or man's purported ability to distinguish between the enemy and a child with a doll in its arms? Or had part of the world really turned the corner en masse, really grown so mad as to think enemy and child were the same? I kept saying "Those bastards!" to myself as the news updates turned into horror stories.

Someone grabbed my arm. Before I registered it, Maris

said in a scared, shrill voice, "Nicholas is out there! He was going to Israel on El Al!"

For an instant I hated her for saying that. We hate anyone who hands us the death sentence, the news that everything is terminal.

We looked at each other and ran out of the store. My car was parked nearby and we jumped in without saying anything. Both of us were silent all the way to the airport, the loud radio news the only words we shared.

A mile outside the town of Schwechat on the autobahn, police barricades blocked the road. I told the first man we came to I was afraid my brother might be one of the dead. He was sympathetic and checked with his boss, but couldn't let us through because things were still going on out there.

After they finished shooting, the terrorists ran out of the airport building, got back in their car, and drove away down the same road we were on. They didn't get far. There was a crazy, moving-car shoot-out between them and the police that resulted in more blood and death. There is a photograph of their stopped Mercedes, its rear window blasted out, one of the terrorists dead on the road, his pants conspicuously soiled. A young policeman is looking at the body with a small smile on his face.

I made a U-turn and drove to the next phone booth, where I called my friend Barbara Wilkinson, who worked in the news department at O.R.F. Luckily I got right through, and she knew what I wanted the moment she came on the line. Nicholas had introduced us years before.

"Walker, Nicholas is dead. I just heard that. His wife was wounded, but that's all I know. Call me back in a couple of hours. Everything is completely crazy here. Call me later. I'm sorry. I'm crying. Call me later."

I realize now that I began this narrative by speaking of Nicholas's and my relationship in the present tense. But that's only because whenever he comes to mind, always several times a day, I think of him as still alive: his late-night calls, the black Valentino suits and pastel shirts, the strange but unique balance of precision and hyperbole of a good man unsure of himself but totally sure of his art. I loved the landscape inside him. Next to Maris, he was the best friend I had as an adult, and perhaps the greatest compliment I can pay him is thinking he is still here. When he died it was the first time I ever had the feeling that life sometimes unfairly takes sides. Possibly the only reason for that relationship was to be happy together then, for that period of our lives. Expecting or wanting more was unwise or greedy.

No, I don't like that. There are too many ways to rationalize the death of someone you love. Many sound good, but none are strong or convincing enough to genuinely console you. Especially when you see someone smoking "his" cigarettes, or a new film you would love to talk to him about . . . if only he were alive.

Not long before this happened, I was reading around in a poetry anthology and came across one entitled "A Space in the Air" by Jon Silkin. The last part of the poem touched me, so that I copied it down and gave it to Maris. She liked it too and put it up on the board above her desk.

> *And I shall always fear*
> *The death of those we love as*
> *The hint of your death, love.*

Why had I discovered that poem then? Why had I thought it "lovely" when all it did was tell a cold truth about life that was best ignored as long as possible? Art is beautiful

until it becomes real or the truth. Keats was wrong—beauty
may be truth, but the truth, once lived, is rarely beautiful.

Neither Maris nor I liked Eva Sylvian. She was a loud, self-
centered woman who never stopped talking about herself. She
lived in the shadow of her husband because she liked being
known around town as Mrs. Nicholas Sylvian. But she was also
the kind of person who fights her way out of that shadow by
constantly trying to dominate any conversation with stories
from her own dull life. Somewhere inside, she knew the most
interesting thing about her was her husband, but that only
made her more strident and desperate for attention.

In the hospital, she was impossible to listen to. After the
first visit neither of us had any desire to be there, because she
went on and on about what she'd seen, how she'd felt when it
happened, what the doctors were doing for *her* . . . but little
about Nicholas. To put it horribly, she had finally gotten hold
of the spotlight and wasn't about to give it up for anything.

But because of Maris, we went to visit Eva every day.
Maris believed in continuity: If this woman was Nicholas's
wife, then it was our duty to help until she was ready to walk
back into her life again. We didn't need to be her friends; only
to continue for a while our friendship with the man who'd
loved her.

In his will he had asked to be cremated, but first they held
a memorial service at his favorite building in town, the Otto
Wagner–designed church on the grounds of Vienna's largest
insane asylum, the Steinhof. That was in the will too, but I
could never figure out whether the request was serious or another sly Nicholas joke. No matter. The Jugendstil church was
filled with people. What was most heartening, the mourners
came from everywhere to say good-bye to him. He would have
loved to see the array.

He'd made films about old Russians, sexy spies, a foolish tour group that got lost on its way to Venice. Some of his movies were dull, others superb. But all of them were made with the greatest love toward whomever he was picturing, and that was evident everywhere. As we were walking out of the church, an old woman with a thick Ottakringer accent and an old loden coat on said to the man next to her, "Nicholas Sylvian knew us. That's why I came. He knew what was in my refrigerator, you know what I mean?"

We drove Eva to the Zentralfriedhof where the cremation would take place. It is an enormous cemetery and you can casily get lost in it if you don't know where you're going. Eva went into the crematorium and we started walking back to the car.

"What do you think of cremation?"

"Not much. I read somewhere that your soul gets destroyed if you do it. That scares me a little. I want to be buried in a nice simple box."

She stopped and looked at me. "In Vienna?"

"I don't know. I love it here, but a small part of me thinks I should be put down in my own country. If there's any life after death, I'd be able to understand the language better."

She put her arm around my back and we walked in silence. On reaching the car, she stopped and said she wanted to wander around the place for a while by herself, if I didn't mind. She would catch a tram home. I understood because I felt like being alone too. We made a date to meet for dinner and I drove off with a quick glance at her in the rearview mirror. I would go home, she would look at gravestones, Eva would wait while her husband slept in flames.

The phone was ringing in my apartment when I opened the door. Dashing to catch it, I narrowly missed stepping on Orlando, who'd come to the door to say hello. I scooped him up and took him along to the phone.

"Hello?"

"Walker, it's Maris. You've got to come back here. You've got to see something. You *have* to. It's incredible!"

"Right now? I just got in this minute. I really don't feel like driving anymore, Maris."

"Have you ever heard of a man named Moritz Benedikt?"

"No."

"All right, I'll take a picture. I've got the Polaroid with me, but it's not the same. When you see this picture you're going to drive out here in the middle of the night, believe me. Can I come over after?"

"Sure. I'll probably be asleep, so use your key."

Real sadness either keeps me up all night or punches me to sleep. This time it was all I could do to put the receiver down and get to bed before going out as if I'd been conked on the head. I dreamed of Nicholas sitting naked on a scarlet stallion twenty hands high in the middle of a beautiful pond. He looked very happy and called out to me, "Bathing the red horse!"

When I awoke, Orlando was asleep on my stomach and Maris was lying by my side. The room was completely dark and warm and smelled of her distant, hours-old perfume. It took some time for my mind to land back on earth. While it was circling the airfield, I gently combed her soft hair with my fingers. It had grown much longer since she'd been in Vienna.

"How long have you been here?"

"About an hour. I'm glad you're up. I've been dying to wake you. You've got to see what I found. Can I turn on the light?"

"Uh huh."

The light burst the air like a flashbulb. I closed my eyes against the white shock. When I opened them again, she was holding a Polaroid photograph in front of me. It was a picture of an ornate black marble gravestone. Across the top, thick gold letters spelled out the name "Moritz Benedikt" and the dates he lived. Below them was a small cameo photograph of Benedikt; a common practice on Austrian gravestones. I couldn't see the photo very well, but before I had a chance to think, she handed me another snapshot, this time a close-up of the cameo.

"Holy shit!"

It was a picture of me. Same hair, soft tired eyes, large nose. It's common to hear people say they know or have seen someone who looks a lot like you. It's different when you're faced with a mirror image of yourself, thirty years dead. It's time blown through a horn—right in your face.

"Who was he?"

"I don't know. I asked every groundkeeper out there I could find, but no one knew. It'd be easy enough to track him down, though, Walker. God knows, Vienna is famous for keeping records. You could probably find out how many sugars he put in his coffee, if you looked hard enough."

I couldn't stop looking at the picture. The light wasn't good and some parts were a little out of focus, but the resemblance was stark and mysterious and . . . exciting in its way. You think you are the sole proprietor of your looks. Once you discover you aren't, you immediately start wondering what else there was in common between you and your double. What kind of life did he live? What were his secrets, what were his dreams? The world is a place of wonders, but the greatest of all is yourself. Finding that someone once walked the earth with your face is incentive enough to send you out searching for answers. But that was one of my greatest mistakes. Wonders don't always have answers or reasons. Or rather, even if they do, those answers are not necessarily what we want to know.

The black stone was so polished it looked like obsidian. The gold letters cut into its face were deep and done with great care and skill. I stood a few feet away and took in the whole thing before moving closer to look at his picture on the stone. A bouquet of not-so-long-dead flowers lay at the foot of the grave. There was someone alive who knew and still cared for Moritz Benedikt. Oddly, Maris hadn't mentioned the flowers, but she'd been right about something else: After her photographs, I'd had to come to the cemetery the next day to see for myself.

The cameo of Benedikt was large and vaguely yellow from age. He wore a dark suit and formal shirt, but no tie. Not only did we look alike, but for the first time I realized he wore an expression halfway between amusement and small exasperation that I often had on. My mother called me Mr. Long-suffering whenever she saw it. So, the last public image of Moritz Benedikt was as Mr. Long-suffering. Too bad for him. It made me smile. I wanted to smile then or just generally lighten up because the more I looked at my . . . self, the more nervous and uncomfortable I became. Besides the impossible similarity in looks, I had a gooseflesh chill going up the middle of my spine from something else as well. Some people, after shivering involuntarily, are asked what's the matter. The common answer I'd heard all my life was "Someone just walked over my grave." How's this, though—imagine coming across your grave, replete with a picture of you on it wearing one of your most recognizable expressions. Only it isn't your grave and it isn't your stone and it isn't a picture of you and the person in the ground there has been dead thirty years. That ground two feet in front of you.

Two old women, both dressed in black, both carrying identical purses, walked by. One of them looked at me and nodded her head.

"*Guten Tag,* Herr Rednaxela."

The name stuck its finger in my ear, but I couldn't remember where I'd heard it before. I smiled at the woman as if I knew her and what she was talking about.

"It took you a long time to get here!"

Her friend looked angry and shook her head. "Leave him alone. He's way ahead of schedule."

Rednaxela. The crazy man on the bicycle the first day in Vienna with Maris. He had called me Rednaxela!

Without really seeing, I watched the two women start walking away.

"Wait!" I ran a few steps to catch them. "What are you talking about? Who's Rednaxela?"

Both women smiled and exchanged glances—they were in on something I didn't know anything about. One of them gave me a little coquettish shrug. "That's your job to find out. You've come this far."

The other one came up and patted my shoulder. "Everybody's proud of you. Don't mind what I said before. I was only teasing."

They began to leave again. I grabbed the one closest by the arm and pulled her around to face me. Her smile vanished. "Don't touch me! Stop asking questions. Fuck off!"

I shook her arm. It was thin as a pipe cleaner through the thick wool of her coat. "What are you talking about? Who's Rednaxela? How do you know me?"

A bunch of birds on the grass started as one and flew away.

The woman saw a young couple nearby and started

screaming in a squeaky voice, "Help! Let me go! Leave me! Help!" Her companion hit me on the back with her purse. The couple came running over and the man pulled me away from the old woman.

"Who's Rednaxela, damn it!"

"You'll find out, shithead!"

"Just tell me now."

"The fuck I will, sonny boy."

I started back at her, but the man held me.

"Hey, man, are you crazy? That's an old woman!" He was strong and wasn't going to let go.

The old women scuttled away, watching me the whole time over their shoulders. At first they both looked terrified, but when they were a safe distance away, one of them laughed like a loon and made a crazy face at me: thumbs in her ears, pinkies pulling out the corners of her mouth, her tongue zipping in and out like a snake's. Her laugh was so strange and loud that the man, his wife, and I all stopped tussling to watch the two women as they turned and disappeared among the gravestones.

"Are you crazy, man? Beating up on old ladies? What the hell for?"

He let go of me and crossed his arms—a father expecting an explanation from his ten-year-old.

"Forget it. It was a mistake." I was embarrassed and angry and wished like hell I knew where the "ladies" had gone.

"You don't shake up old ladies in *graveyards*, man. I don't care what you do in your own country."

I looked at him. "What are you talking about?"

"This is Austria. I don't care how you treat people in your own country. Even if that was your grandmother. Here you do it our way."

His wife came up and gave me a defiant look. "Where *are* you from? What kind of language was that? I used to work out at the United Nations, but I never heard people talking as crazy as that before."

"What do you mean?"

"That language. Those sounds you were using. Both you and the old women. Where are you from?"

Her husband gave a big snort. "The ocean maybe! Maybe they're all three dolphins in drag."

I looked at him, his wife. "What did it sound like?" I was frightened.

She looked at me as if I were putting her on. "You know what it sounded like. You were doing it!"

Her man snorted again. "What did it sound like? It sounded like this." He put two fingers together and started whistling—whistling so loud that it startled a flock of birds out of a nearby chestnut tree. I looked at him, then at his wife. She nodded at me.

"That's it. Just like that. Where do you speak like that? Can you do it again?" She smiled encouragingly.

I didn't tell Maris. What would I say? "I met two old women at the cemetery today. I attacked one and spoke dolphin-whistle to the other. Then they ran away and stuck their tongues out at me." It would have been a funny scene in a film, but in real life it had the ring of cuckooness deluxe.

And what *about* that strange language I was supposed to have spoken with them? Where did it fit in, and why hadn't I been aware of speaking anything other than my good old American German?

Who was Rednaxela? Or if *I* was him, as two nutty old women and a bearded UFO on a bicycle contended, who was he/I? How come I didn't know anything about who "we" were? Or did I?

Finally, what did Moritz Benedikt have to do with it?

Joking, the old woman said it'd taken me long enough to figure out that I had to come to the cemetery to see his grave . . .

How did it all fit in? What screws or pieces or instructions were missing from the kit that would enable me to put things together correctly and understand?

I knew a peculiar American in town named David Buck who spent most of his time in the National Library researching an obscure sixteenth-century German Anabaptist who'd camped out in Austria for a while. Buck was forever broke and looking for ways to make money. So I called and said I'd pay him to research Moritz Benedikt. All I knew about the man were his dates and the fact that he was buried in the Zentral-friedhof, but Buck said that was enough to go on. He would get back to me when he had something.

Nicholas's death and the bizarre scene at the cemetery shook me badly. I spent days just reading, looking out the window, and eating the good meals Maris cooked. She kept me company and shared a comfortable, necessary silence. At first I tried to hide the dark things swimming just below my surface, but she saw them fast and said I didn't have much faith in us if I did that.

"The whole purpose of friendship is to give the other strength when they need it. Don't cheat me out of that perk, Walker."

To complicate things, Eva Sylvian called two or three times a day, every day. The conversations (monologues) were all the same. It struck me she would have been happier taping what she said on a recorder, then playing it back so she could agree with herself. She asked if we would do this or that for her, ranging from helping to choose the inscription on Nicholas's vault to picking up her dry cleaning. The tone of her voice said she expected these things to be done. Maris said it sounded more as if Eva felt she deserved to be loved, if not for herself, then certainly for her loss. Funny how some people

expect the dearest things in life to come to them simply because they exist or because they have suffered.

One night late the phone rang in my apartment and I was
sure it was Eva again. Maris answered, but her eyes widened
when she heard who was calling. Excitedly, she waved me over
to the phone and, pointing to the receiver, said, "It's Weber
Gregston!"

Gregston was the hottest director in Hollywood. I'd read
an interview with him about his newest film, *Breathing You*,
which had been nominated for six Oscars. I knew about him
through Nicholas, who'd once been his assistant on a film.

"Hello, Walker Easterling?"

"Yes?"

"Hi. Weber Gregston. Listen, I called about a couple of
things. I just heard about Nicholas Sylvian. Jesus, I wish I'd
known sooner. I'd've come to the funeral. I just talked with
Eva. Can you tell me more about what happened? I didn't get
a very clear picture from her."

We talked half an hour about Nicholas and I liked everything Gregston said. He was genuinely grieved about the
death. You could easily tell he'd admired and enjoyed Nicholas
very much. What was especially nice was his knowledge of the
Sylvian films. He spoke about shots and angles in them as if
he'd seen each film three times and paid the closest attention.
Our dead friend would have loved to hear the conversation. He
had thought Gregston the only near genius in contemporary
film.

"Listen, Walker, there's something else. I'm right in the
middle of shooting a film out here. It's a little embarrassing to
say, but one of my actors had a heart attack yesterday and I
need someone fast to fill in for him. It'd be about five days of
shooting in L.A. I saw you in Nicholas's film and he said you're
good to work with. Do you think you could get away for ten

days and fly over? I know it's short notice, but you'd get good money besides doing me a great favor."

Maris was sitting right next to me. I put my hand over the receiver and asked if she wanted to go to California for a couple of weeks. She threw both hands up, closed her eyes, and gave the lucky air a big kiss.

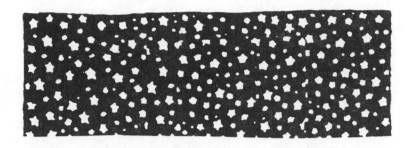

CHAPTER THREE

1.

The bad thing about flying to California was that the trip would have to start at the Vienna airport so soon after the massacre. For some strange reason, I'd . . . forgotten for a while that Nicholas died there. Maybe because I didn't want to think about it, maybe because I'd thought about it too much. The realization struck me on the ride out there.

"God, I completely forgot about where we're going."

Maris was looking out the window and turned to me, smiling. "What do you mean?"

"To the airport. You know. Nicholas."

"Yes, I know. Someone told me they haven't replaced the glass windows yet. You can still see the bullet holes."

"That's not very reassuring, is it?" I put my hand on her knee. She covered it with hers. "I've always liked going to airports before. They're exciting and make me start dreaming as soon as I get close and see the planes taking off and landing."

"Walker, I've got to tell you one thing about this trip: I'm an absolute chicken when it comes to flying. The worst." She reached into her handbag and took out a small pharmacy bottle.

"What's that?"

"Valium. Real strong ones. I took a couple before we left, so if I pass out halfway across the Atlantic, you'll know why."

The bus drove up the ramp to the departure section and stopped. I looked at Maris and took a sad deep breath. "I really ain't looking forward to going in there."

"Me either. Let's do it fast and get it over with."

Unfortunately, there was a long line at the check-in counter and we had to wait. Maris asked if I'd mind staying with the bags a few minutes while she went to buy magazines.

Looking around after she'd left, I noticed there were security police everywhere, "Kobras," in berets and battle dress, carrying stubby gray Uzi machine pistols that looked like strange plumbing fixtures under their arms. What disturbed me most was that these men looked at everyone and everything with completely attentive, suspicious eyes. They trusted no one. And they had probably been told not to. It reminded me of a friend who'd been in Vietnam and said when he was there, everyone was suspect. He'd watched a child hand a bouquet of flowers to the driver of an American troop transport truck and then run away. The truck blew up seconds later.

Maris returned looking as if someone had hit her. "I had to look. Walker, there really are bullet holes all over the windows downstairs! It's unbelievable. One of the soldiers told me there was a shoot-out over there on the escalator."

She pointed off to the left. I told her I wanted to take a look.

"Are you sure?"

"Yes. If I see it, then maybe I won't think about it so much. My imagination is my worst enemy these days."

I walked across the floor listening to the sounds of excited travelers, the P.A. announcing flights to everywhere. A typical day at the airport. The same sounds Nicholas would have heard as he stood at the El Al counter waiting to check in. I looked for that counter but then thought better about really finding it. What did I expect or want to see there? Chalk outlines of the bodies on the ground? Old bloodstains? The shot-out windows would be enough.

The escalator Maris had pointed out was built next to a steep staircase. I started down those stairs because I wanted to come across the windows at my own speed. If I didn't like what I saw, I could turn around and go right back up.

Seeing those bullet holes would be final proof the attack had actually happened and Nicholas was one of the victims. Otherwise, his death for us was only a composite of news reports and hysterical phone calls, a service at the Steinhof church, and dropping his widow off at the door of a crematorium.

I descended the stairs slowly, holding the rail for support. There was an overhang in front of me, so I'd counted fifteen steps before the windows began to come into view. I went down two more before noticing the woman passing me on the right, moving fast down the metal steps of the escalator. She wore a full-length fur coat and sunglasses and had the kind of perfect mood hair that comes with long hours in the chair at the best *Friseur* in town. She jingled when she moved because of all the jewelry she wore. The jingling was distracting, so I stopped to have a look at her. She had that fast purposeful walk and straight-ahead glare of an important person in a big hurry. *Beep-beep*—out of the way for a Hard Charger!

She suddenly stumbled and fell face forward onto the sharp edge of the moving steel step. I grabbed for her instinctively but was too far away. Jewelry clanked hard against metal, then a quiet, thicker sound—skin and bone hitting. She flailed her arms, cried out, somersaulting down one step after another, hitting and rolling. Her coat and skirt flew up, legs spread helplessly. She was wearing peach-colored panties. There was a small purple bruise inside one thigh.

I ran down some stairs, trying to catch up, but by then she was in a heap at the bottom. Her hair was already being sucked into the grate at the foot of the escalator. She lay unmoving as the stairs tore her scalp off.

I heard a scream and unconsciously stuck my arm out to the right. It hit something and I grabbed on to it. Looking quickly, I saw I'd caught the woman by the arm as she was stumbling. The *same* woman who'd just fallen! She steadied herself and smiled gratefully at me. Horrified, I looked at the bottom of the escalator. No one there. I'd seen everything take place before it happened. Stopped it before it continued.

"Thanks so much! It's these damned high heels. I always have so much trouble walking in them. Thanks again." She gave another smile and, standing still, moved slowly down the rest of the way.

I sat down right where I stood, put my hands to my head, and shook like a dog in a bad thunderstorm. Nicholas's death, the old women at the cemetery, Rednaxela, saving this woman from her future . . . I had to tell Maris everything now. I had begun to run out of luck.

"Hey, you, get up! Let's go. What're you doing there?"

Looking up, I saw a Kobra checking me out with both

disgust and suspicion. He gestured with his gray Uzi for me to get going.

For dinner we were offered a precise square of mysterious-smelling beef or mysterious-looking chicken. The stewardess had the face of a woman who'd once come in third in the Miss North Dakota contest. To her dismay, both of us declined the meals and returned to our conversation. I don't like the taste of alcohol, but halfway through the flight I was vaguely drunk on scotch and feeling much more relaxed.

Maris knew it all now. It isn't often in life that you come clean with another person, but I'd tried. What good was it to leave anything out? How could she make suggestions if left in the dark about important, albeit frightening or embarrassing, details?

I looked for some answer on her loved face. From past chats, I knew she liked to think things through before giving her opinion, but my impatience showed too clearly in the way I kept rattling the ice in my glass.

She looked at the glass, then me. "I have my tarot cards here. I'll do a reading for you now if you like, but I'd still rather not. This isn't the place for it.

"The best thing to do is call my brother Ingram when we get in. I was going to anyway, but this is all the more reason to. Remember I told you he's a disc jockey in L.A.? He has this cockamamy talk show in the afternoon called 'Off the Wall' where he interviews every kind of weirdo and lunatic you can imagine. It's funny and odd, but over the years he's met them all—good and bad. I'm sure he'll know someone you can go see. Maybe a really astute palmist or astrologer."

"That's good, but what do you think of all this, Maris?"

"I think it's something to worry about. You have to find out what's happening. If you knew someone strange and mean like Luc, it might be a very elaborate practical joke. It's the kind of joke he liked to play."

"Seeing a woman's future? Looking exactly like a dead man? That's no joke, Maris. It's God!"

"True."

"I'm glad you're calm about it. It makes me feel better."

"I'm calm because there's nothing we can do this minute, ten miles above the earth. Plane rides scare me and I'm just in the middle of praying we get there. Once we've landed we can figure out . . . Oh, forget it."

I sat up and looked at her carefully. "What were you going to say?"

"I was thinking about how magical these last months have been. How we met, how fast we fell in love. But then there's the other magic too—Nicholas's death, your friend Rednaxela, Moritz Benedikt . . . It's really a strange time for us."

"Nicholas's death was magic? That's an odd word for it."

"I don't think so. Magic means mysterious *and* supernatural. We both know he shouldn't have died. Why he died is the mystery. My God, everything is so strange these days.

"You also said something before that isn't true: You're running out of luck? No way! We have each other now. The only two important things in life are real love and being at peace with yourself. You've got one of them. I think what's happening is balance. If you get one, you lose the other. Or it diminishes. You have the love, so you have to lose some peace. It's standard physics: For every action, there's an equal and opposite—"

"—Reaction. But you can have both. Loving someone brings you peace."

"Nope. It makes life interesting and alive, but it doesn't bring much peace."

The first thing I do whenever I return to a town I know is eat a favorite meal there. In Vienna it is *melange* and a *Töpfen golatschen.* In Los Angeles it is a chili cheese dog at Pink's. Within hours of landing in California, we were sitting at an outdoor table in eighty-degree January weather eating America's best with her brother Ingram.

They looked so alike: tall, topped with thick black hair, eyes set wide apart, lips round and perfect as a dark coin. Ingram (Maris called him "Inky") was thin and dressed in typical L.A. wear—T-shirt with the name "Meat Puppets" across the front, baggy/fashionable pants, sneakers. He talked fast, but his hands never moved except to bring the hot dog to his mouth. I kept imagining him at a radio microphone with those still hands, fielding questions from guys selling real estate on the Lost Continent of Atlantis (once it rose). Maris was his best audience and their closeness was self-evident.

After they'd caught up on each other's lives, she told an abbreviated version of our story. His eyes went back and forth between us, and he asked many questions, some of them alarmingly personal. He knew Luc, and angrily kept repeating he'd warned her about that asshole.

"Don't be obnoxious, Inky. I warned you about a couple of your friends, but you didn't listen either. Two of them tried to kill you. I only had Luc."

That made him laugh. He reached across the table and tried to take her bottle of cream soda. She pulled it back and shook her head. It was one of those games brothers and sisters play until the day they die and enjoy every minute of.

"Everything is good between you two?"

"Wonderful. But, Inky, there's something important you can help us with."

While Ferraris and low riders roared by a few feet away, she told him about the "magic" of our last months. This time he asked no questions at all, which made me skeptical. But then anything was possible in his world, including people who talked to Pluto. When she was finished he nodded his head and said more to himself than to us, "Venasque."

"What's that?"

"It's a man. A shaman. He teaches people to fly."

The studio gave us a sunny apartment off Wilshire Boulevard with a couple of long porches and bougainvillea flowers growing everywhere. It was such a pleasure to wear light clothes again and go out of the house without a coat on.

Weber Gregston's company, "Black Lion," gave us a car and the news that shooting would begin for me in a few days. Weber was making a thriller/horror film called *Wonderful* based on three paintings by Eric Fischl. He'd written it together with one of the most famous novelists in America. No one outside the production knew much about the film because it was a closed set and people involved were keeping their mouths shut. The script arrived in the hands of a woman who looked like a prison guard.

I was set to play a professional killer named Mr. Pencil. Although the part wasn't difficult, it was peculiar. While Maris and her brother spent an evening out, I read the script first as an actor and then again as a screenwriter. Both ways it was macabre, perverse, original. Weber was still riding high on the success of his last film, and I'm sure that was the only reason why a major studio agreed to finance *Wonderful.*

That was also the night I called Venasque for the first time. From the first he was garrulous and friendly. The tone of his voice sounded as though he was grateful for someone to talk to. Ingram must have filled him in on my "problem" because the shaman asked for details on the way the woman had fallen down the escalator stairs, the color of the women's faces in the graveyard, how to spell "Benedikt," my birth date.

"And you're here to make a film?"

"Yes. We'll be staying about two weeks."

"It'll have to be longer."

"Why?"

"Because if we work together, it'll take a whole day to drive to the mountains. Then we'll be up there a minimum of a week, another day to drive back . . . I'd say give yourself a good ten days just to be sure."

"Can you help me, Mr. Venasque?"

"I can teach you to fly. That's the first step."

"What do you mean, *fly?* Really, like a bird?"

I almost heard him smile. "Birds don't fly, Mr. Easterling. They live. Part of their way of living is to travel off the ground. But ask a bird how he does that and he'll look at you funny. The same when someone asks you how to walk. Put one foot in front of the other. Sure, that's the mechanics of it, but how do you *walk?* Or find the right balance to ride a two-wheeler bike? You do it. You find it. I can teach you where it is in you."

"And you do this with anyone?"

"Anyone who can pay."

"How much is it?"

"A thousand dollars."

"That's not much to fly."

"It's not such a hard thing to do. If you're not satisfied at the end, I'll give you your money back."

"Why do I want you to live out in the desert, speak like a guru, and tell me it takes years to master the art?"

"You read *Siddhartha* and Castaneda too many times. Come and see me and we'll talk some more. Listen, 'Miami Vice' is on in five minutes. A show I never miss. Come and see me."

My first day on the set of *Wonderful*, I watched Gregston carefully. He was amiable but intense, short-tempered, balanced by a terrific sense of humor. When he wasn't working he sat alone and read a novel by Robertson Davies, or sketched in a leather notebook he kept constantly under his arm. The cameraman, George Lambert, said Weber's whole life was in that notebook, but didn't elaborate.

Over coffee, the director told me about the character I was to play. What he said wasn't special, but spoken with such conviction, and in such picturesque detail, that I got the feeling there really *was* a Mr. Pencil out there in the world who was W.G.'s friend.

The first of my two scenes was shot in the backyard of a gorgeous house in Brentwood. All I had to do was cook hamburgers over a barbecue and smile. The boy playing my son ate fire. He stood in front of the camera, stuck a great burning torch down his throat and belched back flame, while grinning Dad back at the grill and the rest of the adoring family looked on.

On our fifth day of filming, Maris got permission to watch. Unsurprisingly, she and Weber hit it off instantly. He had her sit right next to him, where they talked and laughed like banshees between every take. Even Weber's people were surprised at this, judging by their looks and asides to each other. I was too busy barbecuing and smiling to have any real misgivings, but it was the first time I'd ever felt even vaguely uncomfortable about her with another man.

At lunchtime, we snuck off to a corner of the big yard to eat alone, but hadn't been there five minutes before Weber came over and asked if he could join us.

"Weber says I look like the only woman he's ever really loved. But she won't love him back."

"How come?" I bit a little too hard into a chicken wing.

He smiled. "Her name is Cullen James, and besides looking as great as Maris, she's also too goddamned loyal to her husband. She was the one who gave me the idea for this movie. I had the most extraordinary experience with her a couple of years ago that has kept me thinking ever since." He put his full plate down on the grass and lit up a cigarette instead. "Cullen had these dreams at night. Sequential—one following the other perfectly, night after night. Always in the same place: a fantasy land called Rondua, sort of like in *Lord of the Rings*, but wilder and far more frightening. Right after we met and I was trying to pry her away from her husband, I started having dreams in Rondua, too. Every night I traveled there. We even met up with each other there once. I couldn't begin to tell you what it was like. Take an old-time 'Purple Haze' acid trip, multiply it by about sixty, and you're at Rondua's front door. Giant dogs two stories high wearing bowler hats, a king named Sizzling Thumb, even the fucking *Devil* was around. His name was Jack Chili. It sounds nuts, but it happened. Believe me. Imagine sharing the same *dreams* with someone. Being able to talk about what you've *both* seen the next morning! It was really the only transcendental experience I've ever had, but it made me one hell of a believer."

"What happened to her? Are you still in touch?"

"Yes. She was attacked in New York by an escaped murderer. Killed him with a crowbar when he broke into her apartment."

"Jesus!"

"There's more. She swears she didn't do it. That her child from Rondua, 'Pepsi,' came over and did it for her."

"She sounds mad."

He shook his head vigorously. "No, she's full of magic. After she described what happened, I believed her."

Maris and I looked at each other. She spoke first. "Do you believe in magic, Weber?"

"Yes. Look at you, Maris. How is it possible in one lifetime to meet two women with almost the same face? Don't say coincidence. That's the easy way out."

Maris looked at me and mouthed the name "Moritz Benedikt."

Weber look at the ground. "I've given up trying to understand God. How He works. That sounds obnoxious, but when I saw Maris today, I could only shake my head. It doesn't disturb me anymore, although it used to. In college I majored in philosophy and religion. I was sure that was the way to get to the bottom of things. That, and some thinking on your own." He waved the thought away. "Silly little student. Do you ever read Emerson? He said it best. I like him very much. 'Do not require a description of the countries towards which you sail. The description does not describe them to you and tomorrow you arrive there and know them by inhabiting them.' That's it. That's how it is."

The second shot took place in Malibu. Mr. Pencil sets up a tripod on the patio of someone's beach house. Opening a briefcase, he takes out a sniper rifle, assembles it, and attaches it to the tripod. I didn't like it because the act was too close to what had happened with Nicholas. I told Weber that, but he only said "Use it! Show how Mr. Pencil dislikes what he does for a living, make him even more repellent."

Intercut with this would be shots of a bunch of nudists on a cruising boat. Accompanying them is a Dalmatian that roams the deck sniffing people and things. They talk and laugh and have a lazy, sexy day at sea. Suddenly one of them rears up with a big bullet hole in the middle of his chest, like a bright red carnation. Then the dog is hit too and knocked overboard.

Cut back to Pencil pulling the trigger again as he shoots everyone on the boat. Perfectly cool about it, he stops once to wipe sweat from his eyes before returning to the job. When he's finished, he takes the rifle and tripod apart, repacks them, and leaves.

The part with the people on the boat would be done later. Today was just me and my gun at the beach.

A firearms expert showed me how to put the pieces together without fumbling or looking confused. Luckily I had done something similar in an earlier film, so it wasn't hard after a couple of tries.

Everything went fine until I saw the dragon. I saw it through the telescopic sight of the rifle while looking out to sea, supposedly at my target. The creature was far away in the water, but the scope's magnification put it right on the end of my nose. It was black and long and *essed* up and down in the water, as if on a frolic.

What does a sea serpent look like? Here's the surprise: All that was going through my mind was how beautiful its eyes were. Totally feminine and sexy. Giant and deep, purple, and flecked with coppery yellow. I think there were even long lashes, too. It slowly turned its head toward shore and looked at us.

Someone off to my left screamed.

Another shouted, "Holy fucking *shit!* Look at *that!*"

"It's the Loch Ness monster!"

"Godzilla!"

I kept watching through the scope. Someone tugged at my sleeve.

"Walker, what does it look like?" Weber's excited voice.

"Beautiful eyes. You can't believe the eyes." I stepped away to let him see. He only looked a moment, then told his cameraman to try and catch it on film.

Some of the crew ran down to the water for a better look. The dragon/serpent seemed unbothered and uninterested. It looped and coiled and swirled in the water, once showing a spiked tail that seemed a mile behind its head.

I'd seen blue whales off the coast of South America with heads as big as open parachutes. I'd seen a Super Galaxy transport plane block the view of the entire sky as it left the ground. Colossal things, but this creature lazing in a green sea half a mile away was the biggest of all.

The only reactions I had were awe and a kind of bewildered love. No fear and no real amazement. Somewhere inside, we know wonders like that exist: they *have* to in a world as varied and individual as ours. What's more, we want them to be there, but science and rationality hold tight rein on our reality—if we haven't seen it, it isn't there.

Fine, but twenty people stood on the shores of the Pacific Ocean and the twentieth century watching something they'd been told all their lives didn't exist.

A police helicopter spluttered overhead and flew straight out toward the thing. Raising its monumental head, the serpent looked sedately at the whirring bug. The purple eyes blinked. Like a tall building that's just been dynamited, the sea all around it flew up as the monster dove and disappeared.

The *whop-whop* of the helicopter circling the empty roiling sea, the long crash on shore of high backwash waves; for those of us who'd witnessed it, life had for once broken its silence (or one of its rules) and told us a secret.

Yet it was no use trying to tell others, as we quickly found out. George Lambert offered the film he'd taken of the dragon to the television stations. They dutifully showed it, but also covered themselves by filling their studios with "experts" who unanimously denounced the sighting as either absurd or hilarious.

The only places that took it seriously were the creepy/ wacko newspapers like *The Truth* or *The National Voice. They* ran pictures of the monster next to articles on children who sold their mothers to the Ayatollah, or men who moved cream cheese with their minds.

The common belief was that Weber Gregston staged the whole thing to get publicity for his new film. He was unbothered either by the accusation or the days of craziness that followed.

"Who cares what they think, Walker? We know what we saw! That puts us one up on all of them. They want to think I'm pushing my movie? Fine. Or George's film is a fake? Fuck 'em. We saw it! We got a taste of what the world is really like under its skin. It's my friend Cullen's crazy dreamland, Rondua. That's the real truth. It's what we thought life was like when we were kids. Lying in bed at night, scared and excited about every sound and shadow out there. Remember those days?"

We were having drinks next to the swimming pool of his rented house in Laurel Canyon. Maris was doing slow laps alone while both of us watched her and took some sun. She wore a black swimsuit and, with her hair slicked back and gleaming, against the swimming pool blue she looked like a moving exclamation point.

"There are coyotes up here still. My neighbor told me when there was a fire in the canyon that he saw a whole family of them running away from the flames. Coyotes and maybe even wolves.

"That's like our sea monster. Who the fuck would ever think on a sunny day at Malibu you'd look over the rim of your Ray-Ban sunglasses, Coca-Cola in hand, and see the 'real thing' out there in the surf. Godzilla at the beach! Sounds like a title for a Roger Corman film."

Maris held on to the edge of the pool, listening. Her legs waved slowly back and forth in the water. The silence of the middle of the afternoon. The air smelled of chlorine, mimosa, and lemons. The extension phone nearby rang. With a groan, Weber got up to answer it. I looked at Maris and she blew me a little kiss.

"Philip! How are you? When'd you get back? Sure, I'm home. Sure, come over now. There are some people here you'll like. Come over when you like. Good. See you in a while. I'm glad you're back, you bastard!"

Grinning, he hung up. "You ever heard of Philip Strayhorn?"

"No."

"No one has, but everyone knows who he is. 'Bloodstone.' "

"Bloodstone! You mean in *Midnight?* That's the most hideous horror film I ever saw. *Midnight. Midnight Too. Midnight Always Comes* . . . How many of them have they made so far?"

"Three. He's made a good chunk of change playing Bloodstone in every one. We were roommates at Harvard and started in films together."

"You made *Breathing You* and he made *Midnight?* That's some difference."

Half an hour later, a nondescript balding man with an open, sweet smile walked out onto the patio and grabbed Weber from behind. The two of them danced around in each other's arms, oblivious to us.

When they separated, Strayhorn came over to us with an extended hand and that good smile.

"You're Walker Easterling. I've seen your films."

"You're kidding."

He immediately named four obscure clunkers I had made long ago, and said they were "terrific."

He used that word a lot, but the way he said it made me believe him. Philip Strayhorn was one of those people who seem to know something about everything (and everyone) and love to talk about it. A polymath for sure, but no show-off. He talked in such an excited, compelling, way that you were quickly caught up in both his enthusiasm and information, no matter what the subject.

How he'd gotten to be one of Hollywood's most famous on-screen villains was interesting in itself. Broke and out of work as an actor, he wrote the screenplay for the first *Midnight* and sold it on the guarantee they'd let him play the heavy if the film was ever done. It was made for $400,000 and grossed $17 million. The day we met, he'd just returned from Yugoslavia where they'd recently finished shooting the fourth sequel.

I wanted to know why he thought the films were so successful. He smiled and said one word, "Bosch."

"What do you mean?"

"When I wrote that first one, I had a book of Bosch's paintings in front of me and just kept looking at them as I wrote. You won't find any better monsters anywhere. Bloodstone is a combination of several of his figures. The only hard part was trying to imagine what those monsters would be like if they came to life. People go to the movies to be entertained. The best entertainment in the world is great art. You want to be scared? Look at *Garden of Earthly Delights* under a magnifying glass; it'll give you nightmares. Just don't tell that to the guy who goes to the movies at the shopping mall Saturday night. If he heard where Bloodstone came from, he'd walk out or want his money back. All the *Midnight* movies are Bosch, plus a lot of screaming and stabbing. They're not art, but they come from art.

"Tell me about your sea serpent. That's what I came over to hear."

Weber brought him a glass of ginger ale (he didn't drink alcohol), and between the two of us, we gave him as complete a description as possible. Then we went into the house and watched a video of George Lambert's film. Philip took a piece of paper and pencil off the desk and began drawing. After a while he stopped looking at the film.

He held up the drawing. Even in the flickering gray television light, the figure he'd sketched looked too familiar.

"This is an Elasmosaurus. It lived about a hundred and fifty million years ago, in the Jurassic and Cretaceous periods. Fifty feet long, with a neck on it that stretched about as far as the Golden Gate Bridge does. If your creature were real, that's what it'd be."

"What do you mean?"

Philip pointed at the television. "That thing is not classifiable, all told. That's what's scaring the experts. If they had a name for it, even a dinosaur a hundred and thirty-five million years old, they'd be more confident and willing to accept the possibility it's there. But it ain't a dinosaur. Scientists don't like things they don't know the names for. See the spikes on the tail? No Elasmosaurus had spikes, as far as they know. Its ears were also supposed to be very small. But this one's ears are big. Stop the film, Weber. Look at the size of those ears.

"The Leucrocotta, Catoblepas, Nasnas, sea serpents. All creatures talked about in legend, but no one's seen any of them since man decided they don't exist anymore. Why? Because man's got to be the biggest and smartest. One of modern man's inventions: If I can't photograph it with my super-duper camera, or get a reading on it with my monster meter, or catch it in my helicopter, then it isn't there.

"Okay, but this thing of yours is there because too many goddamned people *saw* it. The experts don't want to admit that, so they're scrambling around. Trying to sound convincingly arrogant and dismissive about things like actual sightings, or even your film there. It's all a big trick! You guys did it with hidden wires. Steven Spielberg did it a hundred times better in his last film. Convenient ways of getting out of it, no?

"You know what I was reading about today? Abtu and

Anet. Have you heard of them? In Egyptian legend, they were
two life-sized fish, identical-looking, that swam in front of the
Sun God's ship and protected it from danger. They swam day
and night, always on the alert. Isn't that a beautiful image? No
Abtu and Anet these days. Only sonar.

"Let's send out for a pizza. I haven't had a good disgusting one since I got back."

While Weber called The Pizza Clinic, Philip turned to
me and said in a quiet voice, "I really came over to talk to you.
Venasque told me he thought it'd be good if we met and talked
a little, if you have any questions or anything."

"Venasque knew I was here?"

Philip smiled and shrugged. "If he can teach you to fly, he
can know where you are."

"That makes me nervous."

"It shouldn't. You'll like him. He's an old Jew who
watches too much television and eats Doritos. It just happens
he's a shaman, too. The best I've ever met."

I leaned toward Strayhorn, already embarrassed about
what I was going to ask. "What exactly *is* a shaman? A teacher
or a holy man?"

"Both. More someone who shows you how to read your
own map. No matter what you learn, you'll come out the other
side of it knowing more about yourself."

"Did he teach you how to fly?" I looked around cautiously
after asking, in case someone might hear and think I was nuts.

"No. He taught me how to swim."

"To *swim?*" I said, too loudly.

He spread both hands and gently breast-stroked the air a
few times. "I never learned how. Never cared about it. So
Venasque taught me how to swim. I needed it."

"But just to swim? You could have gone to the YMCA for
that. Those were pretty expensive swimming lessons!" I was

about to go on, but stopped when I saw his gentle face harden. I'd offended him.

"Forget the cynicism, Walker. A good teacher knows intuitively what you need and gives you exactly that. Sometimes what he suggests shocks you, but then you learn fast he knows better than you. Venasque said I'd spent too much of my life looking inside and had to learn how to look out. Someone I know went to him and learned how to do calligraphy. Now they have the most beautiful handwriting you ever saw. What you need depends on who you are."

"All right, but swimming and good handwriting are one thing, Philip. You've got to admit that learning to *fly* is another! Wouldn't you be skeptical if you were me?"

"I was! Until I met him and talked to him for about an hour. In between his taco chips and Coca-Colas."

"What do you guys want on your pizzas? The works? Anchovies? Extra cheese?" Holding his hand over the receiver, Weber looked at us. Behind him, I could see Maris moving around the kitchen with a couple of green plates in her hands.

Philip got up and started for the phone. Stopping in front of me, he said all he was going to say about the shaman for the rest of the night. "Go and see him. He's waiting for you. Anything else I say will only bias you."

Mansfield Avenue is in the Hancock Park section of Los Angeles. The houses vary in style from Spanish to Tudor to postmodern, but are generally about the same size. What I found most interesting were the front yards. Almost all of them were small, but so perfectly green and mown that I got the feeling a billiard ball would roll unimpeded from one side to the other if only I gave it a small push. Driving slowly down the street checking for the right house number, I also noticed an inordinate number of men walking around in stiff dark suits, yarmulkas, and chest-length beards. Later, Venasque said with a wry smile that they were Secret Service men. When I asked "For which side?" he cracked up.

" 'For which side?' That's good, Walker. You gotta good sense of humor on you. We can use it later."

I don't know what I expected a shaman's house to look like, but Venasque's turned out to be no different from others on the block. A narrow straight driveway bordered one side of the lawn and went to a garage in back. A shiny black-and-silver Jeep was parked in there. The house itself was khaki-colored, with brown metal awnings and decorative wrought iron over all of the downstairs windows. Most of those windows were wide open when I went up the walk. Loud television noise poured out of them and onto the quiet street.

Before pressing the doorbell, I stopped a moment to hear if I could make out what show he was watching. Maybe if I could, it would tell me something about him. As if on command, the theme song for "I Love Lucy" boomed out. I looked at my watch—three in the afternoon. Right on time. I looked through a window and saw a chubby black-and-white bullterrier standing erect on a couch, staring right back at me. I pulled back. He reminded me of the lions in front of the New York Public Library. As soon as I rang the bell, he gave one blunt bark, jumped awkwardly from the couch, and skittered across the floor to the door.

I was nervous, and it didn't help when no one answered for the longest time. I was tempted to ring again but didn't. I would show the shaman patience. Maybe it was one of my first tests.

"Wait a minute, wait a minute, I'm coming!"

The dog barked again. Once.

"Shut up, Big! You know who it is."

I straightened up and quickly tried to decide what expression to have on when he opened the door. A Zen koan I'd once read crossed my mind. "Show me your original face, the face you had before your parents were born."

"Hello, Walker! It's about time you came around."

I don't know how it happened, but the first thing I saw was the pig. It was gun-metal gray and about the same size as the dog. It was definitely a pig, but a scaled-down, swaybacked version. Wagging its stringy tail like a happy dog, it came up and very loudly sniffed (snorted at) my leg.

"That's Connie, and the dog is Big Top. We were just having lunch. You want a sandwich?" He was short and fat, and had white, crew-cut hair. An almost completely forgettable face. He looked either like a retired policeman or the owner of a hot-dog stand. He wore a red polo shirt and a pair of overalls. The only thing that sort of stood out was that he was barefoot. I didn't know how to answer his sandwich invitation, so I said, "That'd be great," although I wasn't hungry. I couldn't stop looking at the pig and bullterrier. They stood next to each other and the pig licked the dog's face slowly and completely.

"Terrific. I got some great pastrami today at Cantor's. Come on into the kitchen. Just watch out for Connie. She likes walking close. I think she's got a thing for legs, or something."

Sure enough, the pig moved right with me as I walked through the place. She leaned heavily against my left leg the whole way.

Venasque's home was a real surprise. Although afternoon shadows had moved in, the rooms were so full of colorful, luminous objects and furniture that it *felt* like there was sun everywhere. The chairs and couches were all soft and round, and covered with tropical flower/exotic bird Lily Pulitzer patterns. Mustard and lime and raspberry carpets sat lightly on the polished blond wood floors. He ate at a white rattan table in a white breakfast room. The pig stopped in that room and collapsed on the white shag carpet as if the long trip to the kitchen was too much for her. Venasque stopped and shook his head when he saw her flop down.

"Give a pig M & Ms and she gets tired halfway through the day. All that sugar goes right to her head. No more candy, Connie. I don't know why I keep letting you have them."

The pig looked at him and squeaked. He shook his head again, and started for the kitchen.

"What kind of pig is she?"

"Vietnamese. An old Vietnamese pig. Over there in Germany they call them 'Vietnamese hanging stomach' pigs. That's not a very nice name, is it? Especially not for someone as smart as her. Besides, she keeps Big Top company when I'm not around."

The kitchen was different. Unlike the frilly, feminine feel of the other rooms, this one was all tile and stainless steel. Very high-tech and "cool," but done in such an interesting, individual way, that I couldn't stop looking around at it while he assembled my sandwich.

"This is a marvelous room."

"You like it? Harry Radcliffe designed it. You know Harry?"

"The architect? Of course." I didn't know much about the subject, but Radcliffe was so famous that it would have been hard not to know who he was. Besides that, he was one of Maris's big heroes, and she had photographs of his buildings up all over her apartment.

"Yeah, well, Harry studied with me a while. Funny, funny man. After we finished, I asked him to design me a kitchen instead of paying cash. But nothing too expensive, you know? Something for an old man who likes a straight line and a clean angle." He looked at me over his shoulder and winked. "I'll tell you something interesting. Harry is one of the biggest hotshot architects in the world, right? But a tin ear on that man like you can't imagine! The only thing he had to learn was how to listen to music. So I taught him how to play the accordion. He has about three of them now. But even after he learned how, you didn't want to be in the same room with him and that instrument when he played. A great architect and a terrible musician." He smiled and went back to stacking pastrami.

"Now where's that mustard? I put it right out here on the counter. Big Top, go get mc the mustard, will you?"

The bullterrier walked straight to the refrigerator and somehow, with a flick of his head (or nose), opened it. He got up on his hind legs, leaned deep into the fridge. Sticking his head forward, he put his mouth around something. A yellow tube of mustard. Jumping down, he closed the door with another head flick, and brought the tube to his master.

Venasque paid not attention. "Thanks, Big."

2.

"You want to rub your back up against my history, huh? Well, that's only fair. You told me yours."

We were sitting out on the small patio behind his house, drinking tea. January night had come and along with it, a coolness that snuck right into your bones. The tea tasted warm and good. Connie and Big Top slept on their respectively named pillows nearby. The pig never seemed to get comfortable: She kept hopping up, grunting as if something had bitten her ass, then trying to settle herself the right way.

"Walker, I'll tell you something. Honesty fades as you grow older. You get better at lying, so you do it more. Specially about yourself. But you want to know about me, okay." He scratched his head, then rubbed both hands over the top of it. "I come from the South of France, originally. My parents were German circus people. They traveled through that area once in their lives on the way to a date in Monte Carlo. They liked it so much they jumped out of their old lives right there and stayed. In the circus they'd had an animal act, which is one of my first memories—funny animals living in our house. They sold the circus caravan they'd lived in, and a couple of horses, and bought a farm out in the middle of nowhere. Do you know France? About fifteen miles from Carpentras and an hour and a half from Avignon. The place wasn't so special, but they loved it enough to work like crazy to get it going in the beginning. Then a little gift from God happened to us; my mother got interested in perfume. She cooked up some kind of special blend that only she knew how to do. That, and what we got from the farm, put us in good shape. Not great, but comfortable, and still happy to be there. Then my sister Ilonka and I were born one year after the other.

"We grew up with perfume smells, funny animals, and that French countryside. It was a heaven, Walker. When I was seven, my father taught me how to walk the tightrope. He tied a horse rope between the two olive trees right in front of our door. In the summer we went into the fields and picked lavender for my mother. Have you ever seen a lavender field blowing in the wind? We spoke German with our parents and French with our friends. When we got tired of one language, we'd switch to the other and have a whole other world of words to use." He stopped and scratched the dog with a bare foot. Big Top looked up sleepily and licked the foot. Once. "You know what I remember? Glasses full of sunlight. Having family picnics and seeing the sun in every glass we used."

My lessons began at the end of that sentence. I blinked once, thinking about his family and their picnics. The moment I closed my eyes, there was a completely different smell in the air. California night is damp and ripe; fresh-cut grass and dew, night-blooming flowers somewhere nearby. This new smell was dry and sunny, hot flowers and earth giving up their scent to two o'clock on an August afternoon. In the South of France, 1920.

When I opened my eyes, the first thing I saw was a boy riding a zebra bareback past a field of lavender. Black, white, lavender, all moving, all movement. He wore white shorts but no shirt or shoes. Both boy and animal had the same serious, thoughtful expression on their faces.

"Do you want some wine?"

A woman with brown flyaway hair and bold green eyes knelt by my side, a glass of wine in her hand. I realized I was sitting in the shifting shade of a (chestnut?) tree with giant yellow leaves as my moving roof.

"The boy knows you're watching, Walker, so he's riding like a good cadet. If you weren't here, he'd go like the devil flying through hell. Here, come on and drink this." She shoved the glass at me with one hand, and pushed the hair out of her face with the other. I took it and, still watching the boy and zebra canter back and forth, forgot to thank her.

"It's Venasque, isn't it? When he was a boy."

"He *is* a boy! What do you think?" His mother's voice was a challenge.

A young girl with something cupped tightly between two small hands came from behind the tree. Smiling, she held it out to us: it was ours if we wanted. She looked very much like the boy.

"Mama, *regarde!*"

"What now, Ilonka, another lizard? Put it down. Show us."

The girl dropped to her knees, hands still cupped. She was eight. "Ilonka" means apple tree in Hungarian. Her husband's name was . . . *would be* . . . Raymond. She would be shot by the Nazis when she was twenty-eight. How did I know these things?

A gray-green lizard sat still between her slowly opening hands. Before she could do anything, it shot out and right up the tree. I watched her while her happy eyes followed it up.

She kept a blue flower in her dresser drawer, pretending it had been given to her by a boy she knew. Just that morning she'd put a finger in her own shit and, electric with guilt, tasted it. She'd been especially good today as contrition for having done such a wicked thing, although no one knew about it, besides the two of us. She looked at me and smiled sneakily. She knew what I was thinking.

I was about to say something unimportant when I heard Venasque's voice. His adult voice fingered its way through my conscious mind.

". . . mother liked the name Ilonka. It means—"

"Apple tree in Hungarian." I'd put my head down and closed my eyes, knowing what would be there when I opened them again: today, California, sixty years later. I was right. Both hands locked behind his neck, Venasque was staring at the night sky.

"Good, you saw! I wasn't sure. It was nice there, huh?"

"Was I really there?"

He grabbed for something in the air and brought his hand down to show me what it was. Sitting in there was the lizard his sister had let run up the tree.

"Walker, there are two important things you've got to know before we get started. You know everything about everyone. We all do. You're surprised you could go back to that day in my life? Don't be. It's an easy trick to learn. Someplace in you is the knowledge of every day of my life. I gave you a little push this time to find it, but soon you'll be able to do it whenever you want. But you won't use it. Know why? Because you won't want to. Even with your own life. Hopefully, by then you'll want to figure out how to live without making stupid mistakes on your own. Do you read mystery novels? Yes? It's the same with them. A fool can read ten pages and then turn to the end of the book to see if the butler did it. But why ruin the whole process? The fun is trying to figure out the mystery yourself. If you get it right at the end then you really feel good and not a cheat."

"Why would I want to learn about this place in myself if I'm not going to use it?"

"For the power and the discipline! Only weak, helpless people learn karate so they can hit someone. Don't you ever watch 'Kung Fu'? One of my favorite shows. Remember I told you I was going to teach you how to fly? Well, I am, but you won't ever do it. You'll never want to, if I teach you right. The satisfaction is knowing you can."

"What was the second thing I should know before we start?"

"That's something else. The second is, we know the past is a few million years old. But the future . . . there's no guarantee it will be even half as long. Right? Well, that's what I wanted to tell you—it *won't* be half as long.

"Connie. Connie! Come here. I gotta lizard for you."

The pig sprang up and waddled over. Venasque put his open hand in front of her. She gave it one fast *shloop* with her wet mouth and the sixty-year-old lizard was gone. She nuzzled his hand to make sure nothing else delicious was there before returning to her pillow. Venasque shook his head in wonderment, as if she had done something special.

"There are a few years left, but that's not important. I think it'll be best when everything is over."

"What do you mean?"

"Us, *life,* man's whole long story will finally have 'The End' written across it. What nobody understands is what comes *after* that. Only some of those who are around when it does happen will be able to find that out. I hope I'm one of them, but I may never come back at that time."

"Come back? You mean reincarnation?"

"They've been talking and writing about reincarnation forever, but no one seems to get the hint, you know? Man is so dumb, down deep. You think people have talked about it for thousands of years because they're making a mistake? No. Reincarnation means coming back and working on life until you get things right, Walker. But even people who do believe in it never think that maybe life on earth won't go on forever. They think you live and die and come back maybe ten or fifty or a hundred years from now. That's wrong. You do live and die and come back, but not always in the future. Know why? Because after a certain date, there *isn't* a future. There's an end to our time here. Pretty soon some idiots will make a big mistake that'll lead to other big mistakes, and then the world will die. And I mean everything will die—man, animals, bugs. Sad, but that's the way it is. Getting back to what I was saying, there's only this certain amount of time available to us humans to live in. You can come back in 1390 or 1790 or 1990, but not so long after that because if you did, you'd be born on a charcoal briquette! So we live and work out our troubles now, or in our past. Sometimes we Ping-Pong back and forth, depending on what we need and where it is in our history. It even happens to animals. That sea monster you saw? Where do you think it came from?"

"Philip Strayhorn said—"

The old man waved away the rest of my sentence. "Phil Strayhorn's read too many books. He should swim more. I'll give you the technical name of that thing if you want, but all you gotta do is look at those old sea maps explorers used. There's a dragon like yours drawn on each one. That part is No Man's Land! Don't sail here! You think guys like Columbus and Magellan were fooling around? You think they were crazy? Hell no! They said don't sail there because they'd seen sea monsters there. But monsters come back too, Walker. From what I can understand, they usually die and come right back to the same time, but sometimes they pop up nearby. Like out at Santa Monica." He smiled.

"Why would a sea serpent be reincarnated?" Did I believe any of this? I did.

"For the same reason man is reincarnated—to work things out. It doesn't matter where we are in time because the problems are always the same. I can imagine the same is true for sea monsters.

"I'm going to show you something now which I shouldn't do yet, but you need it to believe what I've been telling you. Don't get scared, though. Even if it gets bad, try not to get scared."

Before I could say anything (like "No!" or "Help!"), I realized I was putting my hands out in protest, not against Venasque, but some man I'd never seen before. We were in a cold gray room somewhere, and my back was flush against a window. I saw bright daylight coming in from behind me.

The man coming at me was a midget, no taller than my beltline. He was dressed in a natty blue suit that was a little masterpiece of tailoring and had obviously cost a lot. More than his height, the most dismaying (and interesting) thing about him was his face. It had the seraphic, suffering beauty of Christ in a Renaissance painting: long golden hair, wispy beard, and eyes infused with all the scars and joys of life.

"You are *my* son!" he said, pushing me backward through the window.

I didn't have a chance to scream because the next thing I knew, something heavy was standing on my chest, licking my face. The pig.

I looked up and saw its craggy, comical face and sweet eyes against the California night sky. I pushed her off and looked for Venasque. He was standing by one of the flower beds, watering his plants.

"What'd you see back there?"

Weakly, I pushed myself off the ground and into a sitting position. "What the hell was that all about?"

He put the watering can down and stabbed a stiff finger at me. "Don't *ever* ask me questions in that voice, Walker! You either work with me and believe in what I'm doing, or you get out! You gotta lot to learn and not *so* much time to do it in."

"Well what the hell *was* that? You send me back to some-place where a midget pushes me out a window? What is that? Where was I? Come on, Venasque, I don't understand this stuff!"

"It was your last life, Walker. How you died back there. You fell out a window? Did you hit the ground? Did you feel yourself die?"

"Should I?"

"Yes; the most important thing you could've done would have been to stay there and feel yourself die! Who was it that pushed you?"

"I told you—a midget who called me his son."

"Don't you want to know if it was your father? Don't you want to know why it happened? That's the whole purpose of studying. All these magical things that have been happening to you lately all come from that last life."

My heart was beating like a hammer on an anvil. BAM BAM BAM. "Do you know why I died there?"

He pursed his lips. "I don't know. I got a feeling, but there's all kinds of funny stuff coming out of you. Like some-one's turning the channels on you fast and I can't see any one picture yet."

"How will I get back there to find out about it?"

"After we go to the mountains I'm going to have you go through a couple of rebirthings. You know what they are?"

"You hypnotize me and I go back through past lives?"

"Something like that. First you gotta learn some other things. We gotta fix the TV set to stay on one channel before we can watch the Super Bowl, eh?"

That night Maris and I made love—slowly and deeply. After it was over, she said it'd felt like two clouds touching and then moving together as one great whiteness. Later, we figured out that was probably the night she became pregnant. Neither of us was surprised.

Afterward, we lay on our backs, holding hands. She hadn't asked anything about what had happened with Venasque because she knew I'd tell her as soon as I'd sorted the meeting out in my mind.

"Walker, we're good for each other, aren't we?"

"Of course! Why are you asking?"

She squeezed my hand hard, then let it go. "Because I'm letting myself fall more and more for you, and part of me gets scared doing that.

"Did I ever tell you about the fat man I saw in Vienna? We were supposed to meet one day, but I had some time to kill before, so I went into an AIDA for coffee. The biggest fat man I ever saw walked in right behind me and sat down nearby. He was so huge that it looked like he was sitting on a pin and not a chair. You know what he ordered? I counted. Three pieces of cake, two scoops of ice cream, and when he was finished, two coffees with *Schlag.* He ate the whole . . . blop in about five minutes. His hand and mouth never stopped moving: like a big steam shovel. At the end, when he went to pay, he reached for his wallet and took out the only bill in there—a hundred-schilling note. His check was for ninety-eight. I heard the waitress tell him. He gave the hundred and told her to keep the change.

"The first thing I thought was, how sad. This big fat man, who obviously didn't have much else in the world *but* cake to look forward to, used up the very last money he had to buy some. Then I thought some more about it and realized how wrong and condescending to think that way."

"How so?" I took her hand again.

"Because he probably knew sooner or later those cakes he loved so much would kill him with a heart attack or something as bad. But so what? That's what he loved best, so damn it all, he's going to appreciate it to the last cent or breath he had. Isn't that wonderful?" She turned to me while the soft light from the bedroom window fell over her shoulder and the top of her breast. "I can't tell you how envious I was of him. Know why? Because never in my life has there been anything I'd been that crazy about. Nothing. *Except you.* You're the first. So I have every reason to be scared of that, don't I?

"Obsession is nice, but it can also kill you."

"You think I'm going to kill you?" I smiled at her, but she did not smile back.

"I don't know. No, of course not. I'm hoping I know you well enough to believe you're always telling the truth. That's a lot, Walker! I love you. I love you too much sometimes. You've got more of my secrets now than anyone else ever. That makes you kind of dangerous, you know what I mean?"

I leaned over and kissed her gently. "Can I tell you my coffee story now?"

"Don't make fun of me. That story really happened."

"I believe you. I'm not making fun of you, Maris. I only want to tell you my coffee story so you can see how you fit into *it.*"

She pinched my arm, harder than was necessary. "You're not going to make this up just for me?"

"I swear to God not. This happened about a week before we came over. Remember that day I gave you that big bouquet of roses? Then. I went in for a coffee, just like you did. Anyway, I had just ordered when I saw an old man sitting by himself off in a corner. It was a big place, and I had the feeling that was *his* seat every day. His *Stammtisch.* All the waitresses seemed to know him. I don't even know why I kept looking at him after that first glance, except for this great bad boy smile he had on the whole time. Thank God I did!

"The waitress brought him a cup of coffee, and for the first time I saw his hands. Maris, he had the worst case of palsy or Parkinson's disease I think I've ever seen. His hands were shaking so badly that they were out of control. There was no way that man would be able to pick up the cup and get it all the way to his mouth before it spilled all over. But he kept smiling, as if he had a great big trick up his sleeve and was proud of it. What was he going to do? With those crazy shaking hands, he reached into his coat and brought out a straw—"

"A *straw?*"

"Yup. A big, long, yellow straw that he dropped right into the cup. It looked like a little kid was going to use it, but the thing worked perfectly. Think about it for a minute. After it was in, he didn't once have to use his hands, just his lips. But you know what I loved most? After he took his first sip, he looked up with the proudest expression on his face. No double-crossing hands were going to stop *him* from having his coffee."

She slid closer to me. "I like that story."

"I liked seeing it, but you know what struck me after I saw him? The first thing? That I had to tell *you* about it. Partly because I want to tell you everything now, and partly because . . . because you're *my* straw, Maris. Without you, I know this now, there'd be no way I'd ever be able to—"

"Drink coffee?" She giggled.

"Drink my life. I've been trying to think of a good way of letting you know how much I love you. Seeing that guy showed me. Before you, I had such shaky hands. I know you won't, but I love you so much I wish you'd marry me."

She put a hand over my mouth and said "Sssh!" But she also smiled—beamed—so at least I knew she'd been thinking about it, too.

We fell asleep with our foreheads touching. When we both jumped awake later, she said it was because I'd butted her so hard with my head.

I'd been dreaming of a cemetery. A Russian Orthodox cemetery in St. Petersburg, Russia, around the turn of the century. Outside the high walls, horse-drawn sleds, *droshkies*, hushed over the snow-packed streets, with now and then the delicate metal tinkle of sleigh bells. Snow was spinning slowly down, but it was the nineteenth of April, Easter Day.

The place was full of people because this was traditionally the day they came to greet and honor their dead. They had colored Easter eggs with them which they lay on the graves. After that, they opened bags and baskets and took out all kinds of food which they ate while standing around the egg-orna-mented graves, chatting gaily with each other, including their dead in the conversations.

My name was Alexander Kroll. As a child, my father had liked to call me Rednaxela when we played together. I had come today to visit his grave and bring him an egg. He'd died the year before of a cancer that slowly ate his face and showed me what he would look like forever once the disease had fin-ished with him.

He had been a poet, a man capable of taking our endlessly long Russian words and sewing them invisibly together into beautiful quilts of language and imagery. While the cancer squeezed that last of him in its stone fist, he began work on a play about a child who accidentally builds a new Tower of Babel with toy blocks. My father died silent and sad because his body wouldn't permit him to finish the first act. The in-scription on his grave read *Dum vita est, spes est.* While there is life, there is hope. He chose it himself.

I didn't know my mother because she'd died when I was

born. However, my father, who had the very un-Russian name Melchior, was almost enough to compensate for a life without her. He cooked and cleaned for us, showed me off to the world as his greatest achievement and joy, and spoke to me from the very beginning as an intelligent adult who would naturally understand and appreciate the sound of life's thunder.

An old couple nearby stood in front of a small grave and spoke approvingly of how well Nikolai looked. I looked at the tombstone and saw that Nikolai (their son?) had been dead forty years. Father would have appreciated their ongoing love. Like Heinrich Heine, most of his work had been a hymn to the good in life. One of his friends, Nozdryov, said Melchior Kroll admired thieves for their initiative, earthquakes for changing the scenery, and a cholera plague for inspiring artists to their greatest work. But the same Nozdryov fell on his knees and wept the day they lowered my father into the earth.

"We didn't deserve him, Alexi. If he isn't in heaven right now, then God is a whore."

In my pocket was the knife I'd used two nights before to kill the red woman. It was a beautiful Swedish knife and had always done its job perfectly, almost known by itself where that baby-soft spot just below the ear sang out to be cut. If I was in a good mood, the job was finished in two moves: once hard below the ear into the neck, then out again and straight into the heart. The first touch for greeting, the second to finish.

The red woman said she worked in a leather factory, making gloves. I believed her because beneath all her fingernails was the red dye she used in her job. I noticed all their hands. One woman had bitten every fingernail down to the nub, another had black on two fingers from blotting ink in her office. The red woman, the nub woman, the black woman. All of St. Petersburg was talking about it. I had become the celebrity my father should have been. I had the fingertips of each of their thumbs in my pocket. I was writing a play about it.

Bending down to his grave, I took out pieces of bread and cheese. The bread caught for a moment on the knife, so I had to reach deeper into that pocket to free it.

From behind me I heard someone shout, "Look out! It's a mad one. Look at its face!"

I turned and saw the dog. It ran, then stopped and swayed as if dancing to some secret music. People yelled at each other to watch out—it was mad, it had rabies. And of course it did, but that was him now. I stayed where I was and put my hand out for him to come to me. He tried, but his roaring eyes and rubbery legs kept him standing where he was. His thick brown tongue hung uselessly out of one side of his mouth. He saw me and growled, then whimpered. He fell down and got up, fell down again. Poor thing.

"Careful, it'll bite you!" The old man who'd come to visit his Nikolai tried weakly to pull me away. I brushed his hands away.

"Come here."

When he was a meter away, he began speaking to me in German.

"*Vielleicht bist du Rippenbiest, Hammelwade, oder Schnürbein?*"

I put my hand out again to touch him. When I moved, his eyes cleared to a ferocious gold. He lunged, biting deep through my arm into the bone.

"Hello, Papa."

Venasque drove his Jeep like a little old man.

"I *am* a little old man, Walker. What do you expect?"

We were traveling north on the Pacific Coast Highway at thirty-five miles an hour. The car was packed with mysterious-looking boxes, a portable television, and both animals. The two of them either sat at attention next to each other, an inch behind my ear, or lay on their name pillows and snored like propeller planes. Untrue to his word, Venasque had an economy-size bag of M & M candies on his lap that he fed to them over his shoulder.

"They get tired traveling. This gives them some extra energy."

He kept his hands at three and nine o'clock on the steering wheel and never moved them an inch from that position. He checked both inside and outside mirrors constantly. Every hour, no matter where we were on the road, he slammed on the brakes "just to make sure they're working." I found that unnerving, but the dog and pig slept on peacefully or ate their M & Ms in contented silence.

"Why'd you buy such a big car?"

"I travel to the mountains a lot. If you get in an accident in a Jeep, you don't have to worry. Besides, right before I got it, I saw John James driving one down Pico Boulevard. That was good enough for me."

"Who's John James?"

He looked at me incredulously. "Don't you watch 'Dynasty'? Jeff Colby. He's a major TV star."

A 1951 Ford passed us on the left going about twenty miles an hour.

"How much television *do* you watch a day?"

"As much as I can. When I don't have to teach, I try to go *straight* through."

"You watch all day?"

"Don't sound condescending, Walker. Can you remember your last three lives? I remember mine. Can you fly? I can. Can you do this?" He took something off the dashboard—a snapshot of his animals. With one hand, he stood the picture vertically on the tip of his thumb. It stayed there and didn't move. Reaching over, I took it and did the same trick on my own finger. Like the day in Maris's apartment with her photograph of Luc.

"Good! You can do that. It saves me some time. Who taught you?"

"No one. It happened by itself."

He checked both rearview mirrors. "Nope. Lesson number one: Nothing happens by itself. It happens either because you got a special talent, or because you teach yourself. Looks like with this, you found part of yourself in that photo and it said hello to you."

"I don't understand." I put the picture down on the seat.

"You want to hear how it happened to me?"

"I'd love to, but do you think you could first speed up a little and go around this guy? He keeps looking back as though he's afraid we're going to hit him."

Venasque gave it some gas and passed a man struggling along on a bicycle. When we were by, the rider gave us the finger and shook his head. Venasque waved.

"Back in France before the war, I was a kindergarten teacher. The best job I ever had. I sat in a room and watched little kids grow up. The only things I had to teach them were fun to do, and most of the time all we did was laugh. I taught well, too, because if you failed *them*, you failed life.

"It took a long time for the war to reach us because our town was unimportant, but when it did, it was like a knife in the eye. Nice people I'd known all my life started wearing uniforms and flying Nazi flags and saying Jews were shit. We tried to ignore it, but couldn't.

"Then people started taking their kids out of our school because both my sister and I taught there and we were Jews."

"The Nazis killed her, didn't they?"

Venasque licked his lips and nodded. "You know that too? Yes, they shot Ilonka and her husband Raymond in their own garden. Someone told me she had a strawberry in her mouth when they picked up her body. Death doesn't even let you finish your meal, huh? That was the same day they came for me and the children. Do you remember that?"

I looked at him. "Should I?"

"You were there, Walker. I thought you might remember. Yes."

"Benedikt!"

"Yes, sir!" My palms were flat down in the dirt. I could feel the warmth of the earth through them. We'd been walking all day, and the warmth which had felt so good in the early morning was no longer friendly by three o'clock. All our uniforms were sweated through; we smelled hot, rank, and bitter. Marching, the rucksack I carried felt like a bag of cement against my back. I wanted to throw my rifle away and never pick it up again. Never shoot it, never carry it, never see it. What I had seen that day made me tired of everything, including myself.

I wanted to go home. I wanted to sit in the Café Central and read the Viennese newspapers, or perhaps write a letter to someone. The place would be shadowy and cool as stone. When I had downed the last *Schluck* of real coffee, I'd walk out onto the Herrengasse and take an easy stroll down toward the Opera. Sometimes when you passed the Spanish Riding School you saw trainers leading the horses across the street to the performance ring. I loved the sound their hooves made on the cobblestones.

But I wasn't home. I was a German soldier in southern France in the middle of a war that meant nothing to me. Every day we marched from one small village to the next, scaring these quiet farmers for no reason other than malice. If they gave us trouble, we shot them.

That morning someone shot back. We were standing in

the middle of a country road, waiting for our lieutenant to finish pissing, when we heard that high *skak* of a faraway rifle shot. A fat chip flew off a stone wall nearby, along with the *ping* of the ricochet. The entire troop went down and started firing everywhere at random.

An annoying loudmouth named Korbei, who looked like a goldfish with glasses on, shot a woman and her husband. They were sitting in their garden a few meters away, eating lunch. Korbei thought they had American hand grenades on the table. It later turned out to be a bowl of large strawberries. Korbei was unfazed. He went into their house and stole their movie magazines.

"Benedikt, take two men and go down to the school. Get that Jew teacher and whatever kids there who are Jewish. Take all of them to the *mairie*. Make *sure* to get all the Jews, so if anyone checks, we'll be okay. We'll meet you there in an hour. The trucks should be here by then to take them. And be careful! Whoever shot at us is still around, and I'm sure he's got friends. These people are going to shit when they see their neighbors get trucked out of here."

"Lieutenant, the kids, too? Can't we just say—"

He looked at me coldly. "No. Do *you* want to ask headquarters that question? I don't. Do you think those assholes give a shit if it's a little Jew or a big one? Especially after this morning?

"Benedikt, I want to go home when this war is over. I also want to have *all* my arms and legs when I get there. I don't give a shit who wins. As long as they leave me alone, I'll get their Jews and shove them on trucks and even wave good-bye when they drive off. You know that couple Korbei killed this morning? It made me sad, but not as sad as if that sniper had shot me and I couldn't fuck, or walk, or see, or *live* anymore. *That* would make me sad! So we'll all follow orders while I'm in command.

"Today's new orders are to get the Jews in that school and bring them to the *mairie*. You want to talk some more about it? Too bad, because I don't. Finished. Go to the school and be nice to those kids when you get them. Get going."

I had no idea where they would take the Jews after we brought them in. We'd seen kilometer-long freight trains in the railroad yards at both Avignon and Carpentras, but were they for these people? I knew they were sending Jews to work camps in some parts of Europe, but did that mean all of the Jews in Europe? We'd also heard terrible, unbelievable rumors about what went on in those camps, but who knew if they were true? There was too much propaganda about everything these days. You never knew what to believe, or whose word to trust. Everyone had a story, even the stupidest person had "just heard something incredible." At first, we believed everything because everything was possible then, but now it went the other way—believe nothing until it happened or you saw it for yourself. Besides, there was too much to think about right where we were, especially now that these French farmers had begun shooting back at us.

I took Peter and Haider with me because they were smart old-timers who didn't need to be told to think before acting. If something bad happened while we were at the school, they would at least react coolly.

As we walked down the hill out of town, I thought of my father in Vienna. How proud he'd been when I came home in my uniform the first time. His son, a soldier! In his last letter he'd gone on about how great things would be when I got back. We would expand the store because, as everyone knew, a soldier just home from war wants to celebrate his return to normal life with a new suit. He was in the middle of pulling off a deal that would make my "head turn around." There was a warehouse in town full of material confiscated from a Jew's wholesale store. If he talked to the right people, Papa could buy the whole lot of hopsack and serge and loden for next to nothing. And *then* we'd be in business! I could imagine his face as he wrote these words down on the page. The little man with the sad, saint's eyes. He would hold his green Pelikan fountain pen down at the very bottom, and when he was finished, his first three fingers would be all black.

He also said it was so hard getting good shaving material now that he'd decided to grow a beard and see how it looked. He knew people would laugh at a midget with a beard, but my father had been laughed and pointed at all of his life, so it made no difference to him what the world thought.

What would he say when I told him about what had happened with Elisabeth? How he disliked her! He disliked any girlfriend I had, but Elisabeth was truly his enemy. He had tried every trick he had to undermine our relationship, but she saw through them all and ended up laughing in his small face. He was nothing to her except the father of the man she wanted to marry. She didn't even bother to laugh or be shocked by his size. Maybe that was the greatest affront to him: her indifference to his freakishness. She wasn't kind or pitying about it, nor did she overlook it. It simply *was,* but since she didn't care about him, she didn't care about it either.

"There's the school."

Haider unslung his rifle and began loading it as we walked. Peter adjusted his rucksack.

"How do you want to do this?"

"I don't know yet. Let's talk to the schoolteacher first."

"You think he's going to help us? You're crazy."

"Let's just see."

The school was low and made of stone. As we approached, we heard children singing inside. Their voices were all sweet and high and happy. The three of us exchanged looks.

"That fucking lieutenant! Why'd he send us to do this?

The teacher is one thing, but little kids? I don't care if they're Jews. Listen to that! They're little kids."

The veins stood out in Peter's neck and his face was tomato red when he said it.

"How do you know it wasn't a kid who shot at us this morning?"

"Don't be an asshole, Haider. You know what they're going to do with these kids. You saw all those empty trains in Avignon. My brother lives in Linz. He told me they've got one of those camps out in Mauthausen. There's a stone quarry there a couple of hundred feet high. They set them to work cutting rock. If they mess up, the guards throw them off the top of the quarry. You don't think they do that to kids, too? The lieutenant was right about one thing—those assholes in Berlin don't care what kind of Jew it is—little or big. They kill them all the same."

I looked at him. "You don't know that for sure. I never heard about a camp in Mauthausen."

"Benedikt, if you shut your eyes any tighter, you're going to start seeing stars."

As we got closer to the building, I saw someone looking out the window at us. A man with his hands in the air, as if he was directing the music, was looking our way. At the end of the day, when we could breathe again and stop shaking, we heard he was the brother of the woman Korbei shot.

"Is that the teacher?"

"It must be." I took a step forward while the other two stayed back. One of them jacked a shell into the chamber of his rifle.

"Monsieur Venasque?"

The man in the window lowered his hands and looked at me.

"Do you speak German?" The only phrase I knew in French.

"Yes. What do you want? I'm in the middle of a lesson."

"I'm sorry, but would you please come out here and bring all of your students with you?"

He didn't move for a moment, then nodded at me and disappeared from view.

"Should we go in there to make sure? Maybe he's got a gun."

That made sense, so I went forward and entered the building alone after telling the others to be ready.

The place smelled of delicious flowers. There were bouquets of them everywhere, along with children's drawings on the walls, and a blackboard in front of the room with musical notes written on it. The children turned and all of them seemed either pleased or happy to scc me. They looked to be about four or five years old.

The teacher was at his desk, holding an open briefcase. What made me smile was that his plain face reminded me very much of Herr Schleimer, the man who ran the *Würstel* stand at the end of my street in Vienna.

Seeing my smile, the teacher hesitated a moment, and then smiled back gratefully. I didn't want to encourage him, but didn't want to scare him, either. He knew what was going on. If he made things easier for us, that would help.

Closing his briefcase, he told the children to stand by their desks and be quiet as birds sleeping in the nest. He translated the sentence for me.

"Some of them are afraid of you. Their parents told them Nazis are monsters."

"Would you please tell me which of them are Jewish?"

"Why?" He held the briefcase flat against his chest, as if for protection.

"That's not your business. Which of them are Jews?"

Slowly, slowly, he put his free hand out, palm out, and pointed to the first child in the first row. "Céline!"

The little girl, serious and adorable, rose off the ground until she was floating horizontally a foot above her desk. Spreading her arms like a bird, or a child airplane, she veered softly left and glided across the room out the open window.

"Marcel, Claire, Suzy—"

These children, like impossible peasant angels, rose, and flying too, followed their friend out the window. I ran to watch them, not as a soldier but only a man dashing after wonder.

"Look! Look at them!"

Peter and Haider didn't need to be told: they had their heads back and looked as shocked as I'm sure I did. Without doing anything, we watched them fly away over a purple field of lavender.

Remembering where I was, I turned and fixed my rifle on the teacher. Who wasn't there. I looked around the room, but the only ones there were the children. I looked at a little boy and asked him in sign language where his teacher was. The boy giggled and threw up his hands as if they were full of confetti.

"I never knew what I actually did to make it happen. Even today I'm not exactly sure."

We were stopped at a traffic light next to the ocean. A bunch of surfers and their striking girlfriends walked close in front of us, toting their surfboards. Every one of them had long blond hair and third-degree tans.

"Venasque, where did you go? Did you actually disappear? I couldn't find you anywhere. How did you make those kids fly?"

The light changed and he accelerated without answering. It made me mad.

"*Was* I there or not? Was that one of my lives?"

"You know yourself about Moritz Benedikt, Walker. Remember the man on the gravestone in Vienna who looks like you? And the midget who pushed you out the window? That was your life too. You're beginning to find some of the pieces now and put them together. They're your pieces.

"Yes, you were there. Both of us were. That's where we met last. You never stop meeting the same people in your lives. It's necessary. You just connect up with them differently each time."

"What happened that day? Where did you go?"

"I don't know. I disappeared for a while. I only closed my eyes and said 'Help them' to whoever was listening. There was nothing else left to do! It was the first time I ever discovered we've got things inside to save everyone, only you've got to go deep down for it. God gives us a model kit with all the right parts, but no instructions. It's up to us to find that this and that go together. Most people don't do it, though. They glue things together fast and without thinking because they're lazy with their lives. They don't think of working harder and trying to make something beautiful, or maybe even important. Just a nice 'model' they can live in. But sometimes when you're pushed or scared, like I was, you use your model kit better because you have to."

I wasn't in the mood for Kahlil Gibran philosophy. "What about all the people who try to put the kit together right, but still end up in the shit, Venasque? What about all the nice Jews who were gassed, or the little kids who die of starvation in—" His look stopped me.

"Nobody said life was fair, son. None of us ever figure out all the right combinations. There's a way to learn some of them, but no—Hey! You see that girl there? The one eating the sandwich by the black station wagon? Do you recognize her? That was your red woman in Russia, the one you killed. Today she's having a good time at the beach with her boyfriend. She doesn't even *begin* to sense that the man who killed her a couple of lifetimes ago is driving by. Incredible! Do you know how important it is that she realize that? My God, it'd help her so much to get through this life if she went up to you and asked some of the right questions. But she won't. She's so lazy she wouldn't even know you if you walked up and said hello. Maybe she'd feel uncomfortable or drawn to you, but she wouldn't know why. But that funny feeling wouldn't interest her. The poor girl has another bunch of trouble coming up and she could easily avoid it if she put only a *little* time into trying to understand how to do things right. Not easily, but right. She won't. She's happy walking on the beach in California with her boyfriend's hand on her tushy."

"Do you really know what will happen to her?" I turned completely around to watch the girl. She was kissing the boy a foot away from the thundering traffic.

Venasque sighed. "Yes, I think I know."

"Do you know what's going to happen to you?"

"You mean do I know what's going to happen to *you*, Walker? No. That's what interests me like crazy. I haven't met anyone in years I can't read quickly. I'm not going to teach you just because I'm a nice guy. There's got to be something important for me in my students too. I know some things, sure, but I've got a long way to go, too.

"Wow! Look at the figure on that redhead! I love making this drive. You see enough beautiful girls to make you goofy for three weeks."

Outside Oxnard, we sat on the beach eating and watching the animals dabble with the water. The wind was blowing and kept the heat of the day off us.

Venasque loved sandwiches. In one of his mysterious boxes in the back of the car was our lunch, which consisted of two hero sandwiches as big and round as matching 1930s hotel armchairs. They were packed with so many crayon-colored peppers, pickles, hard-boiled eggs, cheeses, and cold cuts that, try as it might, the tongue couldn't single out one special taste or flavor from the others.

I was only halfway through my chair when Venasque got up, brushed his hands on his pants, and said, "Okay, let's begin."

Looking up at him, even knowing what he had done to me already, I couldn't imagine him capable of great magic. I put the sandwich down on a piece of waxed paper and stood up.

"Go find yourself a good thick stick, about so big." He spread his hands about ten inches.

"Anything else?"

"No, only a stick. That's all you'll use." He turned away brusquely and whistled for the animals. They came running.

I found a stick of driftwood a few feet away and brought it over.

"That's a good one. Now, Walker, what I want you to do is make a sand castle right here. You know, the kind kids build near the water where it's wet?"

I looked down at the bone-dry khaki sand where we stood and thought he was joking. Pushing it with a foot, I watched it slide apart, parched and twinkling from the heat and sun.

"Come on, Venasque. It's too dry. It won't stick together."

"I don't want to hear that! Do what I tell you. There's a way. If I tell you to do it then there's a way. Watch me."

Taken aback by his tone and growing rudeness, I watched silently while he went down on his knees facing me. The animals were at his side and remained there without moving or making noise. His silent guards.

The old man closed his eyes and suddenly stuck his arms straight out in front of him, like a sleepwalker.

His hands started to drip water. It came down in fat fast

plops, as if his fingers were open water faucets. It didn't stop. He looked at me without saying anything.

Reaching down, he slid the shining wet hands under the sand and left them there some time. The spot began to darken into brown and spread in all directions. Something below was making everything wet. Dripping fingers.

In a while he pulled them out again and began to mold and shape the wet muck into walls and squared sections, then turrets and what looked like a moat.

When *his* sand castle began to take definite shape, he stood up with a groan and told the animals to finish it. And like hairy architects or giant worker ants, they dug and pushed and pawed things further into shape. I watched while they did these wondrous things. Looking up once, I saw Venasque standing nearby looking out to sea and finishing my sandwich. He wasn't interested in what they were doing.

When it was done, their castle looked very much like the one at the entrance to Fantasyland at Disneyland. They stepped back and looked it over, then walked down to the water to clean themselves.

"You *can* make a castle here, Walker."

"I'm not you, Venasque. I can't make water flow out of my fingers. Or get a dog and a pig to put up walls for me."

"No, but you gotta brain to think of something else. My way is different from yours, sure. But you gotta learn there *is* a way for you too. Even when it's doing something as small and dumb as this. Give me a castle out of dry sand, okay?

"I'm going to take a walk down the beach. We'll be back in an hour or two, so work on it till then. Remember, I only want you to use that stick you found. Don't bring up any water from the ocean because that's the easy way. *And* I'll know if you've done it."

"How?"

"How will I know? Do it and you'll see. Think up something else, Walker. You can do it. If you caused all that magic to happen around you back in Vienna, you can start taking it from inside and using it for yourself."

He whistled again shrilly, and the animals rushed up from the surf to join him. They took off together down the beach, Connie leaning against his right leg. He looked back once and gave a big wave. "Don't use water!"

I waved back, frowning. When he was far enough away, I jammed the stick into the sand and left it standing there while trying to decide how to go about this chore.

Brilliant ideas, like using spit or even piss *(they* weren't sea water!), had me momentarily excited. Yet how many times would you have to spit (or pee) before you had enough sand . . . How much wood would a woodchuck chuck . . .

It was a beautiful day, and I kept wishing Maris had been there to share it. If she had, she'd have come up with a solution. *Maris* was the architect in our relationship, she was the builder. I thought of Howard Roark in *The Fountainhead. He'd* have known what to do, too. Unfortunately, neither Maris nor Howard was around, so it was only me and my stick and a beach full of dry sand that didn't feel like sticking together unless it was wet.

The first inspiration struck. Perhaps if I dug down deep enough, the sand would be wetter and more formable there. I spent the first fifteen minutes digging like a neurotic cocker spaniel in the hot sand. To no avail, naturally. The more sand I pushed away, the more slid, slunk, slipped back into my futile hole. The more it slid and slunk, the more pissed off I got. The more pissed off I got, the more (and faster) I tried to shovel the stuff out. Good luck doing that! Talk about Sisyphus trying to push his rock up the hill. At least the gods let him move it a little before he lost.

About the time my anger was beginning to redline, a man came up and stood there watching me work. I was too frustrated and hot to be embarrassed by what I was doing. All the same, I felt like telling him to mind his own business and take off.

"Not having much luck with that hole, are you?"

I wanted to hit him on the head. His voice carried the annoying tone of a dope who is sure he's on to something profound.

"That's very true! I'm not!"

"Are you doing it for fun, or what?"

I stopped digging and, lips pursed, watched another mini-avalanche of sand slide slowly and sensuously back into my crater.

"Look, can I help you, pal? I mean, is there anything I can do for you?"

"Not a thing. I'm just standin' here watching."

"I noticed."

"But I don't think you're going to get anywhere, digging like that."

"Thank you. Do you have any suggestions?"

"Nope."

A good way to feel stupid is to be doing something stupid and having someone watch you. He wouldn't go away, either. I turned my back on him and started my spaniel bit again. Then I turned so more of my rear end was facing him, and I started tossing huge spumes of sand at him.

"Hey, watch it! Are you crazy?"

I stopped and did nothing. Maybe he was Venasque in disguise, come back to try my patience. I turned and looked at him. He smiled triumphantly and crossed his arms.

The last of my cool blew out to sea. "Get out of here, will you?"

"I'll do what I want! This is a free country!"

"I haven't heard that line since I was in fifth grade." I got up and walked away. I had to get out of his range or else.

I walked down the beach awhile, then turned and went back. Luckily, my audience had taken off. I got back down on my knees and looked once again at my friend, the sand.

And was still looking an hour later when Venasque returned with the animals, and the man, in tow.

"How far did you get?"

"I didn't." I shrugged.

"I asked him what he was doing there and he threw sand in my face. He's crazy, you ask me."

Venasque patted him on the back. "We two made a bet that he couldn't make a sand castle here."

"Sand castle? You can't build no sand castle where the sand's dry like this! You gotta go down near the water where it's wet."

"No ideas at all, Walker?"

"I wanted to use spit or even piss to get it wet. But you'd have to get too much of both. I didn't drink enough at lunch."

The other man made a face as if something smelled bad.

Venasque thought it was funny. He laughed with his mouth wide open—*HA-HA-HA.*

"That's good thinking, but you're not allowed to use them either. No water. Not the ocean *or* yours. *HA-HA.*"

"*You* used it!" It came out sounding like a bratty, whining child. How was I ever going to learn from him? How can you know magic when you can't even control your own voice or emotions?

"I'm sorry for talking like that, Venasque. I want to do it, but I don't see how yet."

"That's okay. Take more time and think it through. We don't have to be in the mountains for a while." He turned to the other man. "Come on, Leo, let's go get a Coke."

I didn't see him again till later that night.

Working all afternoon, I tried different approaches to the problem, but none of them worked. After a few hours I didn't think about Venasque or when he would return because I knew it would either be when I had figured things out or given up altogether.

Sometimes people came by and said hello, but for the most part I was alone. It was better that way because I wasn't feeling very friendly.

If you take the word "car" or "dog" and say it over and over a few hundred times, it no longer means or sounds like anything. The same was true with this puzzle. I thought about it so much, and poked at it from so many different angles, that by the time the sun was going down my brain was empty. The sunset was all smeared brown and orange, and punched-up thunderclouds that looked like pillows on a mussed-up bed.

I watched it and waited for it to tell me something, but it didn't. If only God would speak to us at moments like that. Appear as a snow-white cockatoo on our shoulder and explain the correct way. Or take up the whole sky with a Ronald Colman face and a few choice, brilliant words that make everything resoundingly clear.

I watched the sunset until the light was almost gone and the colors dried into evening. Unconsciously, I tapped the stick on the sand in front of me. When I became aware of doing it, the solution dawned on me. The moment was disconcerting because the answer was so simple.

Jabbing the stick over my head, I started whistling the theme song to *Zorba the Greek*. "Teach me to dance . . . Venasque!" That made me laugh. It felt so good to figure things out. I danced and kicked up my feet, feeling a foot taller . . . or smarter.

The stick touched the sand a sliding scratch. I drew it a long way to the left, then up and over. No real plan in mind, I let my hand do its own moving and design. It was eager to work. When I'd been at it awhile, I jumped when someone put his hand on my shoulder.

"Walker, you got it! Good man. Let's see."

I'd *drawn* a castle, but that was only part of it. It sat at the edge of a group of other buildings. It was so dark on the beach by then we could barely make out what else I'd drawn.

"You did a whole town, huh?"

"My hand did what it wanted. It sort of got carried away."

"I'll say! I can't see everything, but it's terrific. You got a simple answer to a tough question. That's the right way to begin. Sand castles don't all have to be up in the air. Come on, let's get going."

No more than that. I hesitated a moment, sad to be leaving my brainstorm so soon after having done it. Venasque was already a long way up the beach, walking toward the parking lot.

Without turning, he yelled over his shoulder, "Leave it, Walker. That's nothing. Wait'll you see some of the other things you'll be able to do."

"Will you teach me to dance, Venasque?"

I didn't even know he'd heard me until he snapped his fingers over his head and spun around to face me. " 'Will you teach me to dance, Zorba?' 'Dance? Did you say *dance*, Boss? Come on, my boy!' *Zorba the Greek*. Directed by Michael Cacoyannis. Starring Anthony Quinn, Alan Bates, and Lila Kedrova, who won the Oscar that year for her performance as Bouboulina. A great film. I saw it the other day on cable."

"Walker, I miss you. Where are you?"

"The Sleepy Arms Motel."

"You're kidding. Where's that?"

"Outside Santa Barbara. We spent most of the day at the beach."

"That doesn't sound too magical."

I leaned against the headboard of the bed and told Maris the story of my sand castle. Venasque was sitting on the other bed, looking at *TV Guide* and scratching Big Top with his foot. He leaned over and pointed out that a film called *Nude Druids* was playing on the porno cable channel. I rolled my eyes. He shrugged.

"Have you had anything to eat?"

"Yes, we had some sandwiches for lunch and we're going out later. There's supposed to be a pretty good restaurant near here."

"Please eat, Walker. I don't want you coming back ten pounds lighter."

"Okay. How're things there?"

"I went to the radio station with Ingram today and listened to him do his show. There was a woman on who teaches people how to scream."

"That sounds hard. She charges for it?"

Maris laughed. "She wore an army helmet, too. There was a bumper sticker on it that said 'Screaming has Meaning.'"

"I'll try to remember that."

"I'm going to stay at Ingram's place for a couple of days, so call me there, okay? I miss you like crazy."

"Me, too! A thousand times."

"Is Venasque there with you?"

"Yes."

"Tell him to take care of you."

"I will."

"And remember the man who ate all the cake."

"And you remember the man who drank the coffee through the straw. I'll call you tomorrow, Maris. I love you."

"Good night, *mein Liebster.*"

"Good night."

I put the receiver down and sighed. It was the first time we'd been apart at night since arriving in California. I didn't look forward to spending it without her.

"Were you ever married, Venasque?"

"Twenty-seven years I was married."

"What happened to her?"

"She died. You ready to go out?" He stood up and straightened his pants.

I took my sweatshirt off the bed and followed him out of the room. The parking lot was a pale coppery-orange from the lighting overhead.

"Is it okay to leave the animals in the room?"

"Sure. They'll sleep like rocks after running around all day. Sorry I snapped at you. It's hard talking about my wife. I'll tell you more about it at dinner, after we've gotten some food in us. I hear this restaurant's got great king crab, and it's my treat tonight. Our celebration for your sand castle."

There was no reason for Maris to worry about my not eating. The two of us tucked into enough crab that night to make the waiter give us strange looks. We finished with hot fudge sundaes big as catchers' mitts.

"I lived almost thirty years with a woman I loved, but could never figure out. We were happy, but there were too many times we'd look at each other and wonder 'Who's that? Do I know them?'

"When she died, she died badly, Walker. Got a cancer that ate right through her. She died too long, and the only thing left at the end was an empty box of anger."

"Couldn't *you* do anything for her? With your . . . powers?"

"Nothing. Life and death do their own deciding."

That shocked me. "Really? Nothing?"

"Learn what life is, Walker. Dying comes anyway. I

couldn't do anything for Nelia—that was my wife—because the war taught me to concentrate on life and how to make it better. That was something Nelia and I agreed on because both of us went through that war. Living was more important than dying."

"But you just said she died badly."

"She died badly because she didn't learn enough about life. She went back to her other lives again and again, as you're beginning to do, but all she did was look around in them like a tourist in a foreign country. She took snapshots of them so she could show her friends, but not think about them herself. That's why she died badly. The only thing we can really know is what we're experiencing, or what we've already lived. Then we've got to study it like crazy till we understand."

"But you keep asking me after I go back to one of my lives if I felt myself die there. And what it was like."

"Of course I do! Maybe you'll be the one to tell me what I've tried to find out all my life. I told you: I'm as much a student as you are."

"What are *you* still trying to find out? Seems like you've pretty much *found* things."

He shook his head. "What it's like right after. What the experience of death is. I know we come back, there's no question of that, but where do we go in between?"

"Venasque, was that girl we saw today really the red woman in my dream?"

He smiled and signaled for the check. "No. I said that to see your reaction. But you will bump into that red woman sometime in your life. That's a guarantee."

"But why'd you say it today? What reaction was I supposed to have?"

"Exactly what you did. You were interested and intrigued. I said it because you've *got* to start thinking differently about certain things now. You've got to start thinking different *ways,* too. A man who flies has to believe he has wings. Or that he can have wings. You know what I mean?"

"Okay, I accept that, but there's something else I want to ask you about, too."

He looked at his watch. "Is it a short question? It's time we got back to the animals. They get nervous when I'm gone a long time."

"You don't have to answer now, but I have to say it now: Do you know how often you're loud and impatient with me? A lot. And bossy? I *admit* I don't know anything, Venasque. Whenever you use that tone of voice, it either makes me nervous or afraid of you. Teachers aren't supposed to scare their students."

He got up from the table very quickly and threw some bills down next to his plate. I thought I'd really offended him. He looked at me and rubbed his hand over his mouth. "Ah, you're right. I'm sorry. Since I got old, I don't have so much patience anymore. No matter how much you learn over the years, you can't always use it yourself when you need it most. *Eine Schande*, huh? Big irony. You can be the best teacher in the world, but still you get scared when it's your turn, and you know you don't have so much time left."

"Why not? Are you ill?" I stood there feeling helpless and wrong for having opened this can of worms.

"Ill? Ha, no, I'm just old! When you get my age, the only things that happen to you are more hair grows out of your ears and you get more and more alone. 'The night comes everyday to my window. The serious night, promising, as always, age and moderation. And I am frightened . . .' That's what it's like. Not so great. You read poetry? You should.

"That's why I got those two animals with me. They're my last company."

"What about your students?"

"Very nice people, but they can't help when I have to die.

That's why I'm trying to discover what it's like now. Maybe if I do, I won't be so uncomfortable. I'm good at some things, but I still haven't gotten past wondering what'll happen to me when THE END comes. You think too much about 'The Serious Night' when you're my age. It's natural, but it's a sickness, too. You get nervous. You want everybody else to hurry up as much as you, and if they don't, you get angry.

"Something else, too: I spent most of my life teaching people, or trying to teach them important things. But I get to certain points and can't take them any further. That's not a nice thing to know about yourself. Especially when you're too damned old to do anything about it. Nobody likes to fail, huh?

"Come on, we can talk more back at the motel."

Again that uncomfortable, thin orange light lay over the restaurant parking lot. Standing by the car, I looked up at it.

"This light looks like a UFO is about to land here."

Unlocking his side, Venasque looked up. "It's a safety light. They say it gives a wider arc and covers more ground. Lights up the dark corners better."

I was about to comment, when lines out of nowhere pushed their way to the front of my mind and tongue.

> *"The night comes every day to my window.*
> *The serious night, promising as always,*
> *age and moderation. And I am frightened*
> *dutifully, as always until I find*
> *in the bed my three hearts and the cat-*
> *in-my-stomach talking as always now,*
> *of Gianna. And I am happy through the dark*
> *with my feet singing of how she lies*
> *warm and alone in her dark room*
> *over Umbria where the brief and only*

Paradise flowers white by white.
I turn all night with the thought of her mouth
a little open, and hunger to walk
quiet in the Italy of her head, strange
but no tourist on the streets of her childhood."

I finished out of breath and shaken, as if coming down from an epiphany. I knew some poetry, but nothing like that, and not by heart. I also knew I'd never read or heard that poem before tonight, when Venasque had quoted the first three lines in an entirely different context.

When I was finished reciting, we stood there on opposite sides of the Jeep and looked at each other. I no longer needed to be told that part of my education was to accept miracles, to try and leave myself open to whatever wonders Venasque had.

Bending down to get in, he said, " 'The Night Comes Every Day to My Window' by Jack Gilbert. I've always liked his poetry. Let's go."

Back at the motel, both animals barely raised their heads when we came in. Big Top had managed to climb his thick bulk onto Venasque's bed and was resting his ass on his master's pillow. Connie lay directly below him, leaning up against the side of the bed.

Venasque walked over and gently moved the dog off the pillow. Adjusted, the bullterrier slapped its tail twice.

"I don't blame him. Better to have your fanny on a pillow than the floor.

"Listen, Walker. I want to do one more thing with you tonight before we go to sleep. I'm going to help you go back one more time to another of your lives. But it's going to be one of the earlier ones. Maybe even the first. I want you to feel what it was like then. That'll give you something important to think about when we get to the mountains."

"I've got enough to think about!"

"True, but not your beginnings. You saw some of your last life, and maybe a glimpse of the one right before that in Russia. But to start getting the *whole* thing in good focus, you gotta have at least a little look at what it was like for you way back when. Get ready for bed and you'll do that before going to sleep."

I reached down for my bag. Opening it, I realized that no matter what was about to happen (in the hands of this flawed but remarkable man), I was excited. My insides were fluttering and squawking like a box of birds that's just been shaken, but I was on my way to discovery, and that was what I had come to him for.

"Venasque, that Jack Gilbert poem is a love poem. Why did you quote it to me before? You made it sound like something sad."

His head was so deep in his suitcase that I almost didn't hear when he spoke. "For *you* it's a love poem. I don't have any Gianna lying in my bed. Only Big Top and the night at the window."

Two boys were playing catch with a white ball. Holding my father's hand, I stood and watched enviously as they threw it back and forth, calling each other names when one or the other dropped it. It fell regularly, and I couldn't understand that because both of them were good catchers.

It was raining hard, so few people were around to buy father's potatoes. Together we watched the boys, but unlike me, father snickered every time they dropped it.

A man mostly hidden under a cloak, but sweet-stinking of the plague, crept up to our table. He was about to say something when father shook his wooden staff and told him to get away.

The man's eyes were glassy and exhausted by the disease, but held enough energy to flash hatred deep as a rich man's grave.

"I have to eat too!"

"Then eat the dead. Get used to the taste!"

"I have money. I can pay." A long white arm emerged from the folds of the dark cloak and held out several coins.

"Do you really think I'd touch a sweet man's money and get sick too? Go away! You shouldn't even be out on the street."

The dying man stood there as if waiting for my father to change his mind.

I'd forgotten about the boys playing catch until one of them shouted something and their "ball" fell close to the sweet man's foot. I looked and saw it wasn't a ball but the white skull of a small animal. The man looked and reached down slowly to pick it up. Holding the skull in his hand, he regarded it thoughtfully, then, without any warning, threw it at us.

Father stamped a foot on the ground. The skull stopped instantly and hung suspended in the air. "How hard it is to play my game!" He stamped again. Both the skull and the sweet man exploded.

I opened my eyes to the taste of dryness in my mouth. I knew where I was but had no energy to do more than lie there and look at the stippled ceiling of our motel room. Outside, a truck shifted up a gear and grumbled away across the night.

"Venasque?"

One of the animals gave a small, sad whine. The strong

smell of electricity hung in the air, as if some appliance had burned out or a thunderstorm was waiting to pounce.

"Venasque? Are you awake?" He wouldn't have gone to sleep while I moved through a past life. But it was also possible I'd been out so long that he'd given up, closed his eyes a moment and . . .

Then there was another smell in the air—hot, acidic, familiar: piss. I reached up and clicked on the lamp. Squinting my eyes, I looked through the new glare toward the other bed. He was there, but one glance said everything was wrong. He'd been sitting with his back propped against the headboard, but had slumped over awkwardly to one side and lay there, unmoving. My first thought was he'd been shot.

"Venasque!" I got up and moved to him. Both animals were on the floor between us, looking up at me with the bad news in their eyes. The old man's left eye was wide open, his right, only half. I bent over to listen to his breathing, but only small short grunts came that weren't enough to fuel his big body. I put two fingers to his throat for a pulse. It was there, but as off and out of synch as his breathing. Sliding him down so he lay more comfortably on the bed, I then called an ambulance and gave him artificial respiration until it came.

The flashing blue lights of the ambulance strobed through the orange over the parking lot. The night had been full of strange, vivid colors and total darkness. Nothing in between.

The ambulance had arrived very quickly and the attendants worked with the air of people who liked what they were doing and did their job well. They carefully checked Venasque and asked many questions about what had happened. All I could say was I'd fallen asleep and when I awoke he was this way. They were sympathetic, but cool. To them, the old man's collapse was just another set of readings, procedures, forms to fill out. That was understandable, but whenever I looked at him and his shot expression, I disliked their too-calm voices, questions, indifference to his condition.

When they were finished with me I called Maris, told her to contact Philip Strayhorn, and tell him what happened. Fifteen minutes later he called and asked about everything. Said he was coming immediately, but asked me to stay at the hospital in Santa Barbara until he arrived.

"How are the animals?"

"Sad. They know something bad's going on. They haven't moved from the floor."

I sat in a white room and half read an article in *National Geographic* while waiting to hear about Venasque's condition. The room was empty at first, but after a while, a good-looking couple came in and walked over.

"Are you Walker Easterling?"

"Yes."

The man put out his hand. "Harry Radcliffe, and this is my wife Sydney. Phil Strayhorn called and told us about Venasque. How is he?"

"I don't know. In intensive care, but none of the doctors have said anything more yet."

"Ditto. We asked at the desk when we came in, but the nurses weren't talking."

Sydney pushed long expensive hair away from her face. "We were with him only a few weeks ago and he looked great. We went to a Dodgers game."

"How did you get here so fast?"

"We live in Santa Barbara and would've been here sooner but we were out and—"

"Mr. Easterling?"

A woman stood in the doorway to the waiting room in a

doctor's white coat and a clipboard under her arm. "I'm Doctor Troise. You came in with Mr. Venasque?"

"Yes. How is he? No one's told us anything yet."

"He's in a coma and we're still running tests. But there's something important we need to know before we go on. Certain results indicate that what happened to him *might've* been caused by a very strong electrical shock to the body. Some big jolt from something. Do you know if he touched either an electrical socket or appliance before this happened? Maybe a plug whose wires were frayed?"

"I have no idea. As I told the others, I was asleep and found him like . . . that when I woke up."

"And you *heard* nothing? Like a surprised shout? You know, how you yell out when you get a bad shock from something?"

"Nothing like that, but I was sound asleep and having *big* dreams. I remember that vividly, so I really must've been deepout, you know?"

Radcliffe stood up and walked over to her. "Why do you think it was an electrical shock, Doctor?"

She looked at me to see if this man had the right to ask questions. I nodded.

"I'd rather not say anything about that until we've gotten all the results, sir." She made a wry face and turned to leave. "Sometimes doctors have the bad habit of making wrong prognoses before they know what they're talking about. It gets us into too much hot water. We're doing all we can for Mr. Venasque. I'll let you know what we find."

When she was gone, the three of us traded "what-was-that-all-about?" looks.

Strayhorn looked like hell when he got to the hospital. His eyes were red-rimmed and full of harried sadness. He spoke quickly and asked the same question more than once. Mrs. Radcliffe made him sit down next to her and put her arm around his shoulder.

Almost as soon as he arrived, I felt invisible ranks close around the three of them. The waiting room had become *their* room. I knew Venasque and was there when he was "hit," but the shaman had become their sole concern now and I was way on the outside. This was further emphasized when Radcliffe said it was all right if I wanted to "leave things in their hands now"; they'd take care of everything. Although his voice was friendly and grateful, I understood the offer to mean it'd be nice if you left, pal.

"We'll take care of the animals, Walker, but it would make things easier if you drove the Jeep back to L.A. and put it in his garage. Give the keys to his next-door neighbor, Mr. Barr. Sydney will take you over to the motel to get your bags."

Helplessly, I turned up my hands. "Okay, but let me give you my address and phone number in Los Angeles. Make sure to call me if there's *anything* I can do. Okay?"

"Absolutely. And thanks so much for doing what you did, Walker. We'll let you know what's going on whenever they tell us here. And don't worry about his care, either. We'll watch every move they make. If it's necessary, I'll even design a new wing in this place for him!"

We shook hands. Strayhorn held on a long time and looked at me very carefully. "Did anything happen between you two, Walker? Did you do anything that might have caused it?"

"No, Philip, he made me build a sand castle today on the beach, and then when I was asleep, as I told you, he sent me back to one of my other lives."

"Nothing else? Venasque told me you were one of the most intriguing people he's worked with. Said there was an enormous magic in you. He thought your *being* might have brought that sea serpent up."

"He said that? He never told me."

"He always has his reasons. He told me he was really looking forward to working with you. Now this. That's why I'm asking, so don't be offended. You might have done something without even knowing it . . . Possibly while you were asleep?"

"Philip, it's possible, but what are the chances? I don't know what happened when I was asleep. I dreamed I was back in the Middle Ages with my father. He wouldn't sell potatoes to a man with the plague. When I woke up, Venasque was gone."

"Nothing in your dream might have caused it?"

"Nothing that I know of."

It was not until three days later and we were flying back to Vienna that I remembered the part of the dream that could have caused everything: my father making the "sweet man" and the animal skull explode the moment they became dangerous. Why didn't I remember that when Strayhorn was standing ten inches from me, waiting for information that could save Venasque? Why didn't I remember that?

It was three o'clock in the morning when I got home, but a light was on in the living room. Maris was still up, reading a collection of poetry by her favorite, Diane Wakoski. She looked up from the book, then down again with a smile and read:

> *"Metaphors*
> *I kiss you goodbye*
> *for a while*
> *and will talk about my own perceptions,*
> *angers,*

and even the admiration I feel for the beautiful scoundrel."

"Hello, my scoundrel. How are you? How come you're back? What's with Venasque?"

"That's the second time tonight I've heard poetry. Is today still Tuesday? Jesus, it's been a hundred hours long. Venasque is in a coma. It's bad. Strayhorn and Harry Radcliffe are up there with him at the hospital."

"You mean *my* Harry Radcliffe, the architect? Wow!"

"Remember I told you he studied with Venasque, too? Philip and he came to the hospital and made it pretty clear it'd be better if I left. So I did, and drove his car back. What a night, Maris! What a *day!* You once said 'It's a day that tires you out the rest of your life,' and that was it exactly. All I wanted to do was get home to you.

"Hey, how come you're not at your brother's house? I was so glad to see you that I forgot you're not supposed to be here."

She kissed my cheek. "I had a feeling you'd be back tonight. Anyway, I don't like the guy Ingram's living with. Have you noticed how Los Angeles is a T-shirt society? Everyone lets you know who they are on their T-shirt. This guy wore one that said 'I'd love to sleep with you, but I'm taking lunch with my agent.' Tell me about what happened. Don't leave anything out."

"Do you mind if I do it in the morning? I'm really pooped."

She got up and pulled me after her. "Of course. I'm sorry. Come on, let's go to bed. Is there anything I can do? Make you something to eat? You want a back rub?"

"No, thanks. You know what Venasque told Strayhorn? That I have 'enormous magic' in me, quote unquote. He thought that sea monster we saw might've come up because I was there." I sat down again. "What do you think he meant by that?"

"What he said. You went to him because all those strange things were happening to you. He sensed, or knew, where they came from, that's why he wanted to work with you. And that's why it's so terrible this happened. I've been thinking about you and Venasque since you left, and you know what? I'm *sure* the flying lessons were only a metaphor. Maybe he really was going to teach you, but I doubt it. He never told you he taught anyone else how to do it, did he? The others, like Philip and Harry Radcliffe, learned really mundane things like how to swim and how to play a musical instrument. Only *you* were supposed to fly, Walker. That's not the easiest thing in the world to teach a person. I don't know anything about it, but I'm sure it was a metaphor for something else. Don't ask me what."

"But your brother was the one who initially said Venasque taught people to fly."

"I know. I talked with Ingram about that today and found out something interesting: Everyone who has gone to Venasque comes away feeling better or healed. But according to my brother, no one he knows has ever actually learned to fly. People go to him for that because that's what he advertises, but he never taught it. You were going to be the first."

"That's interesting. Sounds like you're probably right." But as I said that, a picture came to mind from the dream (flashback?) I'd had at Venasque's one night: small children flying gently through the window of a stone schoolhouse in the South of France, forty years ago.

3.

Almost at the same time Maris said she would marry me, the airplane yawed hard to one side and began turning. We shared blank "Huh?" looks.

"I don't like it when planes make curves, Walker."

"Maybe the pilot heard what you said and is looping the loop for us." She closed her eyes and tensed her mouth. "Honey, don't worry."

"I won't worry when my feet are on the ground again. How come the wing is below us? What's going on?"

"I don't know."

"What a moment for this to happen! I finally say 'I do' and the plane crashes. That's nice."

"Ladies and gentlemen, this is Captain Monninger. We've run into a small technical problem, so we're going to land at Seattle airport in fifteen minutes to take care of it. Nothing to worry about, though. We've got some freight shifting in the hold and it's got to be secured. Sorry about the inconvenience. We'll get it fixed and be under way in no time."

"You think he's telling the truth?"

"Sure. The fact he said what it was proves it. When there are big problems—"

"—like bombs?"

"They don't tell you anything. I'm sure it's the cargo."

"Stewardess, could I have another brandy?"

I tried to take her hand but she shook me off. "I'm too nervous."

I looked out the window at the gray clouds. We'd both been so glad to leave Los Angeles that we'd all but run onto the plane. I'd been looking at the flight map when she turned to me an hour into the flight and said in a small voice, "Do you still want to marry me?"

Trying to keep my head on, I put the map down and looked at her. "I'd love to marry you, Maris. You know that. I would love that more than anything."

"I've never been married before."

"I know."

Then the plane tipped.

The stewardess brought the brandy and Maris downed it in three big gulps. "I'm terrified. Now that I want to get married, flying scares me even more. That's a good sign, isn't it? Before, I was just scared of dying. Now I'm worried my husband's going to die."

During all the turning and descending, I noticed somewhere in the midst of that a very strange smell in the plane. Because there was nothing else to do, I kept sniffing to try and figure out what it was, but had no luck. It was unpleasantly sweet, thick and stale like an old box of candy.

The plane dropped below the clouds and suddenly the absolute blue and white of high skies gave over to the green of Washington State. Off to our left, the sun cut through a patch of purple-gray clouds and lit a section of the city like an acetylene torch.

"God's flashlight."

"What?" Maris leaned over and looked out the window across my lap.

"Doesn't that light over there look like God's shining a flashlight down through the clouds?"

She kissed my cheek. "That's a nice image. I know a guy who lives in Seattle, Henry Samuel. A real jerk. Maybe we'll crash into his house and I can say hello. What's that smell? It's like room deodorizer."

"I don't know. I've been trying to figure it out."

"Are the engines on fire?" Leaning over farther for a better look out the window, she said, "Walker, I meant what I said about getting married. I'm just not saying anything more now because I don't know what *to* say. Do you understand? But I want it! I realized that when you went away with Venasque. Being alone again, even for that short time, didn't make me feel helpless or moony. Just indignant . . . no, *confused* by your absence. Does that make sense?"

"Uh huh."

"Good." She crossed her arms and nodded once. The landing gear went down with a solid thump. "Uh oh. Ever notice how a clock ticks faster after it's been wound? As if it's grateful to you for doing it? That's how I feel about us. That's why I want to get married. Being with you makes me feel full of energy; like I've been wound up again."

"Ladies and gentlemen, please fasten your seat belts and extinguish all smoking material. We're making our approach to Seattle airport."

We landed so gently that even Maris applauded the touchdown. "This guy can land me any time."

While the plane taxied to a corner of the airport, we were told to stay on board because the cargo problem would be taken care of in about twenty minutes.

I got up to go to the toilet, but the line ahead of me was long, so I stood next to the galley and waited my turn. Two stewardesses sat nearby and I was close enough to hear their conversation, although they spoke quietly.

"It's the craziest thing I ever heard of."

"Who discovered it?"

"Judy, because of that terrible smell. She told Dick and *he* went down to check. Isn't it *weird?*"

"No, it's disgusting. Thank God Dick did it. I'd have fainted, probably."

A fat black woman standing in front of me leaned over to them and asked in a lisp, "What *is* that smell? I been spraying *4711* all around my head to get it away!"

One stew looked at the other and shrugged. Why not tell her the answer, it'll be over soon anyway. The other shrugged okay back.

"Somehow a coffin we're carrying down below broke open when we took off from L.A."

"A *coffin?* My God! You mean it broke open and there's a body floppin' around against my suitcase? My son told me to be sure to fly an American airline because they don't have so many problems! My eye!"

Both stewardesses put index fingers to their lips to hush her. Giggling, one said, "It happens sometimes if they don't secure the cargo well before we take off. Don't worry, though. They're removing it now. It won't be a problem anymore."

"Wait'll I tell my son. He's a diplomat but he don't know nothin'!"

Hmphing dramatically, she marched for the toilet door when it opened, and struggled her way into the small compartment. "We haven't even got to Europe yet and things are already strange!"

Maris was in my seat looking out the window when I got back. "I think they were telling the truth about the cargo. Look at all those guys down there. Wouldn't you love to have one of their little yellow trucks? You could park it in your *Hof.* Hey, uh oh! Look at that."

A Cadillac hearse pulled up nearby on the tarmac. Two men in black suits got out and walked beneath the plane.

"You want to know what's going on?"

Maris turned to me. "You know? Yeah, tell me!"

"A coffin they're carrying got loose on takeoff and broke open."

"Are you serious?"

"Yup. The stewardesses were talking about it when I went to the can."

"That's one way to congratulate us on our wedding." She saw the expression on my face and put her hand on my neck. "I'm not serious, Walker. Not everything is symbolic. Just some poor guy caught up in the twentieth century. Let's watch."

After a long wait and a number of people running back and forth beneath the plane, the men from the funeral home and two airport attendants brought out the coffin. What was queer was its size—not a child's, but not adult size, either. It must have been very heavy, too, because all of them had red faces or veins bulging on their necks. The brown metal box looked undamaged at first, but then I could see a small blaze of red cloth inside at the top where the seal had broken.

"Maris sighed. "Now he knows."

"What do you mean?"

"I've thought that since I was a girl. Whenever I see a coffin, I always think whoever's in there knows the Big Answer now: what it's like after we die. Then I wonder if they're lucky or not *to* know."

"That's what Venasque wanted to know too. But with all his powers, he couldn't find out."

She looked at me. "Maybe we're not supposed to know. Maybe we should just live the best we can and hope we've done it right by the end."

"How do you know you're living the best you can? How do you know your best isn't really bad?"

"I'm an optimist. I don't think God would be that unfair."

"I love you, Maris."

"That's one of the reasons why I'm an optimist."

PART TWO

People create the reality they need in order to discover themselves.

Ernest Becker

A clown isn't funny in the moonlight.

Lon Chaney

HIS OWN TOO MUCH

CHAPTER FOUR

1.

Vienna was in the midst of a January thaw. Islands of snow spotted the dark earth; the airport runway gleamed wetly in warm, late afternoon sun.

Grinning, Maris waited for me at the bottom of the stairs leading off the plane. "I just spoke German again and it felt funny."

"It doesn't feel funny being back here. It's great. When we get home I want to call California and see how Venasque is."

"Walker, you've been calling three times a day. I really think they'll let you know if anything changes."

"It's important to me, Maris."

"I know it is, but I think you're overdoing it. Let it rest a little."

People walked by toward the bus that would take us to the terminal. I took her arm and pulled her toward it. "Come on, it's not worth arguing about. We're home."

"You're right. I wonder how your cat is? I kept thinking about him on the plane."

"He's happy as a clam. Whenever I give him to Frau Noot he comes back five pounds heavier. She feeds him chicken hearts whenever he's hungry."

While we were waiting by the luggage carousel for our bags to arrive, a striking man with bleached white hair and high-tech, punk clothes walked up to Maris and embraced her from behind. She spun around, but on seeing who it was, hugged him.

"Vitamin D!"

"Hey, Maris! Where the hell have you been, damn it? We've been looking all over Munich for you."

"Victor Dixon, this is my husband, Walker Easterling."

"*Husband?* You got married! That's the news of the week. You're living here now, or what?"

"Walker, Victor's the lead guitarist of the group Vitamin D."

"Hey, Walker! You're a lucky man and I hate you. Congratulations. Yeah, we're giving a concert here at the *Audi Max* tomorrow night. You want to come?"

"You've got a hit, huh, Victor? No more playing at Onkel Pö?"

"Hey, we're number nine on the American Hot Hundred. Number one in Deutschland."

"I know. We were just in Los Angeles. Every time I turned on the radio they were playing it. 'Sundays in the Sky,' right? I'm proud of you, Victor. You fought through and did it."

He looked at her with little boy's eyes, loving and longing for her approval. Plainly, something big had gone on between them in the past. I could have been jealous, but felt only pride. Pride in Maris, pride in our relationship. Victor Dixon was right to love her, and I liked him for that.

"Take care of her, Walker, she's true gold.

"I'll leave some tickets at the box office and you can go if you want. Maris, I'm happy for you. Everybody'll be glad to hear you're all right."

With one more look that leaped at her like fire from a flame-thrower, he strode off. She winked at me and didn't see him turn for one last glimpse of her before going out the door.

"What's the scoop on him?"

"A romance from long ago. Victor was more interested in being famous than being kind."

"It looked like it's still a romance in his eyes."

"I know, but he blew it. You're not jealous?"

"No, proud. Proud you love me. He knows what he's missing. His face tells me that."

"That's interesting. He was always so cool. We tried, but he's another person who thinks he *deserves* love."

"It's uncomfortable thinking about you being with someone else."

"There are our bags. It's uncomfortable thinking you were married once."

"Does that make you jealous?"

"Thoughtful."

Frau Noot lived down the hall. Her apartment looked like the inside of Heidi's hut in the Alps. Everything was *Bauern* furniture, deer antlers, and bad paintings of mountain scenes on the walls, along with what seemed like hundreds of yellow photographs of her dead husband Leo, a conductor on the Viennese tram system for thirty years. She had the sweet bad habit of making inedible cakes and pressing them on the nearest victim, who too often was me because of my vicinity. She was also Orlando's other great fan, and gladly took care of him whenever I had to be out of town. He was in her arms when she opened the door.

"Maris and Walker, you're back! Say hello, Orlando."

"How are you, Frau Noot? We brought you a present from California."

"More bubblebath! You always bring me the best kind. Come in. We were just watching television."

Although he was blind, Frau Noot was convinced Orlando liked to sit on her lap and watch television. I knew he liked to sit on her lap and watch television because TV meant snack time, usually pretzels. Orlando didn't need to see pretzels to enjoy them.

"How's he been?"

"Sad, Walker. I fed him all his favorite meals and petted him whenever he wanted. But I think he was mad at me for something. Or else he missed you more than usual." Her face got tight and she looked about to cry.

"Oh, you know how he is. Cats do what they like. He ignores me half the time, too."

She smiled, but her eyes stayed downcast. "That's very good of you, but I didn't do something right this time. Look at how glad he is to see you." He was on the floor weaving back and forth between my legs.

"Hi, Orlando. How are you?"

"My brother gave me a special new recipe for American apple cake, Frau Noot. Let's make it together this week."

"Yes, Maris, I'd like that. Can we do it soon? The

postman's birthday is next week and I'll make it for him if it's good."

"Sure. We'll do it." Maris looked at me and mouthed the words "Tell her." I mouthed "Us?" pointing back and forth.

"Yes."

"Maris and I are going to get married, Frau Noot. You're the first one to know."

She clapped her hands and rocked back and forth in her seat. "*This* is good to hear! I knew it would happen. I'm the first to know? What an honor! When?"

Maris and I looked at each other and smiled.

"I don't know! We didn't talk about that yet."

"Do it on your birthday, Walker. That's coming soon."

"Exactly, Walker! That's when we'll do it. And we'll bake a big apple cake for the occasion."

"*I* will bake it, Maris, but not apple! I have a special cake for weddings. That will be my present to you. *Eine Noot Torte à la Easterling!*"

Unlocking the door to my apartment, I asked Maris what she thought a Noot Torte would be.

"I don't know, but we'll have to eat the whole thing, even if it has lizards in it, or else her heart will be broken."

"Oh boy, home. Smell it. *Home!*" Orlando was the first one through the door, walking jauntily, like a model at a run-way show. We unloaded the bags on the floor.

"Walker, I want to go home for a while and get some stuff. You don't mind, do you?"

"No, I want to take a shower and see if there's anything important in the mail. You want to take any of your things?"

"No, there's nothing important in there. My car's around the corner. I'll be back in a couple of hours."

She came up to me and we embraced. "You smell like a trip."

"That's why I want a shower. Come back soon and we'll go out to dinner."

"I want a schnitzel. I love the idea of getting married on your birthday. How'd she know when it was? Did she guess your sign?"

"No, blackmailed me last year so she could bake a birthday cake."

"How'd she do that?"

"Threatened to bake me one a day for the rest of the year unless I told her."

"That's dangerous. I think I have to go to the bathroom before I leave."

She went off down the hall while I walked into the bedroom to unpack. I'd unzipped one bag and was staring into it tiredly when she returned.

"Does Orlando like to join you in the toilet?"

"Not usually."

"I'd say he was kinky, but he can't see. Followed me right in and lay by the tub while I peed. Now I'm really going. I'll see you in a couple of hours."

We kissed, and she left. Hanging up a suit, I realized I had no desire to do that, so I started to undress. Naked, I padded into the bathroom.

Lying on the floor by the tub was Venasque's pig, Connie.

"Don't be shocked." She spoke to me in his voice.

"Good Christ!" I sat down on the toilet. "It *is* you, isn't it, Venasque?"

"Yes. I died a couple of hours ago. While you were circling Vienna." The pig shifted on the floor to a more comfortable position.

"Why are you here? How can you be?"

Orlando walked in and right over to Connie. He sat down next to her. The pig sniffed the cat indifferently.

"Were you here when Maris came in?"

"Yes, but she wasn't able to sense me. I'm here for you, Walker. I have to tell you some things."

"Is it . . . Is death what you thought it would be?"

"I can tell you one thing. If everyone was innocent, then there wouldn't be so much fear. The innocent don't know evil, so they don't fear it. No, only the guilty and the lovers really fear. The first because of what they are, the second for what they might lose. That's really all I can tell you about it, Walker. Do you have any other questions? I'll answer what I can."

"Why are you Connie?"

"Because she was alive and you know her. And because she's funny. Would you have preferred Big Top? Connie had to die for me to come to you, but animals have a quick passage to heaven anyway, and it's necessary for me to be here.

"You *must* spend all of your time now finding out who you are, Walker. It is the most important thing you'll ever do. I can't emphasize that too strongly. I understand now why you came to me and why all of those strange things happened to you. Believe me, it is more incredible than my being here like this. If we had been able to work together, it would have revealed itself to you then. Too bad—it would have been the greatest achievement of my life."

"*Me?* What am I, Venasque? What are you saying?" I was freezing cold, and realized with no embarrassment that I had an erection.

"Study your dreams. Follow up on what you learn from them. Maris doesn't know it yet, but she's pregnant. You must find your father before the baby is born. Your real father, not the man in Atlanta. He is in Vienna and watches everything you do. He isn't your friend. He loved you once, but doesn't anymore. Be very careful with him."

"Who is he?"

"The potato seller. Melchior Kroll. The midget. All of them before, someone else this time. When he loved you, he gave you some of his powers. They're coming now, that is part of the problem, but you've got to learn to use them right or else you'll lose when you face him. Look at your hand."

There were no lines on my right palm. Or my left. No fingerprints, no lifeline, no love line. Only the soft pink hills of flesh and a purple trace of veins beneath the skin.

"Think of the name Melchior. Think of Caspar and Balthazar. They're next. I can tell you nothing else. I don't know what will happen to you. Fate is an open road. What you're capable of is beyond belief. But so is he. Touch the cat on his head."

I reached down and petted Orlando. Pushing his head up into my hand, he purred. Without warning, his completely white eyes began to grow darker and form pupils, irises. Whatever he saw for the first time in his life made him howl and arch his back as if he were about to be attacked. Spitting and hissing, he ran madly out of the room. I had given him sight.

"It won't last long; he'll be blind again in an hour. You don't have the power yet to make it stay, but you will soon, whether you work on it or not.

"One of my greatest mistakes was refusing to believe I could do things like that, things other people couldn't. In the beginning I made children fly, made myself invisible . . . You were there, you saw what I did. I couldn't accept it. But you have to, Walker, immediately, and work with it. It took me years to figure out only one problem—how to build my sand castle with the tools at hand. You don't have years, plus you have two problems. What does a man do with the power to raise the dead? Or give back sight, or see another person's future?" Both Venasque and his voice began to fade, the Cheshire Cat from Walker in Wonderland. "The first thing to do is believe fully in those powers, no matter how skeptical you are. Because the second problem is much worse and you'll need those powers to succeed: How do you kill magic without killing yourself?"

"Is my real father magic?"

"Yes, but so are you. Even more so, because of your relationship with Maris. Your father couldn't do that. You can, because you're more in this world than his now."

He was almost gone. I wanted to ask something else but couldn't think what. My tongue was thick as a tire. "Where do you go now, Venasque?"

"It wouldn't matter if I told you. You'll go someplace else. Don't miss your chance, Walker. Don't let him hurt your family. He's a jealous son of a bitch. He has been for four hundred years."

The bathroom was empty. The tile floor cold under my bare feet. Somewhere in the other room I heard my cat running and crashing into things he normally knew to avoid.

Orlando lay asleep on the floor, exhausted by his short, nightmarish tour through the land of vision. What would he think when he woke again to the dark world he'd always known? Did cats, like us, think Thank God, it was only a dream! when they woke from monsters, or the color blue, that took form in their sightless eyes?

I'd had a shower and was feeling better. Maris hadn't returned, but that was good because I wanted to think about what I would tell her of Venasque's visit when we were together again. Certainly not that she was pregnant. If it were true, it was her secret and joy to discover first. How long would it be before she knew? How would she tell me?

Lying on the bed in a bathrobe, I tried out different ways

of reacting to it. "You're *what?*" "Pregnant! No, *really?*" How could I keep the news from her? The phone rang.

"Walker? David Buck here. Where've you been? I've been calling you for days."

"Hi. We've been in California. What's up?"

"I've been doing that research for you. You know, about your look-alike, Moritz Benedikt?"

"Right! What did you find?"

"Big scandal. A very interesting story. You want me to tell you now, or do you want to get together? I've got ten pages of notes."

"Both, but tell me the basics now."

"Okay. Moritz Benedikt is a pretty commonly found name in Vienna. One guy was a very famous editor of the *Neue Freie Presse.* But your Benedikt was famous for something else."

"Famous?"

"Yeah, wait, it was front-page stuff. He was born here in 1923 and died in 1955. Worked as a tailor for his father in a shop on the Kochgasse in the Eighth District, Benedikt und Söhne, Schneiderei. The store was right down the street from the building where Stefan Zweig lived. Nothing special there, except he was raised by his father because the mother died when Moritz was born."

"Wait a minute, David, let me get this down." But I wasn't writing. I was thinking about the killer in St. Petersburg, Alexander Kroll. He was also raised by his father because the mother died in childbirth. "What was the name of Benedikt's father?"

"Kaspar. Kaspar Benedikt. The interesting thing about him was he was a midget."

"I know."

Buck paused. "You *knew?* How?"

"It doesn't matter. Go on." I started when something

jumped up on the bed next to me. Orlando, his old calm, blind self. He rubbed against me, wanting to be tickled. Didn't he remember anything?

"From the different accounts I've read, Benedikt junior fought for the Germans in southern France in World War Two. He was taken prisoner by the Allies, held awhile, then let go. When he got back to Vienna, he started working again for his father. This is where it gets interesting. Seems like Moritz had a girlfriend named Elisabeth Gregorovius. She worked as a waitress at the Café Museum. She's still alive, if you want to contact her. I have the address and phone number, but I didn't talk to her. She's probably the one putting fresh flowers on his grave."

"You're sure she's alive?"

"Yes. I called the number when I found out about her. An old woman answered and said 'Gregorovius', so I assumed it was her.

"Anyway, she and Moritz had one of those great, years-long courtships that either end in marriage or both people dying of old age. Real nineteenth-century romance. From what I got, they were engaged forever before they got married. The newspapers said that was the first thing that made the old man crazy: His son was going to get married and leave the house. Remember, though, this was after like *years* of going out together, so it wasn't a big surprise to Papa.

"Elisabeth and Moritz got married in 1953 and lived in her apartment. He continued to work in the tailor shop and she at the café. Everything stayed peaceful for two more years. She and Kaspar didn't get along, but his son loved her, so there wasn't anything he could do *but* accept it.

"In 1955, January, Elisabeth discovered she was pregnant. She told Moritz, and he was thrilled. The first thing he wanted to do was give his father the good news. So he went over to the old man's apartment and told him. You know what Kaspar did? Pushed his son out of a fifth floor window and killed him!

"When the police came to take him away, Kaspar told them—wait a minute, let me read it to you—told them 'He would have loved it more than me.' That was it."

I looked down at Orlando. "What happened to the father?"

"I'm not finished! While they were taking him to the police station, there was a terrible crash and the two cops in the car were killed, along with the driver of the other car. There was a photograph of the accident in the paper. Both cars, *both* of them, Walker, were standing straight up on their noses! How the hell could that happen? It looked like a movie scene. And guess who the only one was who survived the crash? Kaspar Benedikt."

"You mean they never found him?"

"Yeah, they did. You know the Pestsäule, the plague statue down on the Graben? That night, after a big Viennese manhunt, they found him hanging from it, stone dead, with a note pinned to his shirt. The note said 'Two eyes too many.' *Zwei augen zuviel.*"

Orlando's back felt elastic and warm under my hand. He purred like a wound-up spring toy.

"Where did they bury him?"

"*That* was difficult finding out. It took me almost three days of digging. The name Gregorovius is Greek, you know. You've heard about how incredible they are as fighters in war? I guess they're used to it, if you look at their history. Well, old Greek Elisabeth got some kind of small revenge on her father-in-law. Because she was next-of-kin to both Benedikts, the authorities went to her about disposal of the body. You know what she did? Donated it to the medical school to be cut up! Whatever was left of him after they finished was probably burned, but who knows?"

"What happened to her child?" It was the only important question.

"Can't help you there, Walker. I assume it was born and is still around. You'll have to go to Elisabeth for that. I've got pictures and Xeroxes and other things for you. When do you want to get together?" He snorted. "You want to meet at the Café Museum so I can give them to you?"

I decided not to tell Maris anything until after I had spoken with the Gregorovius woman. When Maris returned from her apartment, she was wearing a green dress I had never seen before. With her California tan against it, she looked as though she'd been on the beach rather than a plane for the last twelve hours.

We went to dinner and talked about getting married. What Venasque and Buck had told me sat calmly with its hands folded in its lap, waiting its turn. I felt isolated from her because of the information I'd learned that afternoon, but didn't feel I was keeping anything back because it all had to be thought about first, and put in proper perspective. There was no question about telling her everything—I would. I only wanted some time to get it straight and . . . cooled off before putting it in front of her for the Maris reaction.

"I know what I want to give you for your birthday."

"My birthday? I'm thinking about it as our wedding day now."

"That, too. I got an inspiration when I was home. It's going to take me some time, so don't be impatient if you don't get it on the day. It'll be worth waiting for. I *hope.*

"Hold my hand, Walker. That always feels good. Now, something happened I didn't tell you about. The most prestigious gallery in Los Angeles wants me to do a one-man show for them. It's the big break for me."

My jaw dropped. "That's, uh, pretty important information, Maris. How come you didn't tell me?"

"Because I had to think about it awhile first. It happened right before we left America. Also because you had enough to think about with all that Venasque stuff."

"The biggest gallery in L.A.? That's a hell of a great thing, isn't it?"

She squeezed my hand and blushed. "Yes. I think this is it."

"I'm proud of you. Also a little pissed off that you didn't tell me *immediately.*"

"You like my work, don't you, Walker? That makes me feel surer."

"I love it! Where do they come from? I know you're not supposed to ask the artist that question, but really—where *do* the cities come from?"

"Now? My dreams, mostly. Both daydreams and night dreams." She sat forward and her expression grew more excited. "But dreams aren't dangerous, or thrilling, until we think of them as real possibilities. It's our own fault . . . and responsibility if we let that happen. Dreams make no promises, you know? In mine, I *see* these cities, but then it's up to me whether I can bring them together the way they appear in my head. I want to show exactly what's passed through me. Sometimes I think it's like a hand grenade thrown into my . . . gut. I try to cover it and absorb all of the impact. Does that sound goofy?"

"Inspired."

She sat back. "Did I ever tell you about why I made the first city?"

"Never. What happened?"

"Well, my father is a selfish man and can be pretty cold. But when I was seventeen, he was stabbed and almost died. We were living in New York then. My heart had pretty much closed toward him in a lot of ways, especially since I was going through my own typical teenage hell. But seeing him in such bad shape opened me up pretty damned fast. Suddenly I felt this complete . . . *agony* of love for him. He didn't deserve it, but that's what I felt. Lying in that hospital bed, his face as empty and gray as a beach in winter . . . It almost drove me mad. So, almost unconsciously, I found myself in a store one day buying a LEGO set with this dim idea. I wanted to build him a city where he could live while he was recuperating. I spent a week working on it. I built him the kind of hospital he should be in, the house where he should live afterward. Big picture windows, a veranda, a giant lawn . . . I got so carried away, I even bought in a model train store the kind of *dog* I thought should be at his side while he sat there in a pink chair and waited for his body to return to him.

"It gave me such peace and pleasure to construct I just continued doing it."

"Did it help your father? I mean, after you gave it to him?"

She smiled. "He looked at it once and said it was 'sweet.' It doesn't matter. I don't even know if I was making it for him. I believe my mind was telling me there was a place I could go, or *build* for myself, where I could be alone and happy. It was one of the things that saved me.

"I wasn't so happy when I was young. But now I am because I love you." Her napkin fell on the floor. Bending over to pick it up, she cried out, "Ow!"

"What's the matter?" My first thought was the child inside her.

"Oh, I do that sometimes. I'll make the dumbest motion, like pick up a napkin, and throw my back out. Now it'll be like this for three days. Damn!"

"Can I do anything?"

"You can let go of my elbow. You're squeezing it to death.

Don't worry—it's not major. Just Maris York growing older. Maris *Easterling* growing older. How does that name sound? I keep trying it out on my tongue."

"You're sure you're all right?"

"Yes. You didn't answer me—how does Maris Easterling sound?"

"Good. Like a Southern belle. You don't want to keep your own name?"

"No. Then we'd sound like a British law firm, Easterling and York." Do you think your parents will like me?"

I looked at her and thought about Moritz Benedikt telling his father he was going to marry Elisabeth.

My parents. Would my real parents like Maris? First I had to find them. First I had to find *him.*

Elisabeth Gregorovious Benedikt sounded nervous but interested when I called. I told her I had discovered her husband's grave at the Zentralfriedhof by accident and, amazed by the physical resemblance between us, had done some further research on him. Could I come and talk to her?

"You know what happened to my husband?"

"Yes."

"You know about his father? What happened to him?"

"Yes."

"How come you want to see me?"

She lived on the fifth floor of a walk-up near the Prater. Although it was a good distance away, the giant ferris wheel in the amusement park loomed behind her building. Inside, the place smelled pleasantly of freshly baked bread, which was incongruous because everything else in there was dark and defeated. The second *Bezirk* is a worker's district. Buildings there are either new and dull and functional, or old and dying. Many of the older ones show signs of one-time grandeur or imagination on their faces, whether via Jugendstil facades or the interesting simplicity of the Bauhaus style. But like the old movie queen who has turned seventy or eighty, whatever beauty or appeal remains shows more what has been lost, rather than what is left.

The stairway was wide enough for three people, and at every landing there was a stained glass window of a different kind of flower. Out of curiosity, I opened one and looked down at the courtyard below. Yugoslavian kids were kicking a soccer ball around, shouting at each other in their staccato, brusque language. One of them looked up, waved, and shouted, *"Immer wieder Rapid!"*

Her door was the only one on the floor painted white. A brass nameplate in script letters spelled out "Benedikt." Inside, I heard Peter Gabriel and Laurie Anderson singing "Excellent Birds."

I had to ring the bell twice before anything happened.

I thought she would at least be startled by my resemblance to her husband, but the 60ish woman who opened the door merely looked at me with her head cocked to one side and an amused smile. She had high Slavic cheekbones and green eyes set beneath a tightly curled bonnet of white hair. She was fat and barely contained by a cheap yellow and orange house dress.

"Mrs. Benedikt?"

"Yes. Wait a minute. Lillis, turn the music down! The man is here!" The music remained up. She put up her hand for me to wait, disappeared down the hall, and came back after the music was lowered.

Was Lillis her son?

"Yes, you do look like him. Come in."

The front hall was a mess of snow boots and coats and, strangely, toys: plastic dump trucks, "Masters of the Universe" dolls, one of those large Japanese robots that "transform" into something racy and sleek after ten twists and turns of their silver arms and legs.

"Everything was clean in here an hour ago, but Lillis likes to play everywhere. This way."

If she was pregnant in 1955, then the child would have been born in 1956, making it over thirty years old. The toys, colorful and by the look of them well used, took on a foreboding quality.

The living room was nothing special. A travel poster for Greece was framed on one wall, a Van Gogh reproduction on another. I looked around for photographs but didn't see any.

"You like baklava? I bought some fresh."

Before I could say anything, she gestured for me to sit and left the room. I chose a big padded chair, and without thinking, sat in it and leaned back slightly. It turned out to be one of those reclining jobs, and before I knew it, I was almost flat on my back. The surprise shook me. Struggling to right myself again, I heard a high-pitched laugh that sounded almost animal in its ferocity. Looking for its source, I saw nothing but a fast-moving shadow in the doorway disappear before I was straight up again. Mrs. Benedikt returned a little while later with a tray loaded with coffee things and a plate of shining baklava.

"You're an American? That's funny. I once had an American boyfriend before the war. He was a student at the university and used to come in after classes."

She had beautiful hands: long and white, and tipped by well-cared-for red nails. I watched them while she poured the coffee. A slight frisson of fear walked up my back. Somewhere inside I knew those hands, knew how important they were to her, knew what they did when she made love, knew how she sometimes secretly held them up to the light to admire, as if they were her only small work of art.

"Be careful in that chair. It's a recliner."

I took the cup she offered. "I know. I almost killed myself a minute ago."

Her face brightened, and she laughed deeply. It was completely different from the laugh I'd heard before.

"Yes, I've done that too! Sometimes I forget and go right back in it. Lillis loves it, though. He'd sit there all day if I let him.

"He'll be in, in a minute, so you'd better know. He looks like a normal man, but he's autistic. Do you know what that is?"

I was hesitant to say the word but did anyway. "Schizophrenic?"

"More or less. Lillis lives in his own head. He looks like a man but is really a little boy who doesn't know how to talk yet. He's very strange. Don't be surprised if he comes in and acts crazy. He *is* crazy, but he's my son. You will see."

The tone of her voice was everyday and unembarrassed. She had lived with the problem so long that it was only another part of her life, however difficult. I've always had the greatest admiration for people who appear, at least outwardly, to handle such crushing setbacks with both calm and unnoticed strength. Their burdens would be unthinkable to most of us, and the thanks they get for bearing them is minimal.

"Has he always been like that?"

She put a piece of baklava in her mouth and nodded. "A gift from his grandfather. After he killed Moritz, he called before the police came and told me what he'd done. Said that it was all my fault and the child's. It took me years to remember the whole conversation because you can imagine the shock it gave me. The last thing that little monster ever said to me was I'd better have an abortion or I'd be sorry."

"Do you believe he had that kind of power?"

"Yes, he had powers. I was stupid enough to think I could beat him, but I was wrong. I've been wrong for thirty years."

She continued eating. "On the island where I grew up, Formori, there was an old woman who told fortunes by looking at lamb bones. She was never wrong. Do you know what she told me when I was ten years old? That I would marry a man who was too right for me and that I would lose him because of that.

"When Moritz came back from the war, he told me our relationship was the only thing that mattered in his life. He also told his father that, and the old man hated both of us for it. It had been just the two of them for so many years. Kaspar thought it would stay that way. He wanted to be everything to his son, which is sick. That's all, *sick.* Then when I came along, he saw he couldn't have it that way. That maybe a normal man wants more out of life than a pat on the head from his father. He did everything he could to break us up. But I fought him, Mr. . . ."

"Easterling."

"Mr. Easterling. I fought and won Moritz away from his father because I had more to give than that ugly midget, and he knew it. That way I won." Her voice was full of cancerous disappointment, memories, and acid. It would be that way until the day she died.

I had no chance to react or say anything because Lillis appeared in the doorway.

There are women whose beauty makes you forget where you are, or even who you are. It doesn't happen often, but when you do encounter one of them, it is almost cruel the way they affect you. I have never understood how any man could live with one of these creatures without going mad with either paranoia or desire.

More disturbing still are the men who have the kind of physical beauty that transcends sexual gender. There were a number of them in Fellini's film *Satyricon,* and I remember, even as a young man, being made hotly uncomfortable (as well as captivated) by their unearthly looks. What did God have in mind with them? Are they here to remind us of the possibility of heaven and angels, or to taunt us mortals who are limited to one flesh, one physical way?

Lillis Benedikt was inconceivably beautiful. Long hair, shiny and surfer blond, that swept in a frozen curve over a high ivory forehead. His eyes were large and blue, as deeply set as his mother's, only slightly more curved and Oriental. The rest of the face was long and perfectly proportioned, down to the full crimson lips and teeth white as paper.

He was smiling shyly when he came in—the smile of a small boy who has been called into the living room to be introduced to company. I was so taken by his looks that I didn't realize at first the fly of his pants was wide open.

Looking straight at me, the smile stayed frozen on his face. Normally, a stare like that would have made me uneasy, especially knowing the man was disturbed, but his damned face was so hypnotic I couldn't look away.

"Lillis, pull up your zipper!" She got up to go to him but he ran across the room. Falling to his knees beside me, he grabbed my arm tightly.

"Do you mind? He won't hurt you. If I try to touch him now he'll only fight and make a scene. He'll be okay in a while and I can fix it then."

"It's fine. Don't worry. Hello, Lillis."

"You don't have to pay attention to him. He'll sit there and just look. That's his way of saying he likes you. He's not dangerous." She reached over and picking up a piece of the dessert, handed it to him. He took it and let it drop to the floor, his eyes never leaving my face.

I picked it up and handed it to him again. Taking it, he squashed it between his fingers.

"I think he's the most beautiful man I've ever seen."

"I know. If he were normal he'd have a hard time keeping

the women away. As it is, when we walk down the street they look at him as if they were dreaming. Excuse me a minute, I'll be right back." She got up and left the room.

He pulled my hand to his face and pushed it against his cheek. Rubbing it up and down with his eyes closed, the gesture reminded me of the way Orlando moved when he was being petted.

"Can you speak?"

Like a fish, he opened and closed his mouth several times before speaking. His words came with the slow, high precision of a little girl's voice.

> *"Today I'll brew, tomorrow I'll bake.*
> *Soon I'll have the queen's namesake.*
> *Oh, how hard it is to play my game*
> *For Rumpelstiltskin is my name."*

Mrs. Benedikt dropped something in the hall as she was returning. Lillis looked fearfully at the door. He had shown me one of his secrets and it seemed he was afraid she would discover it. Only after she was back in the room did I remember I'd heard one of his lines before, in one of my dreams—"How hard it is to play my game."

"Is everything all right? Look how he looks at you! He's not usually that friendly with strangers."

"Does he ever speak, Mrs. Benedikt?"

"Yes, once in a while. He likes it when I read to him. The strange thing is, he has a very good memory sometimes. Especially for fairy tales. His favorite is 'Rumpelstiltskin.' When he's in the mood, he can repeat almost the whole story from beginning to end. Now that I think of it, that's the only one he ever says."

Whether he understood her or not, something in what his mother said seemed to anger him. He got up quickly and repeated what he'd said before. Only this time, the lines were spoken so fast and with such force that they ran together in a kind of high-speed gibberish.

" 'TodayI'llbrewtomorrowI'llbake . . .' "

I hadn't realized how small the room really was until he started running around it. He climbed over furniture, hit walls, kept falling down and getting up again. What was he doing? The expression on the woman's face said she didn't know any more than I.

"Lillis, stop!"

" 'TodayI'llbrew . . .' "

"Please, stop him!"

I tackled him around the knees and we went down together. He kept kicking his legs and repeating the same lines. On the floor he brought his face up long enough to kiss me on the lips. When I pushed him away he laughed.

" 'Is your name Rippenbiest, or Hammelwade, or Schnürbein?' "

"Lillis, stop!"

" 'Is your name Kunz? Is your name Hinz? Can your name be Rumpelstiltskin?' "

"Lillis!"

When I got back to the apartment, I saw Maris had done a lot of shifting around to accommodate her growing stash of things there. Although she'd slowly begun bringing her stuff over, she refused to move into my place until after we were married. Nonetheless, I loved seeing her clothes in the closet, her books on the table.

She was working at her computer. Orlando lay asleep on the monitor, his new favorite hangout when it was on and warm.

"Jesus, wait till I tell you what just happened to me."

"Hold it a sec, Walker. Let me finish this. Don't look, either. I'm working on your birthday present." On the screen over her shoulder I saw some brightly colored intersecting lines, but nothing more.

I walked into the kitchen for a glass of water. At the sink I happened to look out the window down into the courtyard below. What I saw made me run out of the room for the front door.

"Where are you going?"

"I'll be right back!"

Taking the stairs two at a time, I was at the bottom fast. A few seconds more and I was in the courtyard, looking at the bicycle.

You see them all the time in big American cities: crazy-looking things, with every inch of their surface covered with pennants and flags, streamers and mirrors, that make the bikes shimmer and wave as they fly erratically down La Brea or Madison Avenue, piloted by riders as outlandish as the machines. Vienna has its share of eccentrics, but not this kind. That was another reason why seeing the thing again was such a shock.

Leaning up against the wall, unmoving, it looked pathetically sad and desperate—a real quack's dream of style and speed. But what kind of style? Flags advertising milk, a Vienna soccer team, and an old OVP presidential candidate stuck out from beneath the yellow banana seat. Two cracked rearview mirrors on either side of the handlebars, with stickers of the cartoon characters Asterix and Obelix stuck in their centers, impeded any rear vision they might have offered. The bike itself was painted like a piece of furniture from the Italian design group Memphis. One fender was orange, one blue, the different crossing bars each another vivid, clashing color. The tires had been sprayed silver, even on the bottom.

I had seen it before. So many weeks before, on the night I brought Maris back to Elisabeth's apartment. The night we first slept together. Standing there with my hand resting on the seat, I tried to remember exactly what the man looked like who rode it. All that came to mind were his broken teeth, scraggly beard, and the fact that he'd greeted me as Rednaxela. And his smell! The smell of a man on fire with madness.

"Walker!"

I looked up and saw Maris's distant face hanging out the window of our apartment.

"What are you doing down there?"

"Come down and look at this."

"What's up?"

"Just come."

I turned back to the bike to see if there was a way of deciphering anything important from the hieroglyphics scrawled and glued and stuck on to it. Still looking when Maris arrived, I briefly explained who it belonged to and what that meant. With no further questions, she got down on the other side of the bike and began looking, too.

"Where's the guy who owns it?"

"I wish I knew. That'd make things a lot simpler."

"You think he knows you live here? What's this?"

"An old fountain pen clip. I'm sure he knows. There aren't many bikes like this in Vienna, huh? It's got to be a lot more than *Zufall* that he parked it in our courtyard."

Frau Noot came through the door with a bag of garbage to dump. Seeing us, she smiled and waddled over.

"What a beautiful bicycle! Did you buy it, Walker? It's very artistic."

"No, it's not mine, Frau Noot."

"We used to do this with our bikes when I was a girl. Don't ask how many years ago *that* was! We even put cards like this, too. To make it sound like a motorcycle." She bent over and, struggling, pulled something off the back wheel. "Kids never change. What does it say, Maris? I can't read without my glasses."

Handing the white piece of paper over, she folded her arms and waited to hear what her discovery said. "They won't mind I took it off. There's another on the other side."

"I think it's a calling card for a tailor. 'Benedikt and Sons, *Schneiderei.*'" She looked at me and held it out. "You better look at it."

All that was on the card was their title and an address I already knew on Kochgasse in the Eighth District. I turned the card over and over, hoping there would be more.

"I guess it's time we went over there."

"He's a playful little shit, isn't he?"

Maris spoke in English, but Frau Noot understood that one word and looked at her with shocked eyes.

Getting off the Number 5 tram at Kochgasse, Maris took my hand and stopped me.

"You really had to tackle him?"

"Yes. I think he would have ended up jumping out the window or something if I hadn't. He was totally out of control. What number is that? The place should be on this block."

"What happened after he went down?"

"The woman wanted me to leave, but he wouldn't let go of my arm. So I hung around awhile and sort of petted him till he calmed down. Then I took off."

"Are you going to go back?" She was walking fast to keep up.

"I don't know. What more could I get from them? Moritz had a beautiful son who's autistic. His mother says it's due to Kaspar Benedikt's powers, and there's nothing to disprove that."

"Kaspar Benedikt's dead."

"Let's hope so. Unfortunately, it's beginning to look like something of him lives on."

The street was narrow and cars were parked bumper to bumper all the way down it. We passed a Turkish bakery and several other small stores before reaching the address. At first we didn't realize we were there because Benedikt und Söhne had disappeared. In its place was a modern stationery store. Maris and I looked at each other and stepped closer. The window was full of Garfield and Peanuts pencil cases and school notebooks, Mont Blanc ink bottles, pocket calculators, and portable typewriters. I looked harder, knowing something was there, that something *had* to be there.

It was. In the lower left-hand corner of the window was a large decal that advertised "Mr. Pencil sold here!"

"Look at this." I tapped the decal with my finger and Maris gave a little gasp.

"How'd he know about that?"

"Let's find out." Pushing the door open, I walked in, half expecting to see the wild man on the bicycle behind the counter selling graph paper.

A very attractive middle-aged woman was behind the crowded counter talking on the telephone and smiling. She saw me and quickly got off.

"Good day. Can I help you?"

I looked at her a long moment. "Yes, I'd like to buy a Mr. Pencil. Or some of them, whichever you've got."

Her smile went from friendly to confused. "Excuse me?"

"The thing you have advertised in the window outside, Mr. Pencil"?

"I'm sorry, but I don't know what you mean. Could you explain what it is?"

"Um, why don't you come outside with me and I'll show you what I mean."

She came around the counter and I held the door for her. We almost bumped into Maris coming in.

"She doesn't know what Mr. Pencil is."

"Interesting."

"It's over here. This decal."

"I've never seen that before! I don't even know who put it there."

"You're sure?"

"I should know—I own the store and do all of the decorating! I've never even heard of Mr. Pencil. Is it an American product? What is it?"

"How long have you had the store?"

Her eyes narrowed suspiciously. "Why do you want to know?"

"Because one of my relatives used to have a tailor shop here, Benedikt and Söhne."

"Then you should know what happened to the Benedikts. My father bought the store from the widow, and we've been here ever since. Did you want to look at the store, or buy this Mr. Pencil thing? You still haven't told me what it is yet."

"Have you ever met any of the Benedikt family?"

"No. It's cold out here and I have to go back inside. Is there anything else you would like?"

Maris spoke. "Is your father still alive?"

The woman looked fed up with us. "Yes."

"Does he ride a bicycle and have a beard?"

"No! He's blind and is retired in Weidling. Excuse me now."

She left us there. As she was about to go back into the store she stopped. Turning, she went to the decal on the window and pulled it off with one long, dramatic *zip*. Crumpling it in her hand, she looked at us and dropped what was left of it on the ground. I was going to pick it up, but what for? There would be others. That was about the only thing I was sure of.

"What do you remember first? The first thing you remember about your whole life?"

"Papa, you *always* ask me that. I don't know. I told you."

"Come on, you must remember something."

"Why do you always want to know?"

"Because I'm your father. I want to know what's in my son's head. The more a boy can remember, the more grown up he is."

"What do *you* remember?"

"How beautiful your mother was. What a nice voice she had."

"I know that. I think I remember when she sang to me. When I was a little baby."

"See, you do remember things. What else?"

We were walking in the forest. Papa said we would be near Vienna by the end of the day, but I was already tired. I asked him to carry me again, but he said I was too big to be carried all the time. I was almost bigger than him.

I liked the forest, but most people stayed away from it because they were afraid of what was in there. Not Papa and me. He said we were magic and nothing could hurt us. He said nothing could kill us, either, because we were so special. We were from someplace else. I didn't remember where, because I was just a little baby when we had to leave.

I didn't want to tell him because it was my own secret, but the earliest thing I remembered was being carried out of the city where I was born on Papa's back, and looking at all the castles and towers. I think he was running, because I remember going up and down and up and down, and maybe I was crying because I was scared. I remember the castles and the towers and horses and people all over the place.

I also remember my mother leaning over my bed one

night and crying because there were so many names in the world and she couldn't find the right one. She had long red hair and I think my bed was made out of gold.

"Do you remember how they tried to stop us? Maybe that was too long ago for you."

"Tell me again. I like that story about how we ran away together."

"All right. Your mother was the queen and she was very beautiful. But her heart was white and cold as a star. She didn't keep her promises. That's one of the worst things in the whole world a person can do."

"That's very bad. I keep my promises, don't I?"

"Yes, you do, Walter, and I'm very proud of you for that. If you promise me you'll go get wood, you always do it. That's a very important quality in a person. Don't ever forget it."

That made me feel good. "But Papa, if you loved Mama so much, why did you take me away from her?"

"Because she loved only herself. Her heart was only big enough for one person. She would have made you sad your whole life. When I first met her, she was a poor girl who would have done anything to be rich. She got her father to lie to the king and tell him she could make gold out of straw."

"You can do that. I've seen you."

"But normal people can't. Your mother thought she would be beautiful enough to make the king forget about gold when he saw her. And he thought she *was* beautiful, but he loved gold more. That's what got her into trouble in the first place."

"The king was my first father, right?"

"Yes, but your first father isn't always your best father. He was as cold and greedy as your mother. That's why they fit so well together. I knew that if they ever did have a child, the only thing they would like about it was that it was theirs, like their gold. When it grew up, they wouldn't treat it any differently than a ring or a bracelet. When they weren't wearing it or showing it off to the world, they'd throw it in a drawer and forget about it."

That made me mad. "But you said Mother loved me!"

"She loved you because you were just another piece of jewelry, Walter, not because you're a wonderful little boy."

I picked up a rock and threw it against a tree. The tree yelled "Ow! Stop that!" and rubbed the place where it got hit. I looked at Papa and told him to stop being crazy. He laughed.

"Don't you like talking trees?"

"Trees don't talk."

"We can make them talk."

"But they don't *really* talk. Now you're lying!"

"You're right. I'm sorry. What a smart boy. Are you hungry?"

"No. Tell me more about the time we left the city."

"Your mother promised me if she got to be queen, she would let me take care of you when you were born. But when that happened, she told me to go away. She didn't 'need' me anymore."

"That's not nice."

He put his hand on my head and smiled at me. "That's what I thought too, son. But I would have gone away because I loved her. But then I waited around till you were born and saw how she treated you. Even as a baby I knew your life would be terrible and sad if you stayed with her. So I went to her and said she'd made me a promise and had to keep it, whether she liked it or not.

"Do you know what she said to me? 'Go away, little man. I already have a court midget.' But I knew her well by then, so I didn't even let that insult bother me. Instead, I pointed at her and turned one of her fingers into gold. I said I would do one more every day until she kept her promise to me.

"Walter, she didn't even know my name! All of the things

I had done for her, and she never once asked who I was. She just used me to get what she wanted and then after that happened, wanted me to disappear like a cloud after the rain."

Was he angry! We walked for a long time before he said anything again. Then he only said, "Go away, little man," three or four times. I knew when Papa was mad that I should be quiet. Once, when a man was making him mad, Papa made a big bird fly out of the man's mouth. But the bird was *really* big and it couldn't get out of his mouth. Papa made me walk away, but I think the man died because he fell down on the ground and was making funny sounds and was hitting his mouth, really scared. I saw that.

"Yet I still gave her a chance. I gave her one more chance to prove she was at least a little human."

"She had to guess your name. I remember that part, Papa."

"That's right. I gave her three days to find out my name. If she could do that, then all right, I'd go. At least she knows the name of the guy who gave her all she ever wanted in life. That's not asking so much. I loved your mother, Walter. Never forget that. I would have stayed with her and helped forever, even though she was married, if only she had shown the smallest kindness or gratitude." He laughed, and that made me happier. I took his hand. I didn't understand everything he was saying, but if he laughed then things were okay. He laughed again.

"She was finally scared! She finally realized she was going to lose something and there was nothing she could do about it. Oh, how she sent them running! They ran all over that kingdom trying to find out who the little man was. The names she guessed were as wrong as she was. Ratbod! Pankratius! Names as old and stupid as stone. Have you ever heard a man with that name? I gave her a chance, but knew she'd never get it right because her imagination was as small as her heart."

"I know your name, Papa."

"I know you do, son. You own the greatest secret I have. That's what gives you your powers. No other people know that name, so no one else can do what you can. There's no other person like you in the world. That's what I do for *my* son: give him everything I have.

"But your mother was too blind to know I'd have done that for her, too. She was too used to buy and sell, I'll give you this if you'll give me that. Not 'I love you, so I want you to have this. It's free, straight from my heart.'

"She guessed over two thousand names in the time I gave her. After those three days her tongue was as red as her eyes, but still she wasn't even close. Do you remember what her last guess was?"

"Rumpelstiltskin!"

"That's right. She thought my name was Rumpelstiltskin. What desperation! I can't even say that name. You know what the funniest part is? All she had to do was ask. All she had to say was 'Please tell me what your name is.' And I would have done it immediately.

"Come on, let's eat. This talking makes me hungry."

We took off our packs and put them down. He took out apples and cheese, and a bottle of water.

"What happened when she couldn't guess?"

"She called me a little frog and said she was going to have her guards kill me. I told her first to look at her left hand and think about that. On her right hand she already had one gold finger. You know what was on her left? A big fat frog instead of her hand. The worst part was, it was alive."

"You really made her hand into a frog?"

"I really did."

"Could I do that, Papa?"

"You can do anything I do. I taught you how."

"Just think your name and then think what I want."

"Right. Eat your apple."

"Can I do it to you?"

"If you want."

I closed my eyes and thought his name and thought I wanted *both* of his hands to turn into frogs. When I looked, there they were—two big frogs! But something was wrong with them because they didn't move.

"What'd I do wrong?"

He smiled and looked at them. "You didn't think clearly what you wanted. You didn't think if you wanted them alive, so you only got dead frogs. And look at their color—that's not a frog's color, because you weren't thinking a special color when you made your wish. You only made dead dream frogs."

I started crying, but he didn't say anything. I cried till I got tired of it and felt stupid.

"Now wish them away, Walter, or else I'll have to live with frogs for hands for the rest of my life!"

That made me laugh and I did what he said. They went away. It was easy to wish something away. Much easier than wishing *for* something.

He reached over and touched my cheek.

"Quit it, Papa. I'm not a little baby anymore."

"Sometimes I forget that. Eat your apple and cheese. They're good."

"I don't want anymore. What happened after you made her hand into a frog?"

"If you eat your apple I'll tell you. That's it, big bites. And please bite the cheese or else it'll get fleas."

"Papa, tell!"

"Okay. While she was looking at her croaking hand, I took you out of your bed and wrapped you in the fur blanket I'd brought. It was the middle of winter and the snow roared like lions outside. The whole city was covered and I knew we'd have a hard time running through it when we got outside."

"Why did we have to run? You could have kept anyone away."

"Probably, but it was midnight, and our powers are much less then. Always remember that, son. Our magic works best in the day. At night most of it goes back to the moon and sleeps there until first light. Animals have their magic at night. That's why it's not safe to travel after the sun goes down where there are animals.

"Now tell me again what I just said."

"Animals are magic at night and we should stay away from them."

"Good." He sat there awhile, sometimes biting his apple or his cheese. There were birds singing, and somewhere far away I heard someone chopping wood.

"How did you get me out of the castle?"

"I turned to your mother and said 'You're too proud and greedy to care what child you have, so long as no one knows the difference. So I'll give you a child to show others. You can pretend it's yours and that you defeated me. But *never* come after us, or I'll kill you. Do you understand?' She understood. All the hatred in her eyes told me she understood very well but could do nothing about it.

"I took the frog off her hand and changed it into a baby. 'There's your child, Queen. The one you deserve.' "

"What happened then?"

"I put you in my rucksack, down deep where no one would be able to see you. Then I ran out of the castle. I'll remember that night as long as I live. The snow was as deep as the sadness after death, but the only thing I could do was run until we were safely away. There was a festival going on in the city, and there were bonfires burning everywhere. People were drunk and singing, and men were racing their horses back and forth across the snowy streets."

"The horses. Yes, I remember that, Papa. I remember hearing all the horses."

He lay down on his back and closed his eyes. "I have no sense of direction at night, but I knew the southern gate of the city because that's where the potato market was. I ran through that gate and into a night with a knife between its teeth. Horrible and cold, white and black.

"But we made it, and here we are about to start our new life in Vienna."

"Why Vienna, Papa?"

"It's a good city for us to start in. Right now it's full of plague, so people like us can live there undisturbed because there's so much other madness around. No one will notice a little man and his son selling potatoes by the side of the road."

"Will we live there forever?"

"On and off. It's where I come from and I like it. You will, too. People there leave you alone. I want to do a lot of traveling with you, Walter, but sooner or later I think we'll always go back there."

"What happened to my mother?"

He laughed again. "Just what I expected would happen. On the road, I've already heard the story three times how that good queen saved her only child from the evil dwarf Rumpelstiltskin by guessing his name.

"Come on, it's time to go."

2.

The dream must have lasted no more than twenty minutes. I looked at the clock beside the bed in sleepy wonder. Maris wasn't there because she'd decided to stay at her place and work on my birthday present.

I had to talk to her about this. I decided to wait awhile and let my head clear before calling. Luckily she didn't mind late night calls, unlike me, who strongly believed they meant bad news was about to arrive.

What a dream! I could still smell the damp pine forest and see the sun reflect yellow off the red apples. My "father" wore old leather boots that came to points at the toe. He had a beard, but it was trimmed close and was a deep, tree-bark brown. He was handsome and about thirty years old. The only thing that made him different was his size. He was a midget. He walked with a kind of strutting lurch that was both comic and distressing. To judge from the way these small people walk, one would think the world is a boat on a stormy sea: The only way to keep one's balance is to walk like a swinging pendulum.

I closed my eyes and tried to remember or see other things from the dream, but it was no use. It had all slipped back into the mind's dark a few minutes ago.

Orlando was asleep on my arm, but suddenly lifted his head and looked around; his inevitable sign that the phone was going to ring. I even started getting up before it happened because his alarm was so dependable. I was a foot away when it did ring.

"Hello?"

"You *finally* had that dream. Now we can begin."

"Excuse me? Who is this?"

"What was my name in your dream?"

"Who *is* this?"

"Okay, we'll do it slowly. What was my name when we got to Vienna that time? Not my real name, but the one I took. Come on, Walter, I'm giving you a big hint. In Russia I was Melchior, right? Last time I was Kaspar, so what's left? What was my name when we came into Vienna the first time? It wasn't Rumpelstiltskin!"

He laughed, and I knew that sound so well.

"Where are you?"

"In Vienna!" He laughed again. "Watching you and your

new girlfriend. You're still such a horny little boy, aren't you? I told you not to do that. You get into trouble every time, but you insist on doing it. What am I going to do with you? *Magic and the mundane don't mix!* Listen to your father. You want to have magical powers? Fine, but you can't have them *and* fuck the girls too. That isn't allowed.

"Look at what that mixing has done to your friends. Nick Sylvian and Venasque are dead. Your other pals in California just lost everything in an earthquake . . . You even disturb the dead! How about that poor fellow in the coffin that broke open when you flew back here.

"Venasque didn't tell you, but you know why he had that stroke? Because of you. That last dream in the motel room? Blew right out of your head and burned his brain! Remember the doctor asking if he'd touched some live wire or electrical source? It was you, Walter; *you're* the live wire.

"How many lives are you going to go through before you realize you can't mix with them anymore? Once you turn my corner, you can't go back. You could have been an *ocean*, but now you're not enough spit to fill a mouth.

"It was so good in Russia. I thought maybe if we stayed there you'd learn something—see that our way together is so much better than yours with any woman. But no, you've got to touch them, don't you? Worse, you gotta touch them and then fall in love with them.

"Stubborn. I've got to say that for you. I drive you mad in one life, then push you out the window in another, but still you don't learn.

"So I bring you back and bring you back . . . But you go out and make the same mistakes!"

"What magic? I have no magic."

"That's right, it's going away fast. But that's your own doing. Still, you could talk our language with the old girls in the cemetery. Then you saw that woman fall down the escalator before it happened. Hey, you even brought up a sea serpent!

"All that magic I gave you *is* a lot for a normal little boy to handle, but I believed in you, Walter! I wanted to give you everything your mother never would have.

"That's one thing I didn't tell you. Maybe it's time I did.

"You know why I took you away from her? I loved you, there's no question about that, and I'd do it again anytime. The years we spent together were the happiest I ever had. I admit it. My own boy." He started crying—long, hoarse weeping, cut with big drags for air in between. It went on for some time. I was holding the receiver so tightly that my hand began to cramp. I switched hands. "Do you remember the time you brought me the stone? The first time you used the magic? You brought that big piece of granite and turned it into a diamond right in front of me. You said that was how big your love was for me. My God, I love you. I would have loved you for the rest of time if you hadn't been so *fucking human!*

"Everything I taught you, everything I gave you would have made any intelligent person fall down on his knees and kiss my feet. But not you. You're just like your mother, you little shit! Selfish and weak. So pleased with yourself. Mr. Movie Star.

"I'll tell you why I took you. Because she promised to love me if I gave her what she wanted. 'Make me queen and I'll love you for the rest of my life.' That's what she said—not fuck, *love.* Why do you think I helped in the first place? Why do you think I gave her all the magic I had? She was so convincing. 'I don't care if you can't do it. Who needs *that?* It only makes people sad. Love isn't touch—it's the mind.' She made me believe her eyes and not think about what was really going on in that rat-filled head of hers.

"My mistake. She couldn't love people—only things. You

think she loved your father? He was king, that was the only thing she loved about him.

"When you were born I saw a glimmer of something in her, maybe love, maybe not. But I knew that was how I'd win. Even if she didn't love her child, just the object that had come out of *her* body had value. And I took that object. I made you love me more than you ever would have loved her.

"The best part was sometimes I'd go back to her in her dreams, sometimes with you next to me. You were such a lovely child. We'd show her what she was missing."

I hung up. The phone rang again immediately, but something told me it wasn't him this time. It absolutely was not him. I picked it up.

"Walker, please come over right now. I started bleeding a few minutes ago and it's not stopping. Please come now. I'm scared."

I drove down the *Gürtel* at eighty miles an hour, running red lights the whole way. It was two in the morning and the streets were empty, but there were several near-misses that sent my heart into the back seat. I fishtailed left on Jörgerstrasse and flew up that narrow winding street, hoping no one would get in my way. At Wattgasse a patrol car appeared and we raced along for several blocks before I realized they might do something professional like shoot me. I pulled over, jumped out, and ran back to tell them what was going on.

Viennese police are notoriously unpleasant and fascistic, but the look on my face and the words that came zooming out must have convinced them I wasn't bullshitting. They said to follow them.

On Döblinger Hauptstrasse we were doing ninety, one right after the other. When we raced past a bunch of men repairing the tram tracks, one of them got so scared he ran across the street. I laughed because there was only that and praying left.

When we pulled up to the house an ambulance was already in front of the open gate. We all got out and ran, as if there was something more we could do.

Her white bed was full of blood. She was lying on her back with her eyes closed while one of the ambulance men worked between her spread legs. Her pajama bottoms were tossed to one side, red splashes over their green. She was such a modest woman, yet here were five men, four of them unknown to her, all staring at her most secret self.

I went over and touched one of her hands holding so tightly on to the headboard behind her.

"Maris, it's me. I'm here."

She kept her eyes closed. "I know. I know. Oh! Just stay here. I know you're here."

I looked at one of the ambulance men and caught his eye. He shook his head. "I don't know."

One of the policemen came up behind me and talked quietly into my ear. "I was with the UN forces in Lebanon. I saw something like this happen over there. It might not be anything. Sometimes they just start bleeding. It's dangerous, but it doesn't mean she's going to lose the baby. Just wait." He squeezed my shoulder and went back to his partner.

The man working on her spoke for the first time. "Okay. I've done all I can here. We're going to take you to the hospital now." He looked at me. "I thought she was bleeding through, but she isn't, so we can move her."

Her eyes opened wide and she looked around crazily. "Walker? Walker, where are you?"

"Right here, Maris. I'm here."

"They're going to take me to the hospital."

"Yes. I'll go with you."

"Okay. Okay. Let's go to the hospital." She looked at the

man bending over her. "It hurts, but I think I can go with you. I think I can go to the hospital because I think I have to go—"

"Sssssh . . ."

It hadn't been so long since I'd been in a hospital at night, waiting for news: in Santa Barbara with Venasque, the night of his stroke.

The Rudolfinerhaus is hidden behind a row of high, thick hedges. The first time I went there to visit a friend, I'd had to ask where it was because it's so well camouflaged. Once you find it, though, it's not at all the scary, doomful place a hospital can be. It's open and airy and full of floor-to-ceiling windows that light even the saddest corners. When we pulled up to the door that night, a smiling orderly came right out and took over.

They wheeled Maris into an examination room and asked me to wait in a room nearby. A few minutes later, a doctor with a large moustache and a good smile came in. His name was Doctor Scheer, and I liked him from the very beginning.

"Mr. Easterling? I'm glad you're here. I'd like to ask you some questions to clear up a few things. If that's all right with you."

"You speak good English, Doctor, but we can also speak German if you'd like."

"No! This way, I get to practice for free. Your friend—"

"Fiancée."

"Oh, let me note that. Your fiancée Ms. York was quite close to shock when she came in, so we've put her on intravenous to start some fluids back into her. Then we'll wait awhile to see if that helps. If it doesn't, we'll give her a transfusion. But there's no need to worry at this point because she appears otherwise to be a strong and healthy woman. That's most important.

"Let me ask you these questions though. Is she pregnant?"

"Doctor, this will sound funny, but I *think* so."

He looked at me blankly, then wrote something down. "Could you be more specific? Did she tell you? Has she had tests?"

"No, but, um, a friend who's a doctor said she looked like she was pregnant. Her face, or her physical presence . . . Whatever it is, I do know she hasn't had her period for a while and normally she's regular."

"Well, we can find that out fast enough. There's a gynecologist in-house and I'll give him a call. I'm sure he'll want to run a few noninvasive procedures on her—"

"What does that mean?"

"Do you know what a sonogram is? It's like the sonar they use on ships to detect submarines or mines beneath the surface of the water. We send sound waves down through the body in a completely harmless, 'noninvasive' way, which then lets us see what's going on inside the person without having to expose them to an X-ray.

"If Ms. York is pregnant, it will show up there. I would think with everything I've seen so far, what we've got is a classical threatened abortion."

"*Abortion?* She didn't—"

He held up his hand to silence me. "Mr. Easterling, the word abortion in medical terms means any kind of termination of pregnancy. Laymen misuse the word all the time, so it has come to have a terrible connotation. In Ms. York's case, 'threatened abortion' only means that her body itself is threatening the abortion. She has had nothing to do with it. However, as far as I can see, although there was a large loss of blood, this has not happened yet."

"You mean she might be miscarrying?"

"A threatened miscarriage. There are two other possibilities that we are going to check out. One of them is called a 'placenta previa' and the other is called 'abruptio placentae.' Both of them mean her body may naturally be saying something is wrong with this fetus, so it refuses to carry it. Do you understand me?"

"I'm getting confused."

"The body keeps constant check on itself. When a woman gets pregnant and then suddenly, naturally aborts, it usually means the fetus was in one way or another defective. This isn't always the case and sometimes, in something like 37 percent of all miscarriages, the woman loses the child for unknown reasons."

"But what if she isn't pregnant? Why would she be bleeding like that? There was a hell of a lot of blood."

"I'm not sure yet, but I still think she *is*, from the brief examination I just gave her. There's a medical saying: 'Rare things occur rarely.' Unless she has some kind of serious condition that's been unknown till now, like a tumor or some other kind of cancer, from her condition I would say she has all the symptoms of what I described to you before."

"Isn't all that blood she lost before dangerous?"

"You'd be surprised how much a body can lose before it gets into real trouble. She's a strong woman. Her body could probably lose almost two liters and still she'd be all right."

"Two liters?"

"Yes. The thing we worry about most with loss of blood is that the patient will then go into shock. This didn't happen here. Ms. York was disoriented and her color was bad when she came in, but we caught it in time. Now let's see what the gynecologist says."

He took out a pack of unfiltered cigarettes and, lighting up, took a deep, happy drag. I smiled and he smiled back. "Don't say anything. I have to live with a wife who's a jogger. I compromise by taking a five-mile walk every day." He paused. "Every day that the weather is nice."

They wouldn't let me see her that night, although they assured me she was better and it would be all right if I went home. I assured them I was quite comfortable in my awful chair in the waiting room. But after two hours of hospital walls and silence, I fell into a deep sleep.

It took days for the train to cross Europe, but I was in no hurry. There was an exhaustion so deep in my bones that all I seemed to do the whole trip was sleep, wake for a few minutes, then fall asleep again. Once, I slept right through a fistfight that happened two feet away from me when a German soldier from Konstanz tried to steal a pack of American cigarettes from my friend Günter.

The only interesting part of the train ride was when we crossed into Switzerland. The rest of the European countryside looked like any place that's gone through years of war, but not Switzerland. Crossing the border was like entering a fairyland, or at least the land you dreamed of returning home to after living in a trench and dirty underpants for three years. It was so clean! Nothing was ruined, nothing destroyed or broken. The cows were brown and wore gold bells in green meadows of grass. There was perfectly white snow on the mountains, white sails on the boats in the lakes. How could anything stay white while a war was going on? In the Zurich station, where we had to lay over while other, 'more important,' trains passed ours, vendors sold chocolate wrapped in silver paper, cigarettes in yellow and red boxes, apples and tomatoes as big as your hand.

The Swiss are horrible people, but they're smart. They take no sides and have no friends, but what do they care? They make it through wars untouched, with their banks full of money and their fat stomachs full. In France we heard they turned away Jews from their borders even when they knew what would happen by sending them back. Sometimes I thought about the French Jews we'd put on trucks. Sometimes, no, a lot of the time I thought about those French children who . . . flew out of that schoolhouse.

They wouldn't let us off the train in Zurich but that didn't matter. All we wanted from them was their food, and between us we had just enough money to buy it. When I ate a chocolate bar for the first time there, I almost got sick to my stomach from the pure beautiful sweetness of it. They had coffee with real milk and sandwiches on dark bread so fresh and warm it kissed the inside of your mouth. There's a funny contradiction here: You dream about food like that when you can't have it, especially when you can't have it for years, but at the same time you completely forget what it tastes like until you put it in your mouth and bite down after a thousand days. When I told Günter that, he said, "Yeah, just like pussy." When I saw the glint in his eye, good man that he is, I felt sorry for the first woman he slept with when he got home to Bregenz.

Naturally that made me think of Elisabeth. Would she be at the station to meet me? I'd written from France, but who knew what happened to letters sent from another country during a war? I kept thinking the post office there took prisoners' letters and threw them away first chance they got. But every once in a while I'd heard from her or my father. His letters were always the same: boring—how great things were going to be when I got back, the newest deal he'd pulled off and how much profit he'd made . . . But her letters were killers. They never talked about the weather or how hard the war was on them in Vienna. They talked only about sex. They talked about what kind of dreams she was having, what she thought about when she masturbated, what sort of things she wanted to do when we could sleep together again. After one of those letters arrived it always kept me hard for a week. I never knew whether I was glad or not to get them. Stupid as it sounds, they also made me nervous and uncomfortable. I'd play with myself so many times I'd get dizzy. When I wrote her that, she wrote back and set a date way in the future when, at exactly the same time, we should both jerk off and think of the other doing it. She was good in bed, but these letters told me things about her I'd never known when we'd slept together before the war. I wondered if that's *all* they were—dreams on paper. When we finally got to touch again, would she go back to being cozy sweet Elisabeth who sometimes purred like a cat when she was really hot, and most nights fell asleep with one leg over mine?

Günter got off at Bregenz. As we hugged good-bye, both of us started crying like fools. We were home, for better or worse, and we were glad of it. The last I saw of him, he was standing on the platform with a scared look in his eye. There were people swarming all around, but none of them went up to him. I knew exactly how he felt, so I pushed the window down and yelled at him, "Come to Vienna if it's bad here. You know where I am. Kochgasse!"

He waved at me. "Okay, but I'll be all right. You take care, pal."

It was another two days before I got home. Across the whole country, foreign troops were everywhere. English, Russians, Americans in Jeeps and tanks, walking by the side of the road . . . A group of them even waved to the train as we went past. A year before we would have been shooting at each other.

From what we heard, Austria had been divided up among different countries. Each *Bundesland* was controlled by someone else. In the train we learned Vienna itself was split up like that, and wondered who would be in charge of the different districts, and what changes would have taken place. More bad things to think about.

The last stop we made before we got there was Linz, which, from the look of things, had been hit hard. What I remember most, though, were two freight cars off on a siding with large Jewish stars painted sloppily on their sides. Below the stars was the word "Mauthausen." In France, I didn't believe the stories until that day I saw the kids fly, the day our lieutenant told us to round them up and put them in the trucks. After that I believed every story I heard about the death camps. But what was I supposed to do? What could anyone do when one word against it would have meant the firing squad, or worse. The lieutenant had been right that day —our job *was* to get our asses home in one piece, no matter what the orders were.

That was one of the few things I wanted to talk to my father about. He was a survivor. If you were his size, you had to find a way to survive in this world. I wanted to hear what he had to say about what the Nazis had done and why. Much of my life he'd been able to make sense of things that had only confused me. Maybe there *was* a good reason for killing all those Jews but I just didn't know it.

When the train pulled into Vienna it took only a few minutes for me to make out both of them waiting side by side on the platform. When they saw me Elisabeth started to run, but my father grabbed her arm and held her there. Then he started alone toward me in that funny side-to-side walk he had when he was in a big hurry.

When we reached each other he pulled me down and kissed my cheeks. "My boy! Moritz! You're home. You're here."

He used the Papa language, the secret words he'd taught me when I was a boy but which I'd always disliked.

"Hello, Papa. Talk to me in German. I want to hear my

own language now." I was crying again. I picked him up and hugged him, but over his shoulder I was looking at Elisabeth, so far down the way. Papa was Papa, but Elisabeth was home.

"Dave? Walker Easterling."

"Hey! What time is it? Christ, what's so important at eight in the morning that it can't wait?"

"Dave, I want you to do some more research for me."

"Right now? Can I brush my teeth first? What happened, did you find another skeleton in your family closet?"

"No, this time it's something more in your direction. I want you to find out all you can about the history of the fairy tale 'Rumpelstiltskin.' I know it comes from the Brothers Grimm, but I want you to really dig into this and find out everything you can."

After checking with the doctor on duty and hearing that Maris was still sleeping, I went home for a shower and a change of clothes. Orlando was indignant that I'd left him alone for the whole night, so I first had to play with him for some minutes before he walked away with his tail in the air, satisfied for the time being.

I was tired and stiff and worried about Maris, but once I was back in my apartment, the *other* phone call from the night before came back and hit me full force. Everything that had happened since then had clouded over some of what he had said, but enough of it returned and gave me a full dose of the creeps. Not to mention the dream I'd had in the hospital waiting room which, along with the other dreams I'd had over the last weeks, was beginning to make some sense.

After I showered, changed, and put the coffee on, I went to my desk and looked for a pencil and paper. While searching around, I happened to notice the computer in the corner and thought that would work just as well. Turning it on, I put in and pulled out the various disks, commands, blah-blah that needs to be done before you can have your conversation with the television screen. While it was thinking, I fiddled with the mouse and thought about the names Kaspar, Balthazar, and Melchior. When the word-processing program came up, I created a new file and typed those names at the top. Remembering that somewhere in Maris's load of books was a copy of *Grimm's Fairy Tales,* I got up to look for it. Unbelievably, it was the second book I pulled out of a big box. "Rumpelstiltskin," page 209.

Although it's a famous story, I didn't realize how short it was. Before reading, I did a quick line count and saw it was no more than 1500 words. Her copy was in English and I knew I'd have to get hold of the German original too, but for the moment this would be enough.

Whether we have better memories, or simply a better capacity for wonder as children, what struck me was how well I remembered the story, although it had been more than twenty years since I'd last read it: The poor miller's daughter who can supposedly spin straw into gold (according to her father), the king's interest, her desperation when it comes times to actually do it.

When she began to weep, the door suddenly opened, and a little man entered.

Not a midget or a dwarf, "a little man."

What I had forgotten was that he first takes a necklace and a ring from the girl before he does any spinning for her. That made no sense, even in the land of fairy tales. If she was so poor, where did she get all the jewelry? I decided to hold off on the cynicism until I'd read the whole story.

Just after that comes the first intriguing part of the story. When the girl has nothing left to give but still must spin gold for the king, the little man demands her first child when she becomes queen. She agrees! Until that point we're obviously supposed to not only be on her side, but feel great pity for both her poverty and helplessness. But if she is so virtuous, why would she accede so quickly to such a terrible and inhuman demand? All that is said to justify her decision is, *Who knows whether it will ever come to that? thought the miller's daughter. And since she knew of no other way out of her predicament, she promised the little man what he demanded.*

Lured to the kitchen by the strong perfume of fresh coffee, I got up feeling like a graduate student at work on his thesis: "A Critical Examination of the Role of Early Germanic Sexism in 'Rumpelstiltskin,' by Walker J. Easterling." There's probably some weenie out there actually writing something like that.

Warming my hands around the coffee cup, I looked down into the courtyard, but today there was no Rumpelstiltskin bicycle leaning up against the wall. I remembered the scene in *The Bicycle Thief* where the little boy watches his father steal a bicycle and then get chased by the mob. My father? The only father I'd ever known was Jack Easterling of Atlanta, Georgia. A tall, quiet man who sold ad space in the *Atlanta Constitution* and liked nothing more than to have a catch in the backyard with his son Walker, who was never a very good baseball player.

Walker, Moritz, Alexander (Rednaxela), Walter.

Easterling, Benedikt, Kroll . . .

What was the last name of the boy in my Rumpelstiltskin dream? My coffee break was over. Before sitting down again with the book, I typed those names into the computer, too.

The king comes in the next morning, and seeing his third haul of new gold, decides to marry the girl. Nothing more is heard of their relationship until a year later when the queen delivers her first child.

The little man had disappeared (?!) from her mind, but now he suddenly appeared in her room and said, 'Now give me what you promised.'

Wait a minute. I knew it was a story, but how in the world could he have 'disappeared' from her mind when from the beginning he'd been the reason for her success? I was chewing on that when a few lines later I found the key to the story.

The queen was horrified and offered the little man all the treasures of the kingdom if he would let her keep the child, but the little man replied, "No, something living is more important to me than all the treasures of the world."

Why would he say that? If he was magical enough to spin straw into gold, couldn't he just as well have conjured up a real child of his own? Something in what he said the night before slid into my mind. Something about how the girl promised to love him even if he couldn't do it. What was *it*, sex? An intriguing notion, and it made sense. I read the line again. . . . *something living is more important to me than all the treasures of the world.*

I put on my screenwriter's hat and started thinking about motivation. The little man falls in love with the girl and does her spinning. He thinks she'll love him for it, even though he's not a "real" man because he's incapable of taking her to bed. But that makes him fight all the harder for her because he hopes that by doing all these magical things, she'll love him anyway.

I sat back in the chair and snorted. What would Freud or Bruno Bettelheim say? This had to go into the computer too. I went over and started typing, not watching what was happening on the screen. When I did have a few words written, I looked up to check.

On the monitor was a picture of a room. It was clear and in color and looked like a movie. A television flickered in a corner of the room and I realized one of my old films was showing there: the film I had made with Nicholas when Victoria and I first came to Vienna. I even knew the scene. It had been so difficult to shoot that we'd had to do it over and over until Nicholas blew his top at me and said, "Start acting like a human being, will you?"

Someone in the room laughed.

The picture bled away and was replaced by one of Victoria and a man in bed, fucking: the actor I'd introduced her to who owned all of the nice Hoffmann furniture. They were moving around like mad dogs, howling and biting, eating each other alive. Despite the passage of time and my great love for Maris, what I saw punched me in the stomach. While my friend humped my wife, she began hitting him on the back with her small fist. She cried out "I hate you! I hate you, Walker!" The man laughed and put his hand over her mouth. She bit it and made him yelp. My memories of sleeping with Victoria were quiet and comfortable. She used to tickle my back with her long fingernails, and laugh when I tried to roll her around or do something different.

The television picture bled away until the screen was empty. Just the room was there now. I heard footsteps somewhere off-camera and then the madman on the bicycle walked into the scene. He had a large bowl of popcorn in one hand and was humming. Sitting down in the room's only chair, he picked up a remote control box from the floor and changed the channel. Another of my old films came on.

"What are you doing?"

Popcorn sprayed across the floor when the man jumped up. He looked all around him but clearly didn't know where I was.

"Walter, are you here?"

"What the fuck are you doing? Where did you get those films?"

"Where are you?"

"I'm here. Here! Looking right at you!"

He smiled, but there was only dark in his mouth.

"You still have your magic. I can't see you but you can see me. That's wonderful. You *can* still do it if you want."

"I don't want anything."

He kept looking around, as if he'd spy me in a corner sooner or later. Giving up, he spread his arms like a minister in front of a congregation. "You're really *not* here. That makes me so happy. My son still has his magic. What's my name? Tell me my name, Walter."

I was about to say something but stopped. "Tell me why you're here. Then I'll tell you."

"I've always been here. Every time you come back, I'm here. Every life you live, I'm here to see if you're ready to come home to me. The biggest mistake I ever made was letting you grow up. I should have kept you little. When you were little you loved me so much. You didn't think about girls then; you only wanted to be with your Papa. Why did I ever let that happen?"

"The dreams are real? I lived those lives?"

He clapped his hands. "Yes! Yes! Do you know how happy I am to hear you ask that question? This is the thirty-first life you've lived. Never once in any of them have you realized what's been going on. This is the first time! It means you're so close. What's my name, Walter? Tell Papa his name."

"No, not yet. Why have I had to live all these lives? What's the purpose?"

"The purpose? You don't remember? You don't remember betraying your own father? You're doing it now with that bitch in the hospital! Only this time it's going to be different if you keep it up, my boy. Oh, yes, this time you're not going to have another chance. Even a father loses his patience after this long. Every life you get more and more like your mother. Both of you promise and both of you lie.

"Maybe it's just in your blood. Maybe I was wrong to think if I taught you, if I raised you right, you'd be different and see how much better it is to be like me. Like your father!"

I spoke as coolly as I could. "My father is in Atlanta."

His answer was cooler. "Oh, really? Watch the television. See for yourself, *Walker.*"

In an instant I knew the place. I'd been there so many times since my parents told me where I'd really come from. The alley behind Conroy's Restaurant in Atlanta. The only things different were a 1956 Chevrolet parked there, and the area looked much cleaner than I remembered. At the far end of it, a midget appeared holding something in his arms. Something large and wrapped in a white blanket. He went straight over to one of the garbage cans behind the restaurant, and after first kissing the thing inside the blanket, laid it down carefully inside one of them.

He hovered over the can and whispered, "This time. Come home this time, Walter." The sound of someone approaching made him pull back fast. After one last tender look, the little man scurried away.

From the other end of the alley a bum slunk in, looking into every garbage can along the way. When he reached this one he looked once, twice, and suddenly his face said everything. He lifted the white bundle gingerly out of the can, and for the first time I saw that there was a note pinned to the blanket. The bum saw it too, his drunken eyes trying to focus.

"Holy shit, a baby! Wait, what does it say? 'His name is . . . Walker? Please take care of him.' Well, holy shit, Walker. Looks like someone doesn't want you." Cradling the baby to his chest, he staggered away. Along the way, the note fell off without his seeing it.

Shortly after he left, a motorcycle roared through the alley and ran over the note. Somehow or other it stuck to the wheel.

"Now tell me my name, son."

Without my touching it, the monitor rose off Maris's table and exploded in midair.

"Fuck you, Papa."

"How are you?"

"Okay."

"You don't look okay. You look very un-okay."

"Worry. It gives you wrinkles."

"Come here."

"I can't move."

"Come here anyway."

I got up and walked over to her bed. She looked both pale and radiant.

"We're going to have a baby. What do you think of that?"

"I think I love you and I'm very happy."

She frowned. "You don't sound excited."

"Maris, I don't know what you're supposed to say when you find out you're going to be a father. I guess I'm in shock."

"That's better. I think I am too, but it's nice, isn't it? I was so scared last night. I thought this is really it, folks. My time has come. Crazy how twelve hours later you can be glad for all that blood."

"What did the doctor say?"

"That it'd be best if I stayed here flat on my back for a couple of weeks. That part I don't like—it means we can't get married till I'm out of here."

"That can wait. Neither of us is going anywhere."

She took my hand and squeezed it. "What shall we name it? I've been thinking ever since they told me. I hope you don't mind, but I don't want to call it either Walker or Maris. I don't like it when people name their kids after themselves."

"I agree. How about Walter?"

"*Walter?* Where'd you get that name?"

"Nowhere. It's a joke."

" 'Walter Easterling' sounds like a fat banker." She squeezed my hand again. "They've given me every test in this hospital. They're very nice about it, but every time someone new comes into the room they want to give me another test."

"Maris, I'm sorry if I'm not good company. I'm sort of stoned right now. You're the one who went through all the pain, but I'm woozy from sleeping in the waiting room, I guess."

"I can see. When they told me you did that I wanted to run out and kiss you. That wasn't necessary, but I'm secretly glad you did it."

Although she'd been through hell the night before, the news of the child had so buoyed her that she chatted away until she was exhausted. It showed in her eyes first—I literally saw something leave them before they dropped closed for a long second.

"I think I have to sleep now, my friend."

"Okay, sure. But you feel better?"

"I feel terrible, but I don't care. We're going to have a child, Walker. You know how much I want that. I never told you before, but once when I was with Luc I missed my period for a couple of weeks and thought I was pregnant. I've never felt so torn in my life. When my period came I was so happy I cried. I've always been ashamed of that, the being happy, but now I know I was right. Now the whole thing is right and I feel like the best is about to begin for us. It's the truth."

"That's a great compliment, you know?"

"It's going to be a good baby. You deserve the compliment."

I called from a phone booth near her building.

"Hello?"

"Mrs. Benedikt? This is Walker Easterling. Mrs. Benedikt, would it be at all possible for you to talk to me for a few minutes? It's really extremely important."

"No. I don't know. I don't want you coming up here again after what happened last time with Lillis. You understand."

"I do, I understand completely. But we can meet in a café. Mrs. Benedikt—"

"Why do you want to talk? I told you everything."

"It's about Kaspar Benedikt. I have to tell you something that I found out about him."

"Like what?"

"Please come and meet me. I'm five minutes from your place. We can go to the café across the street."

"All right, but only for a few minutes. I'll get Herr Lachner to sit with Lillis."

She came into the café wearing an orange housedress and pink bedroom slippers. The waitress knew her and brought over a glass of white wine without being asked.

While she drank I looked closely at Elisabeth's face, trying to find the woman of my forty-year-old dream. Some people keep their looks all their lives. Whether they get fat or thin, the face stays with them, like their fingerprints. Moritz's wife was from the other group. In my dream she was thin and drawn from the war. Since then, she'd traded her face for potatoes and bread, and white wine at eleven in the morning.

"What do you want today?"

"You said you believed Kaspar Benedikt had special powers. Did you mean that?"

She drank and nodded at the same time. Her glass was already three-quarters empty and she signaled for another. "I told you, I come from Greece, so I've seen some people with powers, mister. Believe it or not, I've seen ghosts, and a woman told my future exactly by reading lamb bones."

"Yes, I remember that. If you do believe, Mrs. Benedikt, then I want to tell you a dream I had. It might scare you, but it's necessary that you hear it."

"When you've lived with a midget, then a war, then Lillis, not much scares you. Tell me."

"Okay. In the dream I'm coming into the Westbahnhof on a troop train from France. The train cars are all green brown and they're filled with soldiers coming back after the war. I'm looking out the window of our car but I can't see you or Papa." Elisabeth's mouth tightened when she heard that word. I expected her to say something, but she only closed her eyes and shook her head. "Should I go on?"

"Yes."

"I'm trying to think of what I'm going to say to you if you're there, but my mind is blank. Tonight, or whenever I get you into bed, I'm going to tell you that. I'm going to tell you I'm so excited to see and . . . touch you that I don't know what to say."

"What else?"

"Are you all right?"

"Yes. What else?" The waitress brought her second glass, but she only put her hand around it.

"I get off the train carrying two big duffle bags with me. In one of them are two pairs of red silk underpants I got for you when I was in Paris. As the train comes to a squeaking stop, I see you and Papa standing maybe twenty meters down the platform. You wave to me and start to run, but he holds you back."

Her eyes still closed, she spat out, "The little shit. I'll remember that the rest of my life. What nerve! He grabbed my arm and said so loudly that everyone around us could hear, 'I go first. You think he wants to see you before he sees his father?' I was so embarrassed to be there with him anyway. People would think we were related or something."

"The end of the dream is looking over his shoulder as I hugged him. I wanted to see where you were. You *were* the first one I wanted to see."

She gave one hard laugh, almost a grunt. "I know. That's what you told me that night." She opened her eyes. "You dreamed that?"

"You're not surprised?"

"Why? I believe in reincarnation. I thought something was strange about your wanting to come and talk to me. After I saw your face I was sure something else was going on inside you."

"Then I want to tell you some other things."

We were there an hour. In between she made a phone call to the man watching Lillis and said she would be back soon.

I told her everything but what had happened with the computer and the fairy tale. The dreams, the prophetic visions, the deaths of my friends. Unlike the first time we'd met, she was quiet, but when she did speak, it was to ask an interesting or perceptive question. I began to understand why her husband had cared so much for her. When I was almost finished I described my experiences with the man on the bicycle and how he'd welcomed me "back" as Rednaxela.

"I'm cold."

"Would you like to put on my jacket?" I started to take it off.

"That won't help. I'm cold *inside*. There's nothing you can do about that. My friend Herr Lachner has met his sister from their last incarnation. She lives in Perchtoldsdorf. Now I've met my husband. Looking at you, I'm not surprised."

She was suspiciously calm. Had I gotten through?

"Mrs. Benedikt, let's say it's true. Let's say I am your late husband and Kaspar Benedikt has returned too, as the man on the bicycle."

"That's why I'm cold. I think it's true. I want to know what he'll do to us this time. You've seen Lillis. What more could he do?"

"Do you know why he hurt your son?"

"He was also Moritz's son. Have you ever seen a man with no *Spatzy?*"

"*Spatzy?* What's that?"

"A penis. Prick. Pee-pee."

"No."

"I have: Kaspar Benedikt. A midget with no prick. Can you think of a worse combination? I always wondered how he made Moritz. Once, I went into the store to meet Moritz for lunch. The old man didn't know I was there and walked out of the back room with only a shirt on. No pants or underpants. I couldn't help looking, you know? I saw it for only a second or two, but there was nothing there, or it was smaller than the eye could see. It was only red down there and, I don't know, shiny. Like a scar from a burn."

"Rumpelstiltskin."

"What?"

"Nothing. What did you do when you saw it?"

"Choked. Made some shocked noise because that's when he saw me."

I sat forward. "What did he do?"

"The pig! He pulled up his pants fast but then asked me if I wanted to lick him there. That's when we really started hating each other. I don't let anyone talk to me like that. Nobody."

Almost to myself I said, "He isn't human."

"Whatever he is, or whatever he was, wasn't very human. You don't know how the man treated me, even before we knew Lillis was coming. I tell you, he hated me because he knew how much his son loved me. In the beginning he only ignored me. But when he knew how much love there was between us, he got a million times worse.

"I hate to think he might be back. I was so happy when I heard he'd hung himself. The worst night of my life there I was, laughing and crying because they'd found him with a rope around his neck down on the Graben.

"You know what I did with the body?"

"Yes. Why aren't you more . . . shocked that you might be sitting across the table from Moritz?"

"Because you're not Moritz. You look like him and you remember things about me, but I don't feel anything for you. It's like bumping into an old friend forty years later. Maybe the face is familiar and maybe there are some good memories, but it's not the person you gave your soul to. The only thing that would make me jump or faint now would be to see *him* walk into this room. I'd know it was him just as I know you're not. He'd come over here and say things only the two of us knew."

"I know some of those things, Mrs. Benedikt."

"So what? You don't know them all. That's the difference between you and Moritz. Scattered little pieces don't make a person. It's all the pieces put together that does."

A week later I made a huge mistake. Maris had been doing well in the hospital and they were talking about letting her go home early if she continued to progress.

On the other side of town, I was regressing. One night I dreamed I was a young male prostitute in Vienna at the turn of the century. None of it made sense to me, but on waking I remembered what "Papa" had said about my thirty-one lives and knew this had to be one of them. It was a violent, sensual dream full of homosexual opera singers, barons in drag, and a brothel straight out of a Jean Genet play.

"Come here, little boy. I've bought your breath."

For the first time in those other worlds I'd traveled (lived?) in, I felt thoroughly trapped and afraid. I have never been to a whore, but if their world is anything like that, they have my full sympathy. All that mattered there were orgasms and fantasy. But the orgasms came too quickly (or not at all) and the fantasies were like bad stage sets. I didn't even know my name because the men called me different things. It was not a degrading experience because I felt so distant from what was done to me. No, the fear came from feeling this is it, I'll never leave here. This will be where I end my life.

The morning after, I got out of bed and immediately began looking through Maris's boxes for her tarot cards. After an hour I realized she often carried them in her purse, so there was a good chance she had them at the hospital.

In a great mood when I got there, she hesitated only a bit before agreeing to do a reading for me. How could I have been so selfish and thoughtless? Why didn't I once think that her problem *might* be due to my magic, or "Papa," and not natural causes? So much else had gone wrong because of those things. Perhaps I didn't consider them because I wanted the doctors to be right—it was a baby, this happened often, it was medical, and not unnatural.

From the first card she turned, I knew it was wrong to ask. The Tower. The Eight of Swords, the Nine of Swords, Death . . . Any good card was upside down, the bad cards in every important place. I know nothing about the tarot, but I could read her face and that told me enough. By the time she turned the last one, her hand was shaking.

"Forget it." I started to sweep the cards up in my hand.

She grabbed it. "Don't do that! Don't touch my cards! I have to do it again. Give them to me, Walker. Now!"

"Forget it."

"Give them!"

"It doesn't *matter*, Maris!"

"It does. I have to do it for me too. Don't you understand?"

I handed them back. After shuffling many times, she laid down exactly the same hand.

"Oh, God. Walker, call the doctor. I think I'm bleeding again."

She was, and this time there was a rush of doctors and hurried talk.

Luckily, Doctor Scheer was on duty and explained what was happening.

"It's not good, Mr. Easterling. Everything was going well until now, but this indicates serious problems. We're going to have to keep much closer watch now, especially with that baby inside her. Doctor Lauringer said he's very concerned she might lose it if the bleeding continues."

"Could it have been stress?"

"That is as good a reason as any."

I stood in the parking lot outside, looking up at the sky.

"Help *her*, for God's sake. Use whatever you have to help her. She's your life, Walker. She's in there and she's sick and you're not helping at all. Think about Maris first. Think about the baby. Save them and you save yourself. Save them and you've saved yourself."

Dave Buck looked like a refugee from Woodstock. He wore a full-length beard, American army fatigues, and combat boots. I'd been to his apartment once and the only picture in the whole place was a psychedelic poster of Moby Grape.

If he wasn't deep in the bowels of the National Library looking up facts on his Anabaptist, Buck was walking the city.

He knew more about the place than most Viennese, and would often take me to see some strange Roman ruin or undiscovered junk store way out in the Twenty-third District that sold old war medals and uniforms.

"The problem with the Brothers Grimm is there's been too much written on them. I got your info for you, but I've been in the friggin' library too long. My eyes feel like old headlights. Let's walk the Ring and I'll tell you what I found."

Any guidebook will tell you that Vienna is one of the great walking cities in the world. The streets are either wide and tree-lined, or else crooked/narrow and filled with interesting or odd stores. The automobile is part of the city but doesn't own it yet.

Winter there means cold and mist. It rarely snows hard, but the days are short, cold, and damp. Buck was standing at Schottentor with his bare hands under his armpits and a green camouflage watchcap on.

"You look like you're going on maneuvres."

"Yeah? Come on, I gotta get my blood moving."

We walked in front of the university, past the Burg Theatre and Town Hall.

"Are we going to hike or talk?"

"Talk." Still moving, he took a tape recorder out of one of his many pockets. "I use this when I want a quote from a book I can't take out of the library. Listen."

He turned the machine on and thumbed it to its highest volume. I took it and held it to my ear.

" 'Contrary to popular belief, the Grimms did not collect their tales by visiting peasants in the countryside and writing down the tales that they heard. Their primary method was to invite storytellers to their house and then have them tell the tales aloud, which the Grimms either noted down on first hearing or after a couple of hearings. Most of the storytellers during this period were educated young women from the middle class or aristocracy.' "

He reached over and took the machine away from me. "That's it for that. I've got a bunch of quotes for you that I'll transcribe and send over, but that's the most important one.

"The other thing you should know, and this applies to almost all of the Grimm fairy tales, the men *changed* a hell of a lot of them before they ever saw print. The brothers were big believers in both the unification of Germany and the true German spirit, whatever that is. It meant they took stories they'd heard from their sources and edited them. Took out sexy parts, changed morals around . . . That kind of thing. They didn't want any good German child reading salacious or lewd stuff. Bad for the upbringing. In their way, they really were kind of literary fascists. I never knew that before."

We stopped at the light in front of the entrance to the Hapsburg Palace and watched tourist busses pull in, eyes and cameras glued to their windows.

"Have you noticed that, like, every other tourist in Vienna these days is Japanese? What does that mean?"

"That they have better taste than the Americans who all go to Paris and eat at McDonald's.

"What about 'Rumpelstiltskin'? What did you find there?"

"The names to remember are Dortchen and Lisette Wild. No, don't bother writing them down because I've got it typed for you. The story was told in 1812."

"Where was this?"

"The town of Kassel in Germany. The Grimms lived there for a number of years and I gather that's where they heard many of their most famous stories. The imaginations of all those nice bourgeois girls. Today we'd call it sexual hysteria."

"Go on."

"I looked through fifteen books for you, Walker. Some of them were older than your story. The best I could find was this: The Wild sisters told the Grimms 'Rumpelstiltskin' in 1812 and the only notation I could find about it specifically was it's one of the 'mixed version' stories. That means one of two possibilities: The girls made up or told the story together, *or* after the Grimms heard it, they took what they wanted from the original and threw the rest out."

"Or both."

"Or both, but my guess is the former."

"Why?"

"The brothers got their stories from basically two sources: middle-class girls like the Wilds, or low-lifes like the neighborhood tailor's wife. There was even an old soldier named Krause who gave them stories in exchange for old clothes! Now, the books say the girls got *their* stories from household servants. Even if what they heard was sexy, I can't imagine in those prudish days young girls would have had the courage to tell people of their own class racy stories. Especially if their listeners were of the opposite sex! It just wasn't done. Take a look at what the women wore in those days if you want an indication of their mores. It wasn't the Age of Aquarius.

"No, my guess is Dortchen and Lisette heard a maid tell a story which, with a little fixing, became 'Rumpelstiltskin.' After the girls had cleaned up whatever parts they thought weren't fit for good ears, they went to the Grimms with it."

He stopped and grabbed my arm. "Know why else I think that? Because Dortchen ended up marrying Wilhelm Grimm later on. She didn't want to make a bad first impression, you know?"

"*That's* interesting. What else, Dave?"

"Only one more thing. They never stopped revising the tales. It's like the Folios of Shakespeare. First Folio, Second Folio . . . In 1920 in a place in Alsace called the Ölenberg

Monastery, someone discovered a set of the stories in the brothers' handwriting. Obviously that's become the definitive Grimm, but every scholar I read said they worked and reworked the originals for years. Even when you read them in German, imagine the difference between the 1812 'Rumpelstiltskin' and the last edition that came out in 1857."

"But there's no trace of the original story that the Wild Sisters told?"

"None."

Besides telling me this information, Buck was a quiet walker. If there was a landmark or building worth noting he mentioned it, but otherwise we trudged through the cold in silence. Past the Opera, the Bristol Hotel, the Imperial. At Schwarzenberg Platz we turned right and walked toward the Russian War Monument.

"Where are we going?"

"I found a Yugoslavian restaurant down by the Sudbahnhof that serves good *sarma*. You in the mood?"

"Lead on."

He was quiet awhile longer, but as we passed Belvedere Palace, surprised me by asking, "Why're you so interested in 'Rumpelstiltskin'?"

"A new movie project."

"What's the story?"

"It's an interesting idea. Did you ever read *Grendel*, by John Gardner?"

"Yes. The story of *Beowulf* told through the eyes of the monster?"

"This is similar. The story of 'Rumpelstiltskin' through *his* eyes."

"You're writing for Walt Disney these days?"

"No, but it's got some of the same feeling. In my story,

the reason why the little man spun for the girl was so she'd love him. She promised she would *if* he made her straw into gold. But he doesn't trust her, so he makes her promise to give him her first child, just in case."

"And she says okay because she wants to be queen?"

"Right. Now, when she is queen he comes and says keep your promise. She tells him to fuck off."

" 'Fuck off'? That's up to date. Are you making a post-modern version?"

"Picture this queen as an entirely egotistical, selfish bitch who'd do anything to get what she wants. She dupes the guy into making her gold, but never has any intention of loving him.

"Plus, here's one of the big twists: Since he's a magic man, he has no sex."

Buck laughed. "He's dickless?"

"In sweeter terms, sexless. But he's also a romantic. Believes if they love each other enough, they don't *need* sex."

"He sounds dopey. You sure this isn't 'Snow White'?"

"He is to a degree . . . a romantic dope. But that belief makes him vulnerable, more believable. Much more than a cliché leprechaun who wiggles his nose and makes a pot of gold appear.

"When he sees she won't love him, he's crushed. But then the bitter, spurned lover part in him comes out. 'If I can't have her, then I'm going to hit her right where it hurts.' "

"Take the kid."

"Not only does he take the kid, but treats him like a son and teaches him all his magic. Both to spite Mama and because he grows to love the boy. It makes sense. Since he can't have children this is the closest he'll ever get."

"That's it? 'The End'? Rumpelstiltskin and son walk off into the sunset?"

"Not quite. Rumpelstiltskin takes the child and somehow

moves them both over into real life. How he does that I don't know yet, but I'm working on it.

"In real life they live together happily for a while. Then Papa makes his biggest mistake: He allows the boy to grow up. And when the boy grows up he inevitably starts looking at women."

"The Brothers Grimm wouldn't like it, Walker. You're starting to get sexy."

"Wait. The boy grows up and falls in love with a woman. Papa gets completely pissed off because that was what got him into trouble in the first place—human love.

"Holy Jesus, it's true!"

Buck looked at me. "What's true?"

"Wait! The boy falls in love with a woman. The old man knows that if it goes further, he loses his son. So he threatens him by saying that if he goes with a woman, he'll get him. But the boy's a boy and ignores Papa. He goes ahead and falls in love and Papa kills him."

"*Kills* him? We're still talking Walt Disney here?"

"Kills him, but then brings him back to live another life. Hopes that by doing it, the boy will somehow have learned his lesson and will go back to loving Papa. But Walter doesn't remember his last life. So growing up, he falls in love again . . ." I stopped walking and looked straight at Buck. "Falls in love again and the old man kills him again. Again and again."

"Sounds interesting. There's the restaurant."

The place was smoky and too hot. Tough-looking men with thick moustaches and loud voices sat at tables drinking wine and talking. There was a television tuned to a soccer game in one corner, but no one watched. We ordered *sarma* and beer and checked out the room. No one was interested in us.

"Tell me the rest. The story ends with the old man killing his son, ad infinitum? No happy ending?"

"How would *you* end it?"

"I like sad ends. I'd leave it there. Post-modern *and* existential. It'll be shown at all the film festivals."

"Don't be modern. Tell me how the Grimms would end it."

"What are the essential elements of the story? Love is the big one."

"Bad love, mostly. Selfish or possessive."

"Okay, then the Grimms would make a point of showing you how bad that kind of love is, and how good love should win out."

"Give me an example."

"Am I going to get paid for this if you use it?"

"Sure. We'll take equal screenwriting credit."

"That's good. Maybe I could pay my heat bill then. Let's see, you've got your bad love, but we haven't seen much good so far. What about the kid's magic? You said the old man taught him."

"That's a problem too, because in *this* world, the kid doesn't remember how to do it. Just knows that he has it in him somewhere. When we meet him it's today and he's only discovered what's up. Who he is."

"Then let him be in love with a girl who shows him through love. That's kitschy. They'll love it in Hollywood."

"Too simple. She's just your normal beautiful girl. Reads the tarot, but doesn't know or understand real magic."

"Make the old man threaten her some way. That'll bring out the fighting spirit in our hero."

I started to say something but stopped. "What do you mean, threaten?"

"Go after the girl. You said the boy's finally discovered

who he is? Then have the old man tell him he's going to kill
the girl if he doesn't go back to their old way of life."

That bitch in the hospital.

The baby. The bleeding. The loss.

Even a father loses his patience after a while. This time
you're not going to have another chance.

I stood up. "Dave, I have to go."

"The food hasn't come!"

"Eat mine. Here. This'll cover it."

"You're a strange boy, Walker. Going home to write?
Don't forget my cut."

Out on the street there were no taxis. I stood there feeling as
though I was going to piss in my pants. When I couldn't stand
it anymore, I went looking for a phone booth. There was one a
couple of blocks down. I called Maris's room at the hospital.
She was eating lunch. She felt fine. Said the food there was so
good she was sure she'd put on weight. That did nothing to
stop my worrying.

Hearing her voice cooled some of the fire in my stomach,
but I knew it was only temporary. Would he hurt her? Was
that what he meant by "losing his patience"? Look at what
he'd done to Lillis Benedikt. Did he get madder and more
vengeful every life I lived?

I had to move, go somewhere. Stepping out of the phone
booth, I looked around and saw the Sudbahnhof standing gray
and wet in the mist. I'd go over there and take a train somewhere. To Rax and look at the mountains. Yes, an hour train
ride where I could sit, look out the window, and think about
this newest nightmare.

The traffic was heavy, and it took time to cross it and
reach the building. Inside, hundreds of people in various stages

of their trips bustled by. Two American kids with pastel knap-sacks and Mount Everest hiking boots ran for the two o'clock train to Villach. A group of old men with thin rubber brief-cases conferred under the arrival/departure board. Turkish and Yugoslavian families with many cheap suitcases and boxes wrapped with heavy cord sat disconsolately on them waiting for their train south.

There was no train to Rax, so I decided to take the two o'clock, get off at Wiener Neustadt, and walk around there a while. Good, let's go. I ran up the stairs behind the knapsack kids, enjoying their excited, familiar-sounding voices.

"We'll stay in Villach overnight then catch the morning train to Trieste."

"What's in Villach?"

"I don't know. Mountains. Come on."

Ambling down the stairs toward us was a crowd of foot-ball rowdies dressed in the violet and white colors of the Aus-tria Memphis soccer team. There was quite a bunch of them and they all looked drunk.

"Hey, Phyllis, I want a hat like that. Think I can find one in Villach?" The American boy was middle-sized but weighted down by the sack he was carrying.

"Amerika! Hey, fucking Amerika!"

"Don't say anything. Just walk by them."

The kids looked at me, surprised to hear their own lan-guage.

"What'd you say?"

"Ignore these guys. Don't say anything to them."

It was too late. The giant of the group, who looked like a young Hermann Goering, moved over to block our way. His friends smiled and looked at each other knowingly.

"Hey, Amis! I speak English. Talk to me."

"Buzz off, Bozo."

The giant looked at the girl and leered. "Boat-zo? Was Boat-zo?"

"Just get out of our way."

He exaggeratedly sidestepped, but when the girl moved by him he grabbed her arm. Pulling her close, he licked her face.

Her friend, gallant and stupid, moved up. "Cut it out, man."

The rowdy gave him a hard fast push and the kid fell flailing backward down the stairs.

While he was laughing, I took two steps up and stuck my fingers in the fat guy's eyes. He screamed. Letting go of the girl, he slapped his hands to his face.

"I'm blind!"

Shocked at what had happened, his gang stood where they were an instant, then came for me.

With no thought at all, none, I curled my hand into a fist with the fingers covering the thumb. Then I put it instinctively to my chin. All of the men were wearing long violet and white scarves. As one, the scarves blew up into their faces and already burning, began melting onto their skin.

Screams, black smoke, the smell of cooking meat.

I don't know what I did.

The American boy was standing again.

"Go! Run!"

They went one way, I the other: back toward Vienna, Maris, my father.

At the entrance to the station, I stood a moment to catch up with myself.

A taxi pulled in a slow circle until it was in front of me. It was so close that I had to look. Papa was driving.

"Out of breath? Not you, boy. I told you you still had your magic."

He pulled away with a screech. I ran after him but the

closer I got, the faster the taxi moved. As he drove into traffic, he stuck his head out the window.

"Tell me my name, Walter!"

Orlando leaped into my lap when I got home. I put a hand on his head and stroked his warm fur. He purred. Not looking at him, I made my other hand into a fist, covering the thumb. Putting it to my chin, I tried to remember everything that had gone through my head. I felt the cat's soft paw batting at my arm. Looking down, I saw that his eyes had returned. He could see again.

3.

Dear Maris and Walker,

I'll assume you heard about our earthquake. I once went through a few horrid seconds of one in Peru, but nothing compared to this baby. Strayhorn and I were at the Taco Bell near Beverly Center when it hit. At first I thought it was only my tostada going down the wrong way, but when the walls cracked and the front window blew out I knew we were in for it.

What do you think about when you're watching your own death? Phil kept saying "This isn't a movie! This is *not* a movie!" Good old Strayhorn. I froze but he pulled me out of there in time. We stood in the parking lot feeling the ground do the hula under our feet. We looked at each other. What the hell else can you do?

To make a sad story short, both of our houses slid into the canyon and along with them everything important we owned. So what? We're still alive while too many people out here aren't. Too many friends disappeared and haven't shown up yet. We're assuming the worst, Goddamn it.

God. That's one funny creature, isn't He? Especially when you see all this suffering and loss. Did I tell you that I used to be a regular church-goer? I was.

Naturally things have changed. My perspective is very different. Being a famous movie mogul looks absurd in this context. So no matter what happens, I have decided that when I can square away what's left here, I'm going to flee this ruin (parts of it are that bad) and travel. Appropriately enough, our studio withstood the quake. Most of the studios did. Ain't it perfect for Hollywood? That means I'm obligated to finish *Wonderful*, but that shouldn't take long.

After it's done I'm taking the salary they gave me and travel on it. Strayhorn says I should buy a new house, but I don't want to be around here now. Maybe not ever again. We'll see. All this verbal diarrhea is only to say that sooner or later I'd like to come through Vienna and see you, if that's okay. I'm starting out in New York so I can catch up on news with my friend Cullen James (remember her, Maris? Your lookalike?), then on to Europe. I don't know what the schedule is precisely, but I'll keep you posted. I want to keep a clean dance card in terms of obligations to either clock or calendar.

Why this letter? Because I realized after all the trouble here that I liked you both very much. When you see the shine on the reaper's blade up close, you realize it's important to be with people who make you feel good to be alive. Both of you did that for me and I'm grateful. I hope a little of it is mutual. I'll be in touch. Don't leave Vienna!

My love,
Weber

Dear Maris and Walker,

With you in the hospital and me out of luck here in broken L.A., it seems that we younger Yorks could use a good dose of luck right now. As I told you over the phone, I'm physically okay, but not mentally.

Glenn's death burned a hole through the middle of everything I am. I pray you never have to experience what it's like to watch someone you love die. No matter how brave or strong you think you are, their loss puts a layer of ash over everything that once mattered. His clothes, his motorcycle that made too much noise, his half-finished pack of cigarettes in the rubble call my name and there's no way of covering my ears. You know me—I used to be too distant and amused by life to let it sink its teeth into much of me, but I realize now that Glenn's being allowed me that distance. He compensated for it with his total involvement in everything we knew together. I miss his banging in the door and up the stairs to tell me about the bag lady on Hollywood Boulevard who gave him a chocolate-chip cookie. Best of all, he wouldn't go on about how sweet it was of her to do that. Only how great the cookie tasted on a hot afternoon.

I hope you and Walker are well, notwithstanding the hospital thing. I never said much about it when you were here, but I like your new man very much. I'm only sorry we didn't have more time together. Have his dreams/magic either smoothed out or explained themselves? My experience over the years with people who've been touched by the miraculous is that if they're decent and caring, they will prevail. Many of them prevail *and* use that power to good ends. I don't know what I could do for you here but if there is anything, please let me know.

The earthquake destroyed our house, so all I've been doing recently is going through the ruins for anything that can be salvaged. There isn't much. I'm staying with a friend until I can find another place. But that can wait. No house this time, though. Houses are for more than one person. Alone, there's too much empty room. Empty rooms are never good company.

Not much else to tell. Californians can't believe this has happened. For years people talked about the coming earthquake, but no one really believed it would come. Everyone had a few extra flashlights and canned food stored in a closet, but we were even embarrassed to admit to those precautions. One of the ironies was Glenn's total paranoia about it. We fought more than once about earthquakes. A week before it happened, he said he was seriously thinking of moving out of the state because the possibility scared him more the longer he lived here.

"How can you move out of California when you're so successful?"

"Because you can't be successful when you're dead, Ingram."

Call me if you need anything—the number is below. I miss you and am happy for the Easterlings and the coming child. The hospital is only for a while, Maris. I'm sure of that. The rest, the good things, will be waiting for you when you get home and have all the rest of your lives to enjoy them.

I love you,
Ingram

She looked up with tears in her eyes. "The poor guy. What can we do for him?"

"Make a tape and send it to him."

"Something more than *that.* His whole life is gone, Walker. The closest I ever came to that feeling was when Luc chased me around Munich. It's misery every day. Being in here is dreamy compared to that."

"In your tape tell him to call a guy named Michael Billa. I'll give you the number."

"Who's Michael Billa?"

"A man I know out there. They'll like each other."

"How do you know he didn't get killed in the earthquake?"

"I . . . talked to him the other day. Believe me, Maris. They're right for each other."

"Hmm. You're not telling me something. Your mouth is too flat. It always gets flat when you have a secret."

I kissed her forehead and smiled like a politician.

"I know you, Walker. You're holding lots of things back from me these days. Aren't you?"

"Not so many."

"Enough. What's happening with the bicycle nut? Did you find out anything new?"

"I think he's lying low. Wants me to think about that Mr. Pencil bit awhile."

"What about your dreams? Anything new happening there?"

"Nope."

"Your mouth is tight again."

"Maris, you've got enough to think about now. I'm not holding back anything I can't handle. Sure, the dreams are continuing, and I worry about the bicycle man, but that's not new. You're my greatest concern. You and our child are most important. If you want to help me, take care of yourself. Ingram's letter says it right. Our earthquake was your getting sick. But *we've* still got a chance to beat it. I'm not trying to sound patronizing, but if you can hold on and keep steady till you're well, then we're going to be able to say 'Fuck you, earthquake. Our lives are our own, not yours.' "

I knew no one named Michael Billa. His name and telephone number slid into my mind the way "fist to chin" slid in the day at the train station. I only knew that when Billa and Ingram York got together they would fall in love.

"Can I help you, sir?"

"I'm looking for the children's section."

"Two aisles down on the right. Is there anything special I can help with?"

"I'd like to see whatever editions of *Grimm's Fairy Tales* you have."

"There are a few there. I'm sure of it."

I walked down past the fiction. The new Stephen King novel, *Flash and Blood* (translated as *Schmerz* in German) stopped me and I thought to buy it. But reading the German title *(Pain)* reminded me of how far off translations can be. In homage to King, I decided to wait until the English version arrived in town.

The children's section was small but loaded with those tall, thin, mostly picture books that cost so much and give a kid so little after one or two reads. Ten dollars for eleven words on each page about a lost ball that finds its way home.

Cramped in next to them here and there were standard editions of the classics. Hans Christian Andersen, Perrault, Wilhelm Busch's *Max und Moritz*. As a child I didn't read much, but the books I remembered were these and other oldies that gave you real worlds, rather than long pages, bright colors, and tepid climaxes.

There were two copies of Grimms: one for little readers and the other a no-frills/no-pictures copy printed in the old German script. I chose the second. Remembering Buck's story about the definitive edition found in the Ölenberg Monastery, I turned to the front of the book to see if this was one of them.

"This is what you're looking for."

I turned, knowing the voice. He had trimmed his beard and was wearing a dark blue double-breasted suit that was the twin to one I owned.

"Nice suit."

He looked pleased. "I thought so too after I saw you in yours. Like son, like father."

"Why are you regular size now?"

"Change. Something different. A new perspective. Do you want this book or not? I bought it for you, so you might as well take it. I already know the story." When he smiled, his teeth were white and straight.

"New teeth too?"

"Don't you like them?" He curled his hand into a fist, a familiar fist, and put it to his chin. When he smiled again his teeth and mouth were the brown graveyard I remembered. "Better?"

"Why are you here?"

"You keep wanting to talk to me, Walter. I thought I'd let you do it once." He shot his cuff and looked at a gold wristwatch. "You have five minutes."

"That's not enough, it's too fast. You should give me time to think of what I want to ask you."

"I don't have to give you *shit*, son. You want to talk to me? Do it now."

"Did you make Maris bleed?"

"Yes."

"Why?"

"To remind you of certain things."

"Will you leave her alone if I go with you?"

"I'll leave both her *and* the child alone. It's a boy, in case you were wondering. He'll look more like her than you, if he ever grows up."

"Why would you hurt them? What's the point?"

"Why would you hurt me, boy? That's a better point. I've given you every chance in the world. But this is the first time you've ever known exactly what's happening, so this time it's the finale.

"You stay and try to be human, then I stop you. If you come back to me, you'll leave a happy widow and child. Your son will grow up thinking lovely thoughts about his dead daddy, and your wife will never remarry. She's very much in love with you. This time you chose well. Not like the Greek woman."

"Did you do that to Lillis?"

"Yes. You have a minute and a half."

"What if I go with you?"

"First you die here. We get out of this world and take you back where you belong. Then I'll have to show you again how to become your real self. The self you should be."

"You said in one of the dreams that our place *is* Vienna!"

"Another Vienna, Walter. A city you've forgotten. You've been back here so many times. Every life you've felt a pull to live here, but never once have you understood why. Vienna is your father's city. One more question."

"What if I say no?"

"You won't. You love Maris too much. That's one of the good parts in you. Once you realize there's no choice, you'll come home."

"What will happen if I don't?"

"Maris will die and I'll take the child. There'll be nothing you can do about it, either. Bye-bye.

"No, don't touch me! Until you know my name, your magic only works on them. Sometimes. That once in my room when I couldn't see you was a joke. Don't take it as any sign.

That's why I want you to come home. I want to teach you all the things you've forgotten." He touched my shoulder gently. "The first lesson will be to find out what Papa's name is."

"How long do I have?"

"A month."

"Will you leave us alone until then? Completely alone. No tricks, no spying . . ."

He looked at me. "Yes, that's fair. I'll leave you completely alone. No, I'll give you until your birthday. That's twenty-six days. I'll give you twenty-six days alone to say good bye. That should be long enough."

I carried the new monitor into the living room and connected it to the computer. I went through the box of discs looking for the word-processing one again. I hoped that turning it on wouldn't bring a repeat of what had happened the last time.

The names of the computer programs sounded like buzz words on the Starship Enterprise: "V-Ram," "Copy Star," "Signum."

"I think we should put up the V-Ram shields, Mr. Spock. We're coming to Signum."

"It's only a copy star, sir. Nothing to worry about."

In the middle of these space names appeared "DEGAS."

" 'DEGAS'? What are you doing here?"

I fed the disc into the computer and turned it on. It was one of Maris's art programs. After much fiddling around I managed to bring up from its memory drawings of buildings and cities she'd done.

What talent she had! Talent and humor and a truly distinctive way of interpreting the world. She didn't like to show work that wasn't finished and would have been angry if she knew I was snooping in her files. But I excused myself on the spot and continued looking.

I had never asked if she wished she were an architect and not a visionary in miniature. You always come up with questions to ask when the person isn't around to answer. She believed in magic and she believed in God. But what did she think of heaven and hell? Did she want a boy or a girl for her first child? What things did I do that got on her nerves but she never told me about? What could I do to make it better?

There was a drawing for a clown museum in the form of a magician's hat, a villa by the sea shaped like a woman's hand opening toward the water.

Written below one drawing was the quote from the Jon Silkin poem I'd given her.

> *And I shall always fear*
> *The death of those we love as*
> *The hint of your death, Love.*

Under another, a drawing of a church, was written "The opposite of love was always disappearance." Patricia Geary.

Both Maris and I were inveterate quotation collectors, but what did this one mean? I wanted to turn and ask, but she wasn't there. She wasn't there and never would be again in my life if I did what my father demanded.

How would he make me "die"? What would Maris do after that? Was he to be believed when he said she'd remain true to me for the rest of her life? At first the thought was comforting, but then I realized how utterly selfish it was to desire that. Did he think I would be at peace knowing the person I loved most was living out the rest of her days on "hold," believing there was no other possibility of fulfillment for her?

What a hateful, evil being he was.

I kept looking at the drawings until I got tired.

"One more."

That "one more" was so interesting that I looked at three more.

The fourth would have been the last, but the fourth was the fruit. The fruit that, once inhaled, gave off an answer the way an orange explodes from a color into a world of smells once you have punctured its skin.

It was a drawing of a city. A medieval city, or perhaps one much older. I have never been very good at history, but this city I knew. It was the Vienna "Papa" had alluded to in the bookstore.

"Another city. A city you have forgotten."

I knew the streets, the buildings. I knew the sounds in the air that were the city on any summer day. Her drawing was a series of lines and curves, pillars, statues, fountains, buildings. It was *my* city and where it had come from in Maris could only be attributed to love.

When you love someone deeply, you know secrets they haven't told you yet. Or secrets they aren't even aware of themselves. I had used no magic on Maris. Not that I knew how to use the meager powers I still unconsciously held. This I knew for sure. I'd not bewitched or bedazzled her into loving me. I'd only hoped and worked for her love, knowing that that is the hardest work in life. I loved her for what she was, I loved her for what she was becoming. I couldn't imagine a time in life together when I would turn and think "This is wrong. She isn't the person I loved. She isn't the person I hoped she was." Maris was the person I wanted to share my life with. She was also the person I wanted to share the trivia of my life with, because that too is part of the magic of concern: Whatever you live is important to them and they will help you through it.

Because I knew her so well, I was sure this was how she felt, too. The picture in front of me attested to this, and if our world hadn't already been so filled with equal measures of wonder and abomination, I would have been a very frightened man because of what I saw on the monitor. She had entered a part of my mind that even I owned no key or code word to.

The drawing took up almost the whole screen, but typed small in one corner were the words "Breathing you on your birthday, Walker. I love you." It was the city she'd meant to build for me as a birthday present. What she didn't know was she'd created the city where I had begun. Her love had taken over, however unconsciously, and showed me not only the city, but where to walk through it to find my father's name. My second father.

I had one more dream before I left Vienna.

My father had rented a villa on Lake Maggiore in northern Italy for the month of July. It was an old sunny house with balconies off every bedroom and a wide veranda that looked out over the lake below. Whenever I wanted, I was allowed to walk down the dirt path to our private dock. We had no boat, but the concrete finger that jutted out into the water was a perfect place for looking at fish and dreaming. I had a lot of freedom that summer and used much of it sitting on the dock, feeling the sun on my shoulders and cooling my feet in the brown water. If I looked hard I could see the train far across the lake winding its way in and out toward Stresa and then the Swiss border. Daddy was reading a novel called *A Farewell to Arms*, and one day he read the part to me about the man and woman in love living in the hotel in Stresa.

I'd discovered how fashionable a suntan was to the big kids. So since there wasn't much else to do, I sat a long time in the sun trying to dye my skin as brown as possible and look to see if I knew anybody on the boats whizzing by. We only had a month on the lake because Daddy had to be back at work the beginning of August. I made a promise to myself that I would read three books and get a great suntan before we went home.

Even though the weather was usually nice and sunny in the day, everything changed at night. There were thunderstorms all the time like I'd never seen before. You could hear them coming sometimes two hours before they hit, outside our window. Whenever I heard the thunder rolling in or saw the scary white lightning over the mountains, I'd pick up whatever I was doing and run for the living room.

The room was yellow. All the furniture was yellow, and I think even the lights were yellow. Daddy said the furniture was by Art Deco, but I didn't know who that was. The important thing was every chair in there was fat and round and friendly. You could fall into them from any position and be comfortable. My favorite I'd secretly named "Sinbad" and everyone knew it was my chair. People even got up and gave it to me when I came in. Sinbad and I were friends. When the storms were blowing and hissing like a monster, we'd leave the doors to the patio open because Daddy liked to watch the rain go sideways, not down, outside. The wind blew it in all kinds of crazy directions and sometimes I got scared, but not really.

The best part of the storms was when they got really bad, Daddy always came into the living room, and sitting down at the piano there, would begin playing along to the rain and thunder. He played the piano very beautifully and knew thousands of different songs and classical music. With every bang of thunder he banged out something nice on the piano. When the rain or the wind blew the curtains up high, he played music by a man named Delius who wrote music that sounded like the rain. Daddy said playing the piano like that was taming the storm, and I never had to be afraid of any storm he could play to.

Since I was always the biggest scaredy cat about the storms, I was always the first one in the living room with my comics or coloring book or whatever I was working on at the time. But sooner or later my brother Ingram, or Mommy, would come in too, and all three of us would listen to the rain and Daddy playing the piano, and it would be like living in heaven for me. There we all were—safe and protected and cozy in the middle of the storm, surrounded by yellow light and my Daddy's music. That was the best part of the summer.

"How long will you be gone?"

"I think only three days. It depends on the production. They told me three days."

She looked at me accusingly. "What if I have problems?"

"I'll be on the next plane. I'm only going to Germany, Maris. They're paying me a couple of thousand dollars to hold up a champagne bottle. It's sort of hard to say no."

"I've seen those champagne ads. Lots of beautiful girls in low-cut dresses."

"Are you being serious or just grumpy?"

"Grumpy. I know you have to go. This hospital isn't cheap."

"Don't worry about that. You know we've got plenty of money from the film."

"Plenty of money lasts an hour when you've got someone in the hospital. I don't want you to go because I'll miss you. No other reason. Even if you're not right here, knowing you're in town makes me feel better. Is that babyish?"

"I love it. I love you too for feeling that way. Listen, I wanted to ask you a question about something else. Did you and your family ever spend a summer on Lake Maggiore in Italy when you were little?"

She nodded. "Yes, near a town called Laveno."

"Do you remember much of it?"

"Pretty much. Why?"

"Do you remember 'Sinbad'?"

"Sinbad? No. What are you asking?"

"I had a dream about you last night. I dreamt I *was* you in that house in Italy."

"You *were* me?"

"I was you, and I was in that big yellow living room where you all went when thunderstorms came at night. Your father played the piano to tame the rain."

She sat up fast. "That's *right!* Oh, Walker, I'd forgotten all about that. It's so mystical. Tell me the whole thing immediately. Every detail."

When I had finished her cheeks were flushed and she wore the biggest smile I'd seen in days.

"That is so . . . It gives me little shivers all over. Sinbad! How could you know about Sinbad? You know why I called it that? Because sometimes I'd pretend it was my sailing ship and I was off on an adventure. Sailing past the Island of the Sirens. I would hold my ears and think I needed lots of wax to hold off their screams. My favorite movie when I was growing up was *The 7th Voyage of Sinbad.* Did you ever see it? With the cyclops and the princess who was shrunken down by the evil magician? I even remember the name of the actor who played him. Torin Thatcher."

"You sound like Venasque. He knew the cast of every film made."

"Sinbad. I saw that movie six times. Whenever they asked the genie in the lamp to do something, he'd bow and say 'I shall try, my master, I shall try.'"

"You were me as a little girl in Laveno. Walker, that must mean something good. Maybe it's a turning point. All your other dreams were so strange and disturbing. This one is only childhood and magic."

"*Your* childhood. That's the kicker."

"No, that's the beauty! Wouldn't it be something if that happened to us forever? Dream each other's dreams? We'd know each other so well we could be—"

"Identical twins."

"Ha ha. Not funny."

"How do you feel today?"

"Good. Especially after hearing that. I'm sad you're going away, but I'm okay. Listen, there's one thing, though. You don't have to call me from there as much as you do here. It'd be sweet, but eleven calls a day from Germany wouldn't help our bank account."

"There's a lot to talk about when I'm away."

"That's true. *How* long will you be gone?"

"Three days. I'll take the night train back Tuesday."

"Okay, then five times a day is enough."

The night train to Cologne is strictly business. Night trains to Italy are full of excited tourists and lovers off for a weekend in Venice at the Danieli. Trains north, especially to the heart of German business, are quiet and full of tired men in rumpled suits with their neckties pulled down, looking wanly through their briefcases.

I was in a first-class compartment by myself until a few minutes before the train was due to leave. I had the German edition of the fairy tales on my lap but only because I wanted to read some of the other stories. I had no further need of reading "Rumpelstiltskin."

The compartment door slid open and a woman walked in. When I saw her I thought of a line my college roommate had once said when we were gassing about women.

"Sometimes you see one on the street who's so beautiful you want to walk up to her, put your hand over her mouth, and just whisper 'Don't talk. Come with me.' You take her immediately to bed, never letting her say a word. Because no matter what she says, it's going to spoil that first beauty you saw in her. You know what I mean? Silent, she's perfect."

The woman across from me was that kind of perfect. Dressed in a shimmery black leather coat and skirt, she had a small Oriental face that held a stunning mixture of voluptuous child and innocent woman; long straight hair fell down over her shoulders like a black waterfall. I smiled at her and turned back to the window.

"Is this seat taken?" She spoke English in a high voice.

"No. Can I help you with your bag?"

"That would be very nice."

She was already sitting when I stood to put her Louis Vuitton suitcase onto the rack above. She seemed very used to men helping her through life.

"Thank you very much. You speak English?"

"Yes."

"That's so good. I'm so tired of speaking other people's languages. Are you going to Frankfurt? It's a long trip, isn't it?"

An hour after the train started, Kiko had told me all about her modeling jobs in Europe, an Italian boyfriend who didn't appreciate her enough, and how lonely her life was. She asked if she could sit on my side of the car, and after she did, every few words were accompanied by a touch on my hand, my knee . . .

If it had happened before Maris, I would have been a happy man. As it was, I smiled and was a sympathetic listener, but made no attempt to reciprocate her warmth. Plainly, she wasn't used to that, and her face grew more and more puzzled. After another ten minutes of long looks and long fingernails on my knee, I touched her hand and said I was married.

"So? Is your wife on the train?"

"No, but she's in my mind and that's enough."

Angry as a swatted bee, she stood right up and went for her suitcase. I offered to help, but she gave me the evil eye and said no thanks.

She was a small woman and had to reach all the way up to get hold of the suitcase handle. Giving one hard pull, the bag came flying off the shelf, knocking her back against the opposite wall head first. The bag hit the floor. She cried out and slumped crookedly into the facing seat. She'd cracked the back of her head against one of the metal coat hangers screwed into the wall. Blood was everywhere—dripping down the leather, spotting her white hands, the gray silk blouse.

Her eyes were closed and she mumbled in either shock or pain. I leaned over, put my hand on the top of her head and said *it*. One moment I felt warm blood and wet sticky hair under my fingers. The next moment I felt only warm, dry hair. I pushed her head up and told her to open her eyes, everything was okay.

I sat there awhile calming her, telling her she'd fallen asleep and cried out something about her suitcase falling. But I told her to look—there it was up on the rack. She'd only had a bad dream.

When it was clear she was all right, I got my bag and left the compartment. Before going, I put her to sleep. Nothing was simpler.

In Cologne the next morning, I had a two-hour layover before my next train left. After a bad cup of coffee in the station restaurant, I found a phone and called Maris. I told her I was in the hotel and they'd given me a nice room overlooking the great cathedral.

"How does it look? Is it like St. Stephen's?"

I had never been to Cologne and knew nothing about it. The only things I saw were trains and tracks and commuters. Closing my eyes, I said *it* again and vivid pictures of the Gothic cathedral, the fourteenth-century stained glass windows, and the Magi's shrine inside the church came sliding into my head. I went on to quickly describe parts of the city, including the Roman-Germanic Museum and its million-piece "Dionysus Mosaic," even the cable car over the Rhine. She told me I sounded like a travel guide and she was jealous.

I got off the other train in the afternoon. I needed only three hours to do what was necessary. The only real problem was finding the place.

On the train back to Vienna I didn't dream, but looking out the window at the sun rising over the Austrian countryside, I let my mind go its way and this is what I saw. Or felt. Or knew somewhere inside.

It is summer in East Hampton, Long Island. Victoria Marshall's parents own a house there by the ocean and invited me down for the weekend. That evening we'd gone to a play at the John Drew Theatre. It was boring, but the interesting part of the two hours was Victoria's hand on my thigh. It wasn't like her. At college we'd spent months rolling around on my narrow bed, touching and pushing clothes aside, getting too hot and too frustrated for our own good. She wants to be a virgin when she gets married, but she also loves me and doesn't know what to do. She wants us to sleep together, but she also wants to keep her promise to herself. I love her but she is beginning to confuse me.

Her hand rubbing my thigh in the theatre, inches away from the eyes of her High Episcopalian parents, tells me something is very different tonight. Is this it? Is she saying yes?

The parents know their daughter and don't worry that anything untoward might happen if they're not around to keep an eye on my shenanigans. They have one drink with us after the show and go off upstairs to their bedroom.

Victoria and I are sitting on the couch. I have a drink in my hand but things have gotten so heated in me that the ice has melted. She waits until the toilet flushes twice up there and the familiar sounds of people getting into bed are over before she turns to me, her eyes full of smoke and promises. She says nothing, but when she reaches over to touch me, I almost pull back because the moment has really come and I can't believe it. Not only does she touch me, but pulls me to the floor with her.

She whispers, "Do you have something with you?"

"Yes."

"All right." She begins to take off her clothes. Me too. When we're naked I remember at the last minute to take it out of my wallet. Hands trembling, I tear it open but leave it in its wrapper. I am afraid the floor will squeak and tell on us, but it is a silent conspirator.

We kiss and touch and everything is hot. Plus, everything is not just this, it is leading up to the moment I've been waiting for almost a year. I touch her between her legs and she is wetter than I've ever felt. This is unbelievable. Moving away, I reach for the rubber. It comes gliding out of its envelope and expands into a circle in my hand. I have no trouble putting it on. Turning to her, she is more beautiful than ever. I rise up and gently part her legs. They move open quickly, and already she is moving her head from side to side.

I can't get in. I move and use my hands and she does what she can, but it is no use. I simply can't get in. Her eyes are wide open now and they say something I can't hear. Is she afraid? Have I scared her into thinking she is too small and will be this way forever? Is it disgust? How could I be so bumbling and inept? How could I do this to her?

We try more and more until my penis gives up any hope and says good night. We lie on our sides, fingertips still touching, but we are lost. What now?

I see all this, but it's nothing new. I was there and remember too well that embarrassing night. What *is* different is something else I see with my new eyes. Something outside the house, sitting on top of the Marshalls' Cape Cod roof.

He has been up there the whole time, watching. Squatting like a Fuseli creature, his hand over his mouth, he's laughing and snickering, trying to keep quiet so that no one inside will know something is up on the roof listening to the hopeless silence of two nineteen-year-olds.

I called him on the phone.

"How'd you get my number?"

"I'd like you to come to dinner."

"When? Where'd you get this number?"

"Can you come tonight?"

He was silent, suspicious, but there was nothing he could do anymore. I knew that, but he didn't.

"Tonight? Why tonight?"

"I have to talk to you."

I convinced him. We'd have his favorite meal, done the way he liked it. I told him I'd had a dream and remembered how to cook it. I even called him Papa once and that must have done it. He agreed. Seven o'clock.

I called Maris and told her I'd be home a day early. Then I went shopping.

They wanted to help, but I said they were my guests and I wouldn't hear of it.

At the market I bought *Tafelspitz*, *Kren*, applesauce, the makings for tartar sauce. Two bottles of good red wine from Styria. An old menu but one all of them would feel comfortable eating. If we ever got around to eating. No matter what happened, I didn't think it was going to be a long evening.

They loved television; couldn't get over it. They watched a documentary about famine in Africa, a Bud Spencer film, a choral group from the Vorarlberg that sang some songs they knew. That made them especially happy.

I spent the rest of the afternoon in the kitchen. Maris was such a good cook that I hadn't whipped up a big meal for a long time. I enjoyed the hours putting the pieces together.

I was done at six and went in to take a shower. This was going to be a big evening and I wanted to look right for it.

At six-thirty they insisted on setting the table. I let them because I think they were so embarrassed that I'd cooked the meal.

The bell rang promptly at seven. I walked down the hall, accompanied as always by Orlando. He walked faster now that he could see, but his sweet personality was still the same.

When I opened the door I only saw a big bouquet of flowers wrapped in shiny plastic paper. Tilting his head to one side, he peeked out from behind them and said, "I brought you some flowers. You used to like roses."

I smiled and took them. "I still do. That's nice, Papa. Come in."

I let him pass me and gestured toward the living room. "Dinner's almost ready."

He went forward a few steps, but then Orlando began weaving his way in and out between his feet, almost tripping him. "Get out of here! I hate cats!" He put his hand out, fingers spread. Orlando fell over, dead in an instant.

I put my hand out, fingers spread, and the cat opened his eyes again.

The old man stopped, back to me, and didn't move.

"Your name is *Breath*, Papa. Come on, dinner's ready."

He walked slowly forward. What else could he do?

At the door to the living room he saw the two women sitting on the couch. Both had their hands folded carefully in their laps over the wide spread of their silk dresses. For two such plain-looking women, in that moment with their faces lit expectantly, they were quite lovely.

"Papa, I'd like to introduce you to the Wild Sisters. Dortchen and Lisette."

For the first time he turned and looked at me. "What is this?"

"You're all my guests for dinner."

"What the fuck is this, Walter? Who are they?"

"You don't know?"

"I wouldn't *ask* if I knew!"

I turned to the women. "Please excuse my father, ladies. He must be tired."

He grabbed my jacket and pulled me to him. "What are you doing, Walter? What's going on?" There was no fear in his face, only distrust and malice.

Did I feel any pity for what I was about to do? Pity for the man who'd once upon a time raised me like a son and taught me everything he knew? Taught me everything I knew once again now?

I laughed in his face. "Do you want to eat first, or should the ladies begin?"

He said nothing, only continued glaring at me, holding my jacket.

"I think we should start with the story," Lisette said in her small, cultured voice. "A good story always enhances the appetite."

"I agree," Dortchen said.

"Good. Then please do."

The two women looked at each other. Lisette told Dortchen to begin:

Once upon a time there was a little man whose name was

Breath. It was a strange name, but because he had such strong magic inside, whoever had created him chose a name no human would ever guess.

Papa let go of my lapel.

The little man was content with this magic for a time, but as he grew older, he realized it was not enough in life. What one really needed was love, especially if you happened to be Breath, who was immortal.

One day he was out walking and saw a beautiful young maiden sitting at a spinning wheel in a barn. She was very poor, but so beautiful that the little man fell instantly in love.

"What is your name?" he asked brusquely, not wanting her to know that already he loved her with all his soul.

"My name is Alexandra, but I'm so sad that I have almost forgotten it."

"Why?"

"Because the king is coming tomorrow and I lied to him. I told him I could spin gold out of straw. When he sees that I can't, he'll kill me."

Now Breath could do this kind of magic easily. An idea came to him. Perhaps if he spun the gold for the girl, she would fall in love with him forever.

At the same time, he had had so many bad experiences with love that he was careful about such things.

"What will you give me if I spin for you?"

"My necklace," the maiden said.

The necklace meant nothing to him, but he didn't want her to know that. He wanted her love, but love is a hard fish to catch and one must do it carefully.

The little man took the necklace and sat down at the wheel, and whizz, whizz, whizz, three times round, the spool was full. Then he inserted another one, and whizz, whizz, whizz, the second was full. And so it went until morning, when all the straw was spun, and all the spools were filled with gold.

The girl watched with delight, but never once in those many hours did she ask the little man his name or thank him when he was done. That made him sad, but those hours together with her alone only made his love grow until it was almost too large for his body.

I watched the expression on his face as the story went on. There was a softening there, a sadness for oneself, a sadness for the truth of history. Dortchen spoke quietly, but besides her voice there was no other sound in the room.

So the king had the miller's daughter brought into an even larger room filled with straw and said to her, "You must spin all this into gold tonight. If you succeed, you shall become my wife." To himself he thought: Even though she's just a miller's daughter, I'll never find a richer woman anywhere.

Papa stiffened. "That's right! He didn't want her. He only wanted the gold. I told her that! But she didn't want love either. She wanted to be queen."

Dortchen and Lisette looked at each other, but I gestured for Dortchen to go on. Instead, she looked at her sister and the other continued:

Everyone knows the story. The little man spun gold for the third time on the promise of Alexandra's child. After a year she gave birth. (To me). He returned and told her to keep her promise.

The queen was horrified and offered the little man all the treasures of the kingdom if he would let her keep the child. But the little man knew she had no love for her son because her heart was as white and cold as a star. Breath replied, "No, something living is more important to me than all the treasures in the world."

He looked at me so sadly, nodding yes, that's all true.

Furious that he had denied her, the queen began to rant and rave so much that her true, mean spirit showed itself. Fi-

nally, she said, "Go away, little man. I already have a court midget."

"She hated me so much! She couldn't stand looking at me!"

Lisette was upset by his constant interruptions. She cleared her throat loudly. *Alexandra said other terrible things. When Breath had had more than enough and knew how much she despised him, he turned one of her fingers into gold to remind her of his powers. But his heart still ached for her, so he gave her one more chance. "I'll give you three days' time. If you can guess my name by the third day, you shall keep your child."*

The story continued. The *true* story of Breath that Dortchen and Lisette Wild had made up to tell the Brothers Grimm more than a century and a half before. The difference was that their version was exactly the same as the one Papa had told me so long ago in the woods outside Vienna. Every nuance, every detail was the same; the bed of gold, the frog on the hand that was turned into the human child for the proud queen, everything.

Earlier that afternoon, with embarrassed looks on their faces, the sisters had told me how the Grimms had laughed and laughed at the name Rumpelstiltskin. They wanted to record the girls' story, but felt it was much too sad and wrong in its original form. Little magical men shouldn't be able to get away with stealing human children. It was simply too strange and immoral. No, their story would end with the good and virtuous queen guessing the little man's name because she was so worried about losing her child. Of course his name had to be Rumpelstiltskin because it was the craziest, funniest name either of them had ever heard. Wilhelm asked, "Which of you made that up? It's genius." Dortchen shyly said, "Me."

So Breath ran out of the city with the child into the stormy black night and neither of them was ever seen again.

The effect on Papa was as I'd expected. By the time

they'd "finished" the story, he was leaning against the wall, crying and nodding at the same time. Someone other than himself finally knew and had told the story of his sad life.

The sisters, on the other hand, were delighted by his reaction. Lisette asked if he was all right. He spoke in a quiet, haunted voice. "Yes."

When they were done, I waited a moment before asking them to do my favor for me. Originally, in Kassel, when I'd asked them to do it, both were astonished. That was *all*? I'd brought them back only to do this one little thing?

"Yes, ladies. You created the story. Now continue it. Please do me the favor of adding my small end, or coda, to it. For all time. Forever."

"Do you know who they are, Papa?"

He was so distraught he didn't seem to hear me.

"Papa?"

"What? No. Who are they?"

"They created you, Papa. You're based on a man named Retzner who lived near Kassel. A poor man who once, after having done some work for a farmer's wife, wasn't paid for it. To get even he stole her child. That's correct, isn't it, ladies?"

"Yes. We made it up together."

He looked at me emptily. What was I saying to him?

"They made you *up*, Papa! You're not real. You came out of their heads. Watch!"

"Dortchen, would you finish the story now?"

She straightened her dress in her lap and took a deep breath:

Now, the little man named the boy Walter because he was a human child and needed a human name. But because he loved him so, Breath also taught him all the magic he knew. The boy grew up knowing what it was to be human, as well as knowing what it was to possess great magic.

The two of them lived together happily for many years. But even Breath, magic as he was, made one mistake. And he made it because there were many human things he could never understand. He allowed Walter to grow up! Naturally, when that happened, the boy fell in love with a pretty young maiden. He told his Papa that he wanted to marry and start a family of his own. Breath couldn't accept the thought of losing his only love. He told Walter that if he did marry, he would kill him. But Walter was young and very much in love, as his magical father had once been with Alexandra. Walter ignored his father and married the girl anyway."

"What is this? What do you mean, they created me?"

"Listen."

Dortchen went on: *Breath's anger was as large as an ocean and he struck his son down, killing him instantly. But living without any love at all in this world was too much for the little man. So he brought Walter back to life in another time and place. He hoped that in this new existence, his son would learn that being both human and magical doesn't work. Once mixed, they can be disastrous to everyone concerned. Breath hoped that in this new life, his son would realize that being with his father was all he should want out of life.*

Sadly, though, the same thing happened in this new life too, and again Breath's anger killed his son.

This time I was surprised by the old man's reaction. Rather than blow up, he seemed to slump, as if the truth were sucking him more and more into himself.

I didn't care. He wanted my life. I didn't want his. Maris was my love. I didn't belong to his.

Dortchen sighed. Poor Papa made the same mistake again and again through time and always with the same result. This made him meaner to the only person who *had* ever loved him. It got so bad that, in time, he completely forgot what love meant, only thinking about his own happiness.

"This terrible circle continued to turn round and round

until the twentieth century. There the boy's name was Walker."

Papa looked at me and put out his hand. "Please!"

"Go on."

"In this life, however, Walker found perfect love with a woman who was able to show him secret, lost parts of his soul and being. In them was the answer to the dilemma that had ruined all of his past lives and happinesses.

"He went to Kassel and resurrected the Wild Sisters who had originally created the story of Breath. Walker asked them to come to Vienna to help him fight his father. Because Lisette and Dortchen knew what true love was, they agreed.

"They came and met the father to tell him how they had created him. But there was one thing left. Walker asked them to end the story of Breath differently. He asked them to say, *When Breath heard the end of their story and discovered where he'd really come from, he was so sad that like his heart, he turned to glass and broke. When he died, his magic died with him. The magic he'd taught his son. The magic that had enabled Walker to bring the Wild Sisters back to life to help. When Breath was gone, Walker was only human again."*

There was a delicate *ping,* as slight as a heartbeat, and then the sound of glass breaking on the floor. I jumped out of the way, but some of it flew up and cut me. Brushing it off, I looked at the couch but they were all gone.

4.

It's good being "only human" again. There *are* times when I wish I still had some magic left. For example, the morning I told Maris the story of what really happened, and she got so angry I was afraid she was going to start bleeding again. She didn't, though. After her initial explosion, she sat up in that big white bed and said, "I couldn't have done anything any- way, could I?"

"Maris, you did everything! Your drawing showed me how to beat him."

"Because I wrote 'Breathing you' at the bottom? Big deal."

"No, because you showed me into a part of myself that had been closed through all my lives. If you'd only shown me his name it wouldn't have done any good. That would have only given us equal power. Showing me the city showed me his name *and* what I should do with it. It was clear in an instant. *You* did that. You showed me how. I couldn't have found it alone."

"It's hard finding your way across someone else's heart, isn't it?

"Walker, promise me something. I believe all of this is over. I believe you won. But if *anything* ever comes up again, you must tell me. Will you promise that?"

"It's over, Maris. Nothing else is going to happen."

"I don't care. You have to promise me that."

"Okay."

"Put up your right hand and say it."

"I promise to tell you everything."

"It doesn't have to be only magic, either. If I'm terrible and you hate something I do, you can't hold back. You have to tell. A deal? I promise to do the same with you."

"It's a deal."

I kept my promise. Six months later, the day it happened, I told Maris about the girl at the door.

The bell rang, I answered it. The instant after I knew who she was, I realized again nothing is done without regret.

She was wearing a long red cape that covered her head as

well as her body. She had blond hair, honey-colored skin, lips as red as the cape.

"Once upon a time there was a sweet little maiden. Whoever laid eyes upon her could not help but love her." I looked up the line later.

"Do you know who I am?"

"Yes, I think so."

I'm Little Red Riding Hood. We've heard about you. *All* of us have heard about what you did. We don't like it. You're dangerous."

Our son . . .

About the Author

Jonathan Carroll is the author of *The Land of Laughs*, *Voice of Our Shadow*, and *Bones of the Moon*. He lives in Vienna, Austria.